CW00517749

DEADLY CALLER

A DETECTIVE JANE PHILLIPS NOVEL

OMJ RYAN

1

Just after 9 a.m., Antonia Berry sat alone in her tiny office. The factory, which had been in her family for three generations, was in Sighthill, just outside Edinburgh. She found herself staring at her laptop, and the mirror image of her face in the on-screen window, as she waited for the Zoom meeting to begin. She'd made something of a special effort this morning, donning a full face of makeup – which included a killer red lipstick she had bought at the weekend – all for the benefit of her first meeting of the day, with her rather dishy client, Matthew Rice, a partner and financial director of Ardent Technologies based in Manchester. Unusually, he was late, which gave her a moment to run her fingers through her tousled auburn hair to ensure he saw her at her absolute best once the video connection was made.

Just then, the screen changed and Rice's handsome face appeared next to hers. 'Morning, Antonia,' he said. He gave her an impish smile and flashed his perfect teeth, accentuating his chiselled jaw. 'Sorry I'm late.' He sighed. 'Lesley called me just as I was opening up my laptop.'

He was, of course, talking about his boss at Ardent, Lesley Bailey.

'Everything ok?' she asked.

Rice nodded. 'Nothing that couldn't keep. Honestly, she's driving me mad at the moment.'

'Stressed out about the IPO?' Berry asked, referring to the imminent stock market flotation of Ardent Technologies, somewhat big news in the British construction industry.

'Yep. I've been working from home for the last few days to stay out of her way. Not that it's done me much good. She must have called me ten times a day, at least. I'll be bloody glad when the whole thing is over and done with. Maybe then, she'll leave me in peace.' He lifted a steaming mug to his lips and took a sip of his hot drink.

Berry smiled. She knew, from their previous Zoom conversations, that as a founding partner, Rice held significant shares in Ardent. Once the stock flotation became a reality, he would become a very wealthy man indeed. Not bad for someone in his late forties. He could soon enjoy all the peace and quiet he could wish for, and a lifetime of exotic holidays. The fact that he was still single made him even more appealing. It was such a shame he lived a four-hour drive away in Manchester.

Rice set the mug down on the desk in front of him, then pulled out his pen and opened a small leather folio. 'Anyway, Antonia. I know you're as busy as I am, so let's get down to business, shall we?'

Berry felt herself blush slightly as the double meaning of his words flashed into her mind; oh, how she'd love to *get down to business* with Matthew Rice.

'So, I've sent you the specs and quantities for our next order,' Rice continued, suddenly serious. 'And I'm hoping you can turn it around in the next seven days. We have a new large-scale project going live in Chicago at the beginning of

June, and we'd like to start the manufacturing at our end on the 17th of May.'

Berry felt her face contort. 'I've seen the order requirements, Matthew, and it's extensive to say the least.'

'Is that a problem?'

'No, no, of course not. It's just that delivering the quantity you need within a seven-day turnaround is going to be quite a challenge. Our usual timeline on a job that big would be a minimum of fourteen days.'

Rice nodded. 'I see.'

'I mean, we could certainly look at seven days, but that would require us to hire in additional agency staff, which would then have a knock-on effect on the price.'

Rice said nothing for a moment, his eyes fixed on Berry's. 'Look, Antonia. We're all under pressure to deliver more for less. If you're saying you and your father can't deliver, then maybe it's time I found myself another supplier?' His tone was passive-aggressive, almost threatening, now.

This was a side of Rice Berry had not seen before. In an instant, his charm and boyish good looks seemed to desert him. She swallowed hard, trying to mask her unease. Ardent was their biggest client, and one their small family business could ill-afford to lose. 'No, please don't do that, Matthew. I'm sure we can find a way to make it work,' she said finally.

'That's what I like to hear.' Rice's smile returned, but appeared bereft of any real emotion. His eyes were lifeless and cold.

Just then, the sound of a doorbell ringing echoed around Rice's house. He glanced sideways to a position off-screen as it sounded again. 'Who the bloody hell is that?' he growled before returning his gaze to Berry.

'It's probably the Amazon delivery guy. He practically lives at my house,' Berry said with forced levity as she attempted to lighten the mood.

'Will you excuse me for a moment,' said Rice. He didn't wait for a response. He stepped up from his chair and disappeared off-camera.

In Rice's absence, Berry's eyes were drawn to the room where he'd set up his laptop for the meeting. It appeared to be positioned in a relatively compact living space that led into a modern open-plan kitchen at the far end of the house. From what she could see, it was all very tastefully decorated in greys and blues; quite minimal and masculine. Out of shot, she heard Rice's footsteps as he made his way to the front door and opened it. There was the sound of a brief exchange, followed suddenly by raised voices. Then a blood-curdling scream exploded through her laptop speakers, followed by another, and another, and another.

'Matthew?' Berry shouted instinctively into her laptop as her adrenaline spiked. 'Matthew? What's happened?'

As an eerie, deadly silence descended on the room, Berry stared at the empty chair. Her heart pounded in her throat so loudly, she thought it would burst. She leant in close to the laptop's microphone. 'Matthew? Are you there?' she whispered, as loudly as she dared.

The room remained silent for a long moment. Then the sound of footsteps began to filter through.

Berry held her breath.

Then the laptop screen was pushed shut from behind. A moment later, the Zoom link was severed.

2

DCI Jane Phillips let out a frustrated sigh as she dropped the thick report of crime statistics onto her desk, then removed her glasses and swivelled her chair to face the window. Beyond the glass, the sun shone brightly, and a light breeze caused the treetops to sway. Her office was on the third floor of Ashton House, the headquarters of the Greater Manchester Police. Rubbing two fingers against her right temple, she attempted in vain to ease the tension headache that had been building since she'd arrived at her desk three hours ago, just after 8 a.m. If anything was guaranteed to stress her out, it was paperwork, and, in particular, the raft of Excel sheets the GMP top brass obsessed over in order to gauge the successes or failings of her Major Crimes Unit. Sadly, data analysis – as opposed to on-the-ground detective work – seemed to be the way modern policing was headed: a mind-blowing array of quarterly progress reviews, input vs output ratio charts, and arrests vs conviction graphs. Tedious didn't even come close.

Letting out another loud sigh, she replaced her glasses, then stepped up from her chair and wandered over to the window. 'There must be more to life, Jane,' she muttered under her breath as she stared down at the large car park below for a long moment.

A knock on her open door broke her train of thought. She turned to find her second in command, Detective Sergeant Jones, standing in the doorway. They were enjoying unusually warm weather for May, and Jones was without his customary suit jacket. His shirtsleeves were rolled up, exposing the heavy scarring on his skinny left wrist, a recent, and unwanted, memento of the job.

'You got a minute, Guv?' he said, his accent thick South London despite having lived in Manchester for over fifteen years.

Phillips nodded. 'What's up?'

'I've just taken a call from a uniform team out in Lymm saying a man's been murdered, stabbed to death on his doorstep. The description of the scene sounds pretty nasty. I was gonna take Bov over there and have a look.'

Phillips felt her eyes widen. '*I'll* come with you.'

'There's no need, Guv. It's just a preliminary walk-through at this stage.'

Phillips shook her head as she reached for her suit jacket on the back of her chair. 'No. I want to come with you. I'd much rather do a prelim than stare at bloody paperwork for the rest of the morning.'

Jones chuckled. 'I'll get my car keys,' he said, then headed back to his desk.

The journey from the GMP's north-Manchester HQ in Failsworth to the location of the stabbing took just over half an hour. The village of Lymm, nestled in the heart of the Cheshire countryside southwest of Manchester city centre, was famous for its well-heeled residents, as well as its large SUVs and expensive real estate. The style of the houses varied from large, purpose-built executive homes to extensively modernised traditional cottages. Their destination was located on a quiet, leafy street on the outskirts of the village, and easily identifiable by the patrol car parked outside. Jones pulled in behind it and switched off the engine.

Phillips felt reenergised, being back at a crime scene. 'Right. Let's get to it,' she said enthusiastically as she stepped out of the car. Jones followed suit.

As they made their way past a large, gleaming silver BMW and up the short, gravelled drive towards the quaint stone cottage covered in green ivy, one of the two uniformed officers stepped towards them. His stab vest badge identified him as PC McCoy.

Phillips flashed her ID.

McCoy nodded. 'Ma'am.'

'What have we got?' asked Phillips.

'A deceased white male,' said McCoy, 'with what looks like multiple stab wounds to the chest.'

'Location of the body?'

'He's lying on his side, just past the front door.'

'Any sign of a forced entry?' asked Jones.

'No. The door was wide open when we arrived, and the locks intact. The body and the scene are as we found it.'

'So, you haven't been inside the house yourselves?'

'No, Ma'am.'

'Good. Any idea who our victim is?' said Phillips.

McCoy nodded. 'According to Control, we think he's the homeowner, Matthew Rice. Apparently, someone he worked with in Edinburgh called it in.'

Phillips furrowed her brow. '*Edinburgh?*'

McCoy continued, 'Yes, Ma'am. It seems Rice was on a Zoom video call with her when he broke off to answer the door, and was subsequently attacked.'

'So, she witnessed it?' asked Jones.

'I don't know. As the only car in the area, we got a call

from Control at around 10 a.m. asking to check out the reported attack. We arrived about ten minutes later and found him like this, and immediately called you.'

'Do you have contact details for the witness in Edinburgh?'

'Sorry, Ma'am, I don't. Like I say, it was just top line details on the original job.'

'Get back onto Control and get everything you can on her, will you? We'll need it when we come back out of the house,' said Phillips, then locked eyes with Jones. 'Let's take a look at the body, shall we?'

To all intents and purpose, the house appeared untouched, but as they drew closer to the front door, extensive blood spattering could be clearly seen against the white wooden frame. A moment later, the body of a man came into view, lying, as McCoy had described, on the left side, just inside the small hallway.

'Jesus. There mustn't be any blood left in him,' muttered Jones as he took in the macabre scene.

'Looks like a frenzied attack,' added Phillips as she pulled on a pair of purple latex gloves and blue shoe coverings. Jones did the same.

Next, she placed her feet carefully on the gravel and stepped forwards to get a closer look. The tiled hallway was typical of such small cottages; compact, with limited floorspace, and connected directly to the stairs up to the next floor. The clothes covering the body were saturated with blood, which was already turning a rusty shade of brown in the warm morning air.

'There's too much blood in there for us to go in this way,' said Phillips. 'Let's see if we can get in around the back.'

Jones nodded.

A minute later, Phillips and Jones were at the back door. Luckily, it appeared as if the cottage was a listed building, retaining many of the original features, including the tiny rear door with thin, single-glazed glass. Picking up a rock from the garden, Jones made light work of smashing out the small panes above the lock, then carefully reached in and released the door.

Phillips took the lead and headed through to the small open-plan kitchen, where everything appeared untouched. 'This is the police,' she shouted. 'If there's anybody inside the house, please make yourself known to us.'

The house remained silent.

Phillips repeated the instruction, again without response.

Moving through to a small dining area that annexed the living room, she noted the laptop power cable lying across the smoked glass dining table, alongside an empty coffee cup and open notepad; a Montblanc pen rested on the page.

Jones pointed to the table. 'Looks like that's where he made the Zoom call.'

'I'd say so, but if that's the case, where's the laptop?' said Phillips.

From their position, they could see the open door to the living room, which connected the combined space to the hallway and the location of the body. Phillips carefully followed the trail of bloody footprints towards the door, to where she was once more able to see the blood-soaked body.

'Looks like one set of footprints going in both directions, Guv,' said Jones.

'Judging by the state of the victim, I'm guessing the killer left them.'

'Do you want to take a look upstairs?'

Phillips shook her head. 'The body's blocking the only access route. We can't risk contaminating the scene.' She scanned the room for a long moment. 'We need an urgent forensic sweep.'

Jones was already pulling his phone from his pocket. 'I'll call Evans.'

'Thanks,' said Phillips as she led the way back out into the garden. 'I'll see if McCoy has found out anything on our witness, then I'll call Entwistle. We need to find out if this guy really is Matthew Rice.'

Jones nodded. As they returned around the outside to the front of the house, he stepped away to call the forensics team.

Phillips made her way back down the drive to the patrol car, where McCoy stood ready, an open notepad in his left hand. 'What have you got?'

'Ma'am. The person who called it in is a woman named Antonia Berry from Sighthill near Edinburgh. According to Control, after hearing Rice being attacked on the Zoom video link, she contacted the local police in Edinburgh, who pointed her in our direction. That's when she called us.'

'Do you have her contact details?'

'Yes, Ma'am,' said McCoy, ripping a page from his notepad and handing it to Phillips.

'Good work,' said Phillips. She stepped away and pulled out her iPhone. It was time to bring in the rest of the MCU team.

Her call connected a moment later, Detective Constable Entwistle, as ever, answering promptly. 'Guv? How's the stabbing?'

'A total bloodbath. One dead male that we can see, but we haven't been able to get upstairs because of the position of the deceased. We're calling in the CSIs as we speak.'

'What can I do?'

'Can you pull up all the information we have on file for Matthew Rice? The address is 48 Baird Lane in Lymm. See if there's a photo ID so we can be sure he is actually our victim.

'Will do.'

'Can you email it through to my phone once you have it?'

'Of course. I'll be as quick as I can.'

As Phillips ended the call, Jones reappeared. 'What's the ETA on Evans?' she asked.

'Within the hour, Guv.'

'Ok, that's good.' Phillips handed him Berry's contact details. 'Read out that number, will you?'

Jones obliged, and Phillips keyed the digits into her phone. A moment later, it began to ring.

'Time to find out what our witness has to say.'

3

L ater that day, back at Ashton House, Phillips
gathered the core team of the Major Crimes Unit in
her office. As she and Jones took seats, the man-
mountain that was Bovalino wandered in, cradling a huge
sandwich and chewing a large mouthful.

'Eating again, Bov?' Phillips chuckled in quiet admiration
at the sheer volume of food it took to keep her enormous
detective constable sustained daily.

Bovalino nodded and smiled as much as he was able to
without losing any of the precious quarry from his mouth,
then took a seat opposite her, next to Jones,

Entwistle was last in, carrying a Manila folder. As ever, he
looked fresh, athletic, and as if he belonged on a catwalk as
opposed to at a crime scene. His light brown mixed-race skin
was accentuated by his crisp white shirt.

'So, Whistler. Have you managed to find anything on
Rice?' asked Phillips, using Entwistle's new nickname,
awarded by Bovalino – a man who believed every copper
should have one. It had stuck surprisingly quickly among the

team, and now she found herself using it more and more often. She liked it – and so did he, it seemed.

'See, I told you that nickname would stick,' said Bovalino with a wide grin. 'Even the guv is using it now.'

Entwistle smiled and shook his head. 'It could be worse, I suppose.' He pulled out an enlarged printout of a driver's licence, which he handed across to Phillips. 'This is what he looks like according to the DVLA records. That picture was updated just a couple of years ago.'

Phillips stared down at the solemn face looking back at her, then presented it to Jones. 'Looks like our guy.'

Jones took a long look. 'Yep. That's him.'

Entwistle placed the folder on Phillips's desk before hitching his buttocks onto a cabinet a few feet away. 'Well, in that case, our victim is Matthew Joseph Rice, aged forty-seven. He's lived at that address for over fifteen years, and has a mortgage on it with ten years left on the term. According to council tax records, he lives alone, and as far as I can see from his social media profiles, he's single, but also very sociable.'

Phillips leafed through the documents in the file.

'Any kind of record?' asked Jones.

'Nothing. Spotless.'

'So, what did he do for work?' asked Phillips.

'He was the chief financial officer for a company called Ardent Technologies Ltd. based out of Stockport. They're into construction, from what I can tell, and the address is in the file. I'm sorry it's just top-line info at the moment, Guv, but with time I should be able to get a lot more.'

'No, no, this is good.' Phillips closed the file. 'Ok. So, just before Jones and I left Rice's place, I spoke to our so-called witness, Antonia Berry.'

'How was she?' asked Bovalino.

'Quite shaken, to be honest. She couldn't see what happened because of the position of the laptop camera, but it sounds like she heard the attack in all its glory. She describes a pretty standard business meeting, via a Zoom call, before Rice broke away to answer the door. There were raised voices, followed by someone screaming repeatedly before everything went silent. She panicked and began asking Rice if he was ok, but got no response. A few moments later, someone closed the laptop, ending the call.'

'Did she see who it was?' asked Entwistle.

'No. The killer was smart enough to not be caught on camera,' said Phillips. 'Plus, we believe they also nicked the laptop.'

Jones cut in. 'But not *that* smart. They did leave behind a shitload of bloody footprints at the scene. Forensics are doing a full sweep of the place as we speak.'

'That's right,' added Phillips. 'Evans called us in the car when we were on our way back here. He'd done a full sweep of the house and confirmed Rice was the only person there, which is what we expected, to be honest. And having witnessed the scene for ourselves, it looks as if all the action happened at the front door.'

The room fell silent for a moment as the team processed the information.

'So, from our initial intel, it seems Rice answered the door without any obvious caution, was fatally stabbed on the doorstep in broad daylight, then left for dead as our perp entered the property and removed his laptop.'

'However,' Jones cut in, 'they did leave the power cable behind, so we can assume they left in a hurry.'

'*Or* they know their tech-kit and realised it wasn't worth the hassle of carrying it,' said Entwistle. 'Most standard power cables are interchangeable these days, or at the very least you can pick them up for almost nothing on Amazon.'

Phillips nodded. 'The question is, what was on that laptop that was so important?' She reopened the Manila file and, a

second later, scribbled down the address she was looking for
on a Post-it note, then stood. 'Bovalino. Can you find out
Rice's next of kin and organise a uniform team to break the
news?'

'Sure, Guv,'

'Whistler, get me a full background on Rice, will you?'

'On it.'

Phillips turned her attention to Jones now. 'Let's take a
trip out to Ardent's offices, see what they can tell us about Mr
Rice and what, if anything, on that laptop was worth killing
him for.'

PHILLIPS AND JONES had worked together for so many years
now, they had no issue with long moments of silence between
them. In fact, the quiet time served a valuable purpose,
allowing them to think, to process the intricacies of their, very
often, complex investigations.

As they made the thirty-minute journey to Ardent Technologies, Phillips stared out of the window and tried to
imagine the last moments of Matthew Rice's life. Her mind
was awash with questions: was he aware of the danger he
faced before that fateful knock interrupted his call with
Antonia Berry? Had he recognised his killer, or were they
looking at a stranger murder? And was the content of his
laptop worth killing for?

Right now, they had very little to go on, but she knew – as
she always did – that in the days that followed, her team
would do whatever it took to find the answers she was
looking for.

Her mind was drawn back to the present as Jones pulled
into the car park of Ardent Technologies headquarters,
comprised of a cluster of large, modern buildings on an

industrial site in the town of Stockport, seven miles south of Manchester city centre.

After parking up in a visitor's bay, they followed the signs to the main office reception, where they were greeted by a smartly presented receptionist who appeared efficient, if a little dour.

Phillips flashed her identification. 'We'd like to speak to someone in charge, please.'

The woman behind the desk raised an eyebrow, then pointed to a large sofa to the side of the reception area. 'If you'd like to take a seat, I'll see who is available.'

Phillips and Jones followed her instructions and a few minutes later, a blonde-haired woman strode towards them with a wide, fixed grin. Surprisingly tall, her long limbs were accentuated by her navy trouser suit.

Phillips and Jones stood as she approached.

'I'm Cherie Howard, the marketing director. How can I help?' she said, offering her outstretched hand.

Phillips shook it firmly, then presented her ID. 'Is there somewhere private we can speak?'

Howard's brow furrowed. 'Er, yes. We can use one of the conference rooms,' she said, and gestured for them to follow her.

A few moments later, Phillips and Jones were led into a spacious room replete with a large, polished wood table surrounded by executive chairs. The motion-triggered lights flickered to life as they entered, illuminating the almost chilly air-conditioned room.

'Can I get you a tea or a coffee?' asked Howard, taking a seat.

'Not for me, thanks,' said Phillips as she sat.

Jones shook his head, following her lead. 'I'm fine too, thank you,' he said. He placed his open notepad and pen on the table.

'So, how can I help you?'

'We understand Matthew Rice is listed as a director here?' said Phillips.

Howard flinched slightly. 'Matthew? That's right, but why do you ask?'

Phillips sat forward in her seat. 'I'm sorry to have to tell you this, Ms Howard, but Matthew is dead.'

Howard's eyes bulged and her mouth fell open. 'What?'

'His body was found at his home in Lymm this morning. He'd been stabbed to death, and we think he was murdered.'

'I don't believe it!'

Phillips continued. 'As we understand it, he was on a video call with one of your suppliers, an Antonia Berry from Edinburgh.'

'I know the name, but I've never met her,' said Howard, clearly still in shock.

'We believe that whoever killed Matthew stole his laptop. We wondered if there was anything on it that might explain why he was murdered?' asked Phillips.

'I have no idea.'

'No business secrets. Valuable information?'

'I very much doubt it,' said Howard. 'I mean, we make industrial foam for the construction industry, which is all very standard stuff. We own the patent outright, so it's totally copyright protected. Plus, it's in the public domain, so it's no secret how we make the stuff, either.'

'I see,' said Phillips. 'We understand Matthew was Ardent's chief financial officer?'

'That's correct.'

'What did that entail, exactly?'

'Erm, well. As the title suggests, he was in charge of all the finances, including procurement and negotiating contracts with suppliers,' said Howard.

'Was he well liked?' asked Jones.

Howard shrugged her shoulders slightly. 'Yes, I guess so. He was widely known as a tough negotiator, but at the same time was charming and very easy to be around.'

'Do you know if he was single? Girlfriend, boyfriend, maybe?' Phillips said.

Howard released a sardonic chortle. 'Matthew was very much a ladies' man. He seemed to have a new girl every week, but none of them ever came to anything. Probably because he had a thing for married women.'

Phillips raised an eyebrow. 'Oh?'

'He said there was less chance of them getting serious on him. Plus, I got the impression he enjoyed the clandestine nature of affairs. Liked the excitement of sneaking around.'

Jones scribbled in his notepad.

'Were you two close?' asked Phillips.

'Not particularly. We worked well together in a business sense, but our lives outside of work were very different, and we had little in common.'

Phillips nodded, then changed tack. 'You mentioned you make industrial foam here for the construction industry. What's that used in?'

'Well, it's rapidly replacing the use of concrete in high-rise buildings. It's ten times lighter than the traditional mix, which makes lifting it into position at height much easier, but with the added advantage that it's just as strong as concrete and steel. Plus, it's more eco-friendly to manufacture. We ship it to markets all over the world, such as the US, China, and more recently, the Gulf states and South East Asia. Not bad for a small business set up in Stockport.'

'Very impressive,' said Phillips. 'So, who owns Ardent? Who calls the shots here?'

'We have a board of directors, which is made up of the four partners: Lesley Bailey, the CEO and founding partner, David Nelson, partner and managing director, me as marketing director and partner, and Matthew...' Her words tailed off.

Phillips cut in. 'So, Matthew was a partner too?'

Howard nodded as she bit her bottom lip.

'I know this is a lot to take in.'

'Like I said, we weren't close, but it's still come as a shock.'

'I'm sure it has. I just have a few more questions, if that's ok?'

Howard took a deep breath in through her nose. 'Yes. Whatever I can do to help.'

'Can you tell me when you last spoke with Matthew?'

Howard took a moment to think. 'Erm, it would have been Monday at 10 a.m. He'd been working from home since Thursday on a special project, so I hadn't seen him for a few days, but we always made time for a quick catch-up call at the start of the week.'

'And how did he sound on the call?'

'Fine. Normal, I guess.'

'Can you tell me anything about the special project he was working on?'

Howard shook her head. 'I'm afraid it's confidential. You'd need to speak to Lesley or David for any details on that.'

Phillips's eyes narrowed. 'I thought you said there was nothing of value on Matthew's laptop?'

Howard stalled momentarily. 'Well, of course, the work he does has value...' She suddenly caught herself. 'Sorry, *did* have value. But what I meant was that I can't imagine anyone would want to kill him to access the contents of his laptop. Like I said, we manufacture industrial foam.'

Phillips stared at Howard for a long moment, trying to figure out if she was lying. She certainly didn't appear to be, but she knew better than to write anyone off so early in an investigation. For now, she changed tack. 'So, where can we find Lesley and David?'

'Ordinarily they'd be here, but Lesley's in London today and David is on annual leave. That's why you got lumbered with me.'

'I see. Well, in that case, I think we have everything we need for the moment.' Phillips offered her a soft smile as she passed over her business card. 'If you think of anything that might be relevant – any reason why someone would want to hurt Matthew or steal his laptop – call me, any time.'

'Thank you,' said Howard, standing as she took the card. 'What about Matthew's parents? Who will tell them about what's happened?'

'It's already been taken care of. No need for you to worry,' Phillips said.

Howard's shoulders sagged and she let out a heavy sigh. 'That's a relief.'

Phillips and Jones nodded in unison.

'I'll show you out,' offered Howard.

Once outside, as they walked side by side across the large car park to the visitors' bays, Jones ventured a theory. 'If he was as much of a ladies' man as she suggested, could it have been a jealous husband?'

'It's certainly plausible, and might explain why the killer took the laptop. I mean, if it were you, would you want images or videos of Sarah sitting on another man's computer?'

'No, I bloody wouldn't,' Jones replied gruffly.

Just then, Phillips's phone beeped in her pocket, indicating she'd got an SMS. Pulling it out, she stopped in her tracks to read it.

Jones continued walking for a moment, before turning to face her. 'Everything all right, Guv?'

Phillips tried her best to hide the smile on her face as she returned the phone to her pocket.

'You look like the cat that got the cream,' said Jones.

Phillips felt her cheeks flush. 'Shut up and get in the car, will you?'

'Hot date, is it?' he teased.

'Never you mind, Jonesy,' said Phillips with a grin. 'Never you mind.'

4

People, in general, are creatures of habit. They like routine, the comfortable, the familiar. They buy from the same shops each day, eat at the same cafes, drink at the same bars and restaurants. But – he wondered – would people be as keen to live a life so rich in routine if they knew it made them vulnerable to acts of crime?

This morning, for example, he had waited patiently as the old lady parked up her car after returning home from her daily trip to the local shops. Parked in its usual position, her anonymous-looking vehicle was out of sight of CCTV cameras or overlooking neighbours. Both of which meant he was able to break into the car and drive it away in a matter of minutes, without being spotted. And, having studied the old lady's habits for several days, he was also confident the vehicle would not be missed until her next trip out, at eleven o'clock tomorrow morning, by which time the car would have served its purpose.

This evening, routine was once again playing a vital role in his activities. Right on cue, as had been the case over the last few nights, he watched his next victim leave the office at 7 p.m. sharp.

Sitting in the stolen car, parked on the main road opposite their workplace, he switched on the ignition and prepared to follow them home. However, something different was in play tonight. Instead of walking to their car in the office car park, as normal, they walked to the main road and flagged down a black cab, then jumped in the back. A few moments later, as the taxi pulled away, he moved out into the traffic and began to follow at a safe distance.

Driving a stolen car always presented the risk of being pulled over by the police, so, in order to minimise any unwanted attention, he was careful to stick to the speed limits as he followed the black cab for the next twenty minutes.

Where were they going tonight, he wondered. It certainly was a break from the routine he had witnessed over the last week.

Eventually, the cab came to a stop outside what appeared to be a trendy bar, packed with revellers standing out on the street, enjoying their drinks in the warm night air. He pulled up to the kerb a few car-lengths farther down the street and watched as they stepped out of the cab and headed for the entrance to the bar.

'Damn it!' he muttered as they disappeared inside. This was not what he'd planned, and this changed everything.

Sitting in silence for a few minutes, staring at the entrance to the bar as he contemplated his next move, a new plan formed in his mind's eye.

'Maybe things don't have to change at all,' he said as a broad smile spread across his face. 'Not at all.'

5

———

Against her wishes, Cherie Howard's best friend, Angela, returned from the bar with another double gin and tonic for her, along with a large glass of red wine for herself, and a Prosecco for the third member of their group, Maggie. As she set them down on the table in front of them, Cherie checked her watch. It was approaching 10 p.m. and they'd been out since 7.30. After hearing the tragic news of Matthew's death the previous day, she'd called Angela in the evening, intending to excuse herself from their monthly after-work drinks. However, the forthright Angela had insisted she still come, reasoning it would do her good. Even Cherie's husband, John, had told her over dinner that she should go, suggesting that a few drinks would allow her to relax, and an evening out with her mates might help her to process the events surrounding Matthew's death.

Thanks to the constant stream of drinks that had flowed since her arrival, her head now felt foggy. The enormity of the news was also starting to finally sink in; *her colleague had been murdered on his doorstep.* A shiver ran the length of her spine. Despite the fact Angela had been talking in a loud voice directly at her, she'd heard nothing of what she'd said. Suddenly, all she wanted was to be at home, safe in John's arms.

'What do you think, Cherie?' asked Angela, her voice at last cutting through.

Cherie locked eyes with her best friend. 'Sorry, what?'

'You haven't heard a thing I've been saying, have you?' said Angela, flashing a wide grin. Her dark hair and perfect skin giving her the look of the British actress, Minnie Driver.

Cherie blushed. 'No, sorry. I was miles away.'

'Thinking about Matthew?' said Maggie, the final traces of her bright red lipstick now attached to her empty glass in front of her.

'Yes. I think it's just starting to hit me.'

Until that moment – at Cherie's request – they'd purposely avoided any direct discussion around Rice's murder, preferring instead to keep the topics of conversation a bit more light-hearted. Unsurprisingly, however, it had been impossible to ignore.

Angela placed a reassuring hand on Cherie's wrist. 'I can't imagine how shocked you must have been when the police told you what happened. I mean, I only met him that one time when I called into your office, and I was gobsmacked when you told me what happened to him yesterday.' Angela took gulp of her gin and tonic. 'It strange, isn't it? You never imagine bad things happen to good-looking people.'

A tear streaked down Cherie's cheek, which she swatted away as she flashed a weak smile. 'I know what you mean, and I feel so silly and guilty for getting upset. It's not like we were close or anything. I mean, we only ever really talked about work.'

'You're not being silly,' said Angela firmly. 'You don't have to be best mates to get upset. Plus, he seemed like a really lovely guy.'

'Angela's right,' added Maggie. 'And let's not forget, he was murdered in broad daylight, for God's sake. Why *wouldn't* you be upset?'

Images of Rice being repeatedly stabbed flashed into Cherie's head, causing her to shut her eyes.

'Oh, God. I'm sorry. That was insensitive of me,' said Maggie. 'I think I've had too many Proseccos.'

Cherie opened her eyes. 'I should probably go.'

'Please don't,' pleaded Maggie. 'I didn't mean to upset you. You know I'm a complete gob-shite after a few drinks.'

Cherie shook her head. 'It's not you, Mags. I've had enough, that's all, and I just want to go home. It's been a big day, plus Lesley has called a board meeting for first thing in the morning to discuss how we handle Matthew's death. I need to be ready for that.'

'Well, at least finish your drink,' said Angela.

'You have it,' Cherie replied, pushing it across the table towards her friend. 'I'm done.' With that she gathered her jacket and bag, then stood.

Angela and Maggie stood with her, and they embraced and kissed her in turn, both promising to call the next day to check-in. Cherie nodded, and offered a faint smile before she pulled on her jacket and headed for the door.

Once outside, she retrieved her phone from her bag, checked the time and typed out a text to her husband.

God, I need one of your hugs. Just getting a cab. See you about 10.30. Love U! Cx

She pressed send, then dropped the phone into her bag and set off along the pavement towards the taxi rank, five hundred yards farther along the road.

It had been a beautifully warm day, and the night air was so close, she could sense the onset of a thunderstorm was just a few minutes away. With only a light jacket, and without an umbrella to hand, she hoped she would make it to the cab rank before the heavens opened.

Walking as briskly as her heeled work-shoes would allow, she was making her way through the rafts of people milling along the pavement when the first raindrops landed on her head. 'Shit,' she muttered, picking up the pace and stepping onto the road for a moment to avoid a large group, before returning to the pavement as the taxi rank came into view. She was nearly home and dry.

Suddenly a woman's scream echoed across the evening air, followed by the sound of an engine revving at top speed behind her. Then came a cacophony of screams and shouts. Instinctively, she turned on her heels and was shocked to see panicked pedestrians scattering in all directions as a car raced towards them. She opened her mouth to scream – her feet were rooted to the spot as if cemented into concrete – but no sound came out as the car drew closer. A split second later, it mounted the pavement and surged in her direction.

The car wasn't stopping. She needed to get out of its path!

The speeding vehicle was so close now she could see the driver's wide eyes, locked onto hers. All she could think of in that moment was John, and never being able to see his smiling face again.

Finally, her feet began to move as she tried desperately to get out of the way, but it was too little too late. A sickening thud followed a split second later, then nothing but darkness.

6

As the clock on the wall of her living room rolled past 11 p.m., Phillips stretched out on her large tanned-leather sofa as she enjoyed a cuddle with her Ragdoll cat, Floss. She was holding up her end of an ongoing WhatsApp conversation with Adam, an old junior doctor friend of her big brother, Damien. Just over a week earlier, she and Adam had met at a dinner-party hosted by Damien. As the only two single people attending, they'd been seated together – her sister-in-law, Vanessa's none-too-subtle way of attempting to matchmake. Initially, Phillips had felt awkward and embarrassed, blushing slightly as she took her seat, feeling expectant eyes watching her whilst Vanessa made comments to the room as to what a cute couple they'd make. Her worst nightmare.

But, much to her surprise, within a few minutes – and against her better judgement – Phillips had found herself appreciating Adam's effortless charm, which oozed from his athletic physique. His prematurely balding hair had been cropped close against his skull, perfectly matching the dark stubble that surrounded his thick jaw. However, by far his most striking feature was his deep blue eyes, which sparkled when he laughed.

Over the meal, Adam had shared his life story since qualifying as a doctor over twenty years previously: working overseas in Australia, a whirlwind romance that ultimately ended in a painful divorce down under, before returning to the UK five years earlier with every intention of remaining single for the rest of his life. These days, he reasoned, he was married to his work. Phillips knew exactly how that felt, and the emotional toll that level of dedication could take on a person. Ironically, she suddenly found herself having romantic feelings for the first time in as long as she could remember. And so, as the party came to a close, she was delighted when Adam had asked for her number, then called just a few days later to see how she was doing.

Since that first call, they'd spoken a couple of times and sent flirty messages through WhatsApp – as and when their hectic work schedules would allow. Currently he was messaging her while on a quick break from working the night shift in the A&E department of the Royal Liverpool University Hospital, just under an hour away from Manchester.

Her phone pinged once more, signalling the arrival of a fresh message.

So, when can I see you again? A xxxx

Her pulse quickened at the thought of spending more time with him. A wide grin spread across her face as she typed her reply.

Which bits would you like to see? Jx

Her finger hovered over the send button as she considered whether or not to send the message. It was the first time she'd hinted at being physical with him. The longer she stared at the words, the less confident she felt. A second later, she shook her head and deleted it, before staring at the screen for a long moment as she considered a more cautious response.

Just then, her phone came alive in her hands as an unidentified caller appeared on screen. She pressed the green answer icon. 'DCI Phillips.'

'Ma'am, this is Sergeant Blackwood at Control. Sorry to ring you so late, but I have you down as the on-call SIO for Major Crimes.'

Phillips's heart sank. Her cosy night in with Floss was about to end. 'That's right. What have you got for me?' she asked, sitting upright.

'Reports of a car used as a weapon in a hit-and-run on Wilmslow high street. Apparently, the car mounted the pavement and deliberately targeted a young woman who was walking up the road. The victim has been taken to the Manchester Royal with life-threatening injuries.'

'Do we know her name?'

'Yes, Ma'am,' said Blackwood, and paused for a moment. Phillips presumed he was looking for the case-file details on his computer screen. *'Er...one of the witnesses named her as Cherie Howard.'*

Phillips felt herself do a double take. 'Cherie Howard? Are you sure?'

'That's what is says down here, Ma'am.'

Phillips jumped up from the sofa and headed for the door. 'I'm on my way to the hospital now.'

After hanging up, she called Jones.

'Guv?' he answered promptly.

'We've got a job. Suspected targeted hit and run.'

'Really? Where?'

'Wilmslow.'

'*Just goes to show, scumbags can show up in even the nicest parts of town.*'

'Yeah, exactly. And get this. Control said the victim's been identified as Cherie Howard.'

'*You what? As in the woman we spoke to at Ardent yesterday?*'

'I'm guessing so.'

'*Well, if it isn't, then that would be one helluva coincidence, wouldn't it?*'

'Yeah, and you know how I feel about them.'

Jones let out a chortle, laden with irony. '*Of course, Guv. Coincidences don't exist in the world of Major Crimes.*'

'No. No, they bloody don't.'

'*So, where do you need me to be?*'

'A&E at the MRI, as soon as you can.'

'*I can be there in twenty minutes.*'

'Me too,' said Phillips. She ended the call and closed the front door behind her.

Twenty minutes later, as she pulled the squad car up to the MRI's Accident and Emergency unit, she felt her phone vibrate in her pocket. Retrieving it, she was consumed by guilt as she read the new message on screen.

Was it something I said? A xxx

Phillips cursed herself for failing to reply. A wave of sadness washed over her as she wondered whether work was always going to come first.

Her attention was drawn to Jones up ahead, walking at pace across the car park towards her. She quickly typed out a message.

Sorry. Been called out on an emergency. Chat soon. Jx

She hit reply at the exact moment Jones tapped on the

driver's window, which caused her to jump slightly. Plunging her phone into her jacket pocket, she climbed out of the car and attempted to act natural.

'Everything all right, Guv?'

Phillips produced a weak smile. 'Yeah, fine.'

'It's just you seem a little jumpy.''

Keen to change the subject, she gestured towards the entrance to the A&E. 'Never mind me. Let's go find our victim, shall we?'

Jones nodded and led the way.

Once inside, Phillips explained the reason for their visit to the receptionist, who directed them to the cubicle where the hit-and-run victim was being treated. A few minutes later, they looked on as a raft of medical staff swarmed around a woman lying on the mobile treatment table. Despite her body being locked in various protective braces and hooked up to a cluster of IVs and machines monitoring her vital signs, there was no doubt the victim was the same Cherie Howard they'd spoken to at Ardent the previous day.

One of the male staff decked out in purple scrubs and wearing glasses turned to face them. 'Who are you?' he asked curtly.

Phillips presented her ID. 'Detective Chief Inspector Phillips, and this is Detective Sergeant Jones.'

The man stepped towards them, out of earshot of the patient. Phillips could see from the badge on his chest that he was the emergency room consultant, Doctor Ashworth. She got straight to the point.

'As we understand it, initial witness reports suggest Mrs Howard was deliberately targeted by the driver of the car that hit her. Is there any chance we could speak to her to confirm this?'

Ashworth shook his head. 'I'm afraid not. She's in a very bad way and about to go into surgery. But you could speak to her husband. He's in the relatives' room along with a couple of her friends, who arrived in the ambulance with her.'

At that moment, two more staff, this time wearing green scrubs, appeared in the cubicle.

Ashworth glanced over his shoulder. 'That's the surgical team. I must go,' he said, before stepping back into the room.

Phillips took that as their cue to leave and made her way along the corridor to the relatives' room, Jones alongside her. They found a man sitting, head in hands, flanked by two women with tear-stained cheeks who appeared to be offering him words of comfort. The woman sitting to his right had dark wavy hair, while the one to his left was blonde.

'We're the police. May we come in?' asked Phillips softly.

The women nodded in unison as the man raised his head, revealing eyes red and puffy from crying.

Once again, Phillips presented her credentials and introduced Jones as they both took seats opposite the trio. 'You must be Mr Howard?' she asked.

The man nodded. 'John,' he said, almost whispering.

Phillips looked at the two women in turn. 'And you are?'

'I'm Angela Morgan,' said the one with dark hair.

'And I'm Maggie Cook.'

'The doctor said you were with Cherie when she was brought in. Were you with her when the accident happened as well?' said Phillips.

Morgan shook her head. 'Not quite. She left us just before ten. We both wanted to stay out, and were still in the bar when we heard some sort of commotion outside—'

'So, I went out for a cigarette to see what was happening,' Cook cut in. 'I could hear lots of shouting and saw a large group gathering farther up the street. Then I overheard someone saying a car had mounted the pavement and hit a woman up by the taxi rank. I don't know why, but I just knew it was Cherie.'

John Howard dropped his gaze to the floor once more.

'I rushed back inside to tell Angela, and together we ran up the road, where we could see her lying in on the pavement, surrounded by loads of people.'

'Someone had already called 999,' said Cook, 'so, we pushed our way through and put our coats over her to keep her warm, then waited for the ambulance to arrive.'

'Did she say anything to either of you?' asked Phillips.

'No. She was already unconscious at that point,' replied Morgan.

'It's *my* fault this happened,' said Howard suddenly.

Phillips felt her brow furrow. 'Why do you say that?'

Tears welled in Howard's eyes once more. 'She found out yesterday that a colleague at work, Matthew, had been killed. She was really upset about it last night when she got home, saying he'd been murdered, and told me she was cancelling her night out with the girls tonight. But *I* said she should still go. If I hadn't, she'd have been at home with me instead, and none of this would've happened.'

Morgan cut in now, placing her hand gently on Howard's wrist. 'Don't blame yourself John. It was *me* that insisted she come tonight, not you.' Sadness oozed from her eyes.

'Try not to torture yourselves with what might or might not have been,' said Jones, gently. 'There was no way anyone could've known this would happen to Cherie.'

Phillips nodded. 'DS Jones is right.' She paused for a moment before continuing. 'Look, I know this is a very difficult time for you all, but some of the initial witness reports at the scene suggested the car may have deliberately mounted the pavement and targeted Cherie?'

'Yeah. I heard a few people saying that,' said Cook, nodding.

'Me too,' said Morgan. 'Do you think it's true?'

'At this stage we don't know, but we certainly intend to

find out.' Phillips pressed on. 'Do you know of any reason why someone would want to hurt Cherie?'

Morgan and Cook shook their heads in unison

'No,' said Howard, his shoulders sagging. 'She's a wonderful woman.'

Phillips eyed him for a long moment as she tried to assess whether his grief was genuine. After all, most victims of violent crimes are known to their attackers. But in Howard's case, his pain seemed all too real.

'What's going on?' he asked, his lips trembling. 'The doctors aren't telling us anything.'

'We don't know any more than you, I'm afraid,' said Phillips, 'but she's in good hands. The team here is the best. DS Jones and I can both personally vouch for that.'

Howard nodded silently as tears streaked down his cheeks.

'I think it's best that we leave you to it,' said Phillips, standing.

Jones did the same.

Phillips glanced at Morgan, then at Cook. 'We'll probably need to speak to you both again once we have the full facts from the scene – and you've each had time to process what happened tonight.'

'Ok,' said Cook.

Morgan nodded.

Phillips led the way out.

Once they were safely back in the car park, she stopped to debrief. 'Seriously, Jonesy. Two directors from the same company are attacked within two days? They *have* to be connected.'

'I'm with you on that, Guv. But why attack two people from a building firm that makes industrial foam?'

Phillips blew her lips. 'I dunno, but we need to find out.' Pulling out her phone, she clicked on the email icon, then stared in silence at the screen as she read a message. Eventually she looked up at Jones. 'The report's come through from the uniform team who took the statements at the scene tonight. Looks like the majority of witnesses believe the car was deliberately aiming for Howard.'

'Anyone get the car's registration?'

'Yeah, a few people actually. Says here it's registered to an Edna Harrington in Hyde, aged eighty-three.'

'Could she have been the driver? It's not unheard of for an elderly lady to lose control of her car?'

Phillips shook her head. 'If she'd stayed at the scene, I could buy that, but the witness report states that whoever hit Howard didn't hang around to see the damage. Quite the opposite, looking at these statements.'

'So we're likely looking for a stolen car, then.'

'Yeah, and I'm sure uniform will verify that in the next few hours after speaking to Mrs Harrington.'

'Which means it's probably already on fire somewhere,' Jones said.

'Yep, along with any trace evidence.' Phillips sighed and stretched her arms, then checked her watch; it was approaching 1 a.m. 'God it's late. I'm hoping we don't get any more calls tonight, but whatever happens, can you pick me up at 8 in the morning?'

'Sure thing.'

'I wanna pay another visit to Ardent, see if there's anything else going on there that might be worth killing for.'

'I'll bring you a coffee from that place near your house,' said Jones.

'Mochachinos?'

'I don't remember the name of it, but the barista has a huge braided beard.'

Phillips grinned. 'That's the one. Miguel makes a mean double espresso.'

Jones shook his head. 'Bloody Chorlton. The place is full of pretentious pricks,' he teased.

'Oi. Are you taking the piss out of where I live?' Phillips replied playfully.

'Never, boss. Never.'

Phillips grinned. 'Right. In that case, I'll see you in the morning.'

With that, they said their goodbyes and headed for their cars.

7

As usual, Jones arrived bang on time, parking up outside Phillips's Victorian terraced home in the bohemian suburb of Chorlton-cum-Hardy. She waved to him as she stepped outside into the early morning sunshine, closed and dead-bolted the door, then walked up the short path to the car. As she dropped down into the passenger seat, Jones handed her a steaming hot coffee in a cardboard cup, the rich aroma pervasive.

'Your usual, Guv.'

'You are a bloody legend, Jonesy. I *so* need this, this morning.' Phillips took a tentative sip of the scalding liquid before placing it in the cupholder in the central console next to her thigh. 'I don't know about you, but I hardly slept a wink last night. I couldn't stop thinking about yesterday's attacks.'

Jones pulled the car away from the kerb as they set off towards Stockport. 'I didn't sleep either. To be fair, I never do when we're on call, but last night was worse than usual. I can't decide whether the two attacks *were* connected or just freak coincidences.'

Phillips's top lip curled into a snarl as she shot him a look of mock disdain.

'I know, I know, there's no such thing in the Major Crimes Unit, and Rice's murder was no accident. But maybe that's exactly what Howard's hit and run was. I know some witnesses said the car deliberately targeted her, but what if the driver just lost control, hit her, then drove off? I mean, the car was stolen after all. He was hardly likely to stick around, was he?'

'That's true, but what are the chances of two senior directors from the *same* company being fatally and critically attacked within forty-eight hours of each other in unrelated incidents?'

Jones glanced sideways at her. 'Slim.'

'Very slim.'

'Yeah. But then I go back to the methods of the attacks. They couldn't be more different – a knife, and a hit and run. Killers who strike more than once usually use the same method each time.'

'Exactly. And that's one of the reasons why I couldn't sleep. My head's jumping all over the place with these two cases.' Phillips pulled out her phone and dialled Entwistle's mobile.

'*Morning, Guv.*'

'Morning, Whistler. Are you at your desk?'

'*Just got in. Bov's here, too.*'

'Great. So you'll have seen my email about Cherie Howard's hit and run last night?'

'*Yeah, we've just been talking about it. How weird is that?*'

'Very. Jones and I are on our way over to Ardent in Stockport to talk to the MD and the CEO. While we're doing that, I need you to look into Ardent for me. So far, all we know is that they make industrial foam. See if there's anything in their history that might explain why two of their directors have been attacked.'

'*No problem, I'll get straight onto it.*'

'And tell Bov I want full backgrounds on Rice and Howard by the time we get back, ok?'

'*Consider it done,*' said Entwistle.

Twenty minutes later, they pulled into the car park of Ardent Technologies and into one of the spaces reserved for visitors. Soon after, Phillips and Jones stood in reception, waiting patiently to be seen, separately, by the CEO, Lesley Bailey, and the managing director, David Nelson. Phillips would chat with Bailey, Jones with Nelson.

Nelson was first to arrive, striding into reception, the sound of the metal segues fitted to the heels of his brown leather brogues causing his heavy footsteps to echo around the space. Phillips placed him in his early fifties, and he cut a foreboding figure at around six feet tall, with a broad frame that appeared bloated around the middle. His attire seemed more country gent than inner-city construction boss, with his tweed jacket over a mustard waistcoat and cream chinos.

'Which one am I supposed to be seeing?' he asked the receptionist in a loud voice.

She replied and pointed in Jones's direction.

Nelson marched towards him, arm outstretched. 'David Nelson, managing director.'

Jones shook his hand firmly.

'Let's get this over with, shall we? Follow me,' said Nelson, sounding like a school master as he turned on his heels and headed in the direction of one of the conference rooms that annexed the reception area.

Jones glanced at Phillips with raised eyebrows before setting off after him.

It was another five minutes before Lesley Bailey arrived. Standing at around five-feet-six, she carried a strong air of masculinity, with her short blonde hair and no-nonsense expression. She walked briskly into the reception area and headed straight for Phillips. Stopping just a few feet away, she stood with her hands behind her back. 'You must be the inspector,' she said dispassionately.

'DCI Phillips.'

'You'd better come to my office.'

A few minutes later, Bailey led the way into her large office, which could best be described as efficiently decorated; it had everything needed for the job, and nothing more.

Taking a seat behind her desk, she offered the chair opposite to Phillips. 'How can I help you?'

'Well, I'm sure you're aware that Matthew Rice was murdered the day before yesterday—'

'Yes. I am. terrible business,' Bailey cut in.

'But I also wanted to make you aware that, last night, Cherie Howard was the victim of a suspected hit and run attack.'

'I know that too.'

'Oh?' said Phillips. 'How so?'

'Her husband, John, called me last night from the hospital,' said Bailey, very matter of factly.

'That must have come as a huge shock, especially given what happened to Matthew just a few hours earlier.'

'Yes, it was.'

Phillips scrutinised Bailey's face, searching for any signs of emotion or empathy, but found nothing. 'We have reason to believe the driver of the car was deliberately trying to run her down.'

Bailey recoiled. 'Why would they want to do that?'

'I was hoping you might be able to shed some light on that for me.'

Bailey scoffed. 'Me? How would I know?'

'Well, it seems something of a coincidence that two partners in the same firm would be attacked within two days, leaving one dead and the other fighting for her life. My first instincts would be to suggest the attacks were in some way connected to Ardent.'

Bailey appeared incredulous. '*This company* has nothing to do with what happened to them.'

'How can you be so sure?'

'Well, why would it? We make industrial foam, for God's sake, and as good as it is, it's hardly worth killing for.'

Phillips nodded. 'When I spoke to Cherie yesterday, she mentioned that's what you do here. Can you tell me a little bit more about the business?'

'What do you want to know?'

'Well, when was Ardent founded, who makes the decisions, that sort of thing.'

Bailey, barely able to hide her impatience, exhaled heavily through her nose. 'I bought Ardent in 2008 from the previous owner, Michael Marshall, when he retired. At that point he was CEO, and I was the MD. It was a medium-sized operation making prefabricated concrete slabs for commercial buildings, with a turnover of around a million pounds a year. I had bigger ideas, and set about bringing the business into the new millennium, switching from concrete to foam, using a technology we developed in-house. These days we turnover around a hundred million a year.'

'Very impressive.'

'I have a board of four directors—' Bailey caught herself. 'Well, three, now Matthew's gone – which consists of me, David and Cherie. We each have shares in the business. That said, as the majority shareholder, I have final say in all areas.'

'So, you're the ultimate boss?'

'Correct.'

Phillips nodded. 'I know you said that it's unlikely Ardent was the reason for them being targeted, but is there anything that has happened here in the past that could explain why two of your directors were attacked?'

Bailey cleared her throat and said nothing for a long moment. 'I'm sure it's not relevant, but there may be something.'

'Really? What?'

Bailey pulled open one of the drawers in her desk and rummaged around for a moment before pulling out a pile of envelopes stuffed with letters. She placed them on the desk between them. 'We've been getting threatening letters for almost a year now. Well, when I say *we*, I mean *me*, specifically.'

Phillips's pulse quickened. 'May I?'

'Of course, but I must warn you, the handwriting and spelling is atrocious.'

Phillips pulled on a pair of latex gloves and removed one of the letters from its envelope, then began reading aloud. 'Bailey U bitch! You'll pay! Yor gonna die bitch!'

'They all pretty much say the same thing,' said Bailey.

Phillips cast her eyes over the pile of envelopes. 'There must be twenty letters here.'

'Yes. I get about two a month.'

'Any ideas who might have sent them?'

Bailey shrugged. 'A disgruntled employee? Environmentalists who don't like what we do, maybe? They've never made themselves known, so I have no idea.'

'I thought your foam was eco-friendly. Why would the environmentalists have issues with you?'

'It's all relative, Chief Inspector. The foam does produce less CO_2 than concrete when it's made, but the eco-warriors want everything to be carbon neutral, which is impossible. Because Ardent's foam is in a large proportion of the UK's new-builds, they claim we're still a major player in global warming.'

'Have you reported the letters to the police?'

'Yes. They sent a couple of officers out late last year, but nothing came of it. They said we should keep an eye on things, that if the messages escalated or became more frequent, we should get back in touch. They also suggested we upgrade our security system, which we did. We're now linked directly to the police.' Bailey checked her watch impatiently. 'Look, is this going to take much longer? With Matthew gone and Cherie in hospital, I have a lot on my plate.'

Phillips offered a thin smile. 'I understand. Just a couple more questions.'

Bailey's frustration was palpable.

'You mentioned it could be a disgruntled employee. Does anyone spring to mind?'

'We have a large workforce with over five hundred members of staff, Inspector. Sometimes people need to be moved on. It could be any one of them.'

Phillips nodded, but said nothing for a moment. 'Right. Well, as you're so busy, I'll let you get back to it.'

'Thank you.'

'Can I keep these for the time being?' Phillips asked, pointing to the letters.

'Be my guest. They're of no use to me.'

Phillips pulled out a plastic evidence bag from the inside pocket of her suit jacket, and placed them inside, before sealing it. 'Thank you. I can see myself out.'

When she returned to the car a few minutes later, she found Jones leaning against the passenger side of the bonnet, soaking up the sun.

'How was Bailey?' he asked.

'Well, let me put it this way: she certainly wasn't winning any awards for sympathy when it came to Rice and Howard. Reminded me a lot of our beloved Chief Constable, actually.'

'Fox? What? You think Bailey's a sociopath too?'

'She certainly has a lot of the traits. Lack of empathy, self-centred, driven, etc.'

Jones nodded. 'Sounds a lot like Nelson, actually.'

Phillips raised her eyebrows. 'Really?'

'Yeah. He seemed more interested in getting back to work than trying to find out who attacked his partners. To be honest, Guv, he was a bit of a knob.'

'God, that does sound like Bailey. But she did at least give me these.' Phillips held up the evidence bag so he could see it. 'Threatening letters from someone with the handwriting of a madman, and a habit of telling her she's a bitch. Having spent a bit of time with her, I can see why someone could have that opinion of her.' She smiled wryly.

'Could the author of those be our killer?' asked Jones.

'I dunno, but it's a start, at least. I'll send them over to forensics and see if they found anything similar at Rice's house, or anything that might be linked. We'll also need to speak to John Howard – find out if Cherie received any. In the meantime, let's get back to base and see what Bov and Entwistle have come up with.'

BACK AT ASHTON HOUSE, the core team took seats around the large table in the MCU conference room.

Entwistle wasted no time. 'I thought you'd want to know, Guv. They've found the car used in the Howard hit and run. It was left abandoned and burnt out in Salford.'

Phillips exhaled loudly. 'Naturally.'

'Do you want me to organise forensics to take a look at it, see if we can trace the driver?'

'Yeah, you'd better. For all the good it'll do, though. No doubt the fire will have destroyed everything.'

'I'll call Evans after this meeting.'

Phillips nodded and turned to Bovalino. 'So, what did you find out about Rice and Howard?'

'Well, Guv, they're both quite unremarkable, I'm afraid. I'll start with Rice. As we know, he was forty-seven, single, and lived alone in his home in Lymm at the three-bed cottage where we found his body. He had a mortgage on the property with just under two hundred grand left to pay off. He drove a silver five-series BMW that was leased on his behalf by Ardent, where he was the chief financial officer. He had minimal credit card debts, and various savings accounts totalling twenty-five grand. He's never been married and has no children, and not so much as a parking ticket on his record.'

'Squeaky clean, then?' said Jones.

Bov nodded.

'So why would someone want to kill our Mr Squeaky Clean?' asked Phillips.

The room fell silent for a moment as each of them pondered the question before the big Italian continued. 'As for Cherie Howard, she's forty-five, married to John Howard for seventeen years. Like Rice, no children, and she and John own a three-bed apartment in Handforth with a mortgage of three hundred grand. As the marketing director for Ardent, she also has a five-series BMW leased through the company. Again, she has some debts and a bit of savings, neither of which tops five grand.'

Phillips tapped her pen on her teeth for a moment. 'So, nothing of any note to explain why someone would deliberately try to mow her down in the street.'

'Nothing.'

'This case is downright odd,' Phillips said.

'I did find something that caught my eye, Guv,' offered Entwistle.

Phillips raised an eyebrow. 'Oh?'

'Yeah. Looking into Ardent's history and financials, it's doing very well financially with an annual turnover of almost a hundred million a year—'

'Lesley Bailey mentioned that this morning,' Phillips cut in.

'Did she also mention the fact they're about to be listed on the stock market for half a billion pounds?'

Phillips sat forward. 'No, she bloody didn't.'

Jones whistled sharply. 'That's a lot of money.'

'More than enough to kill for,' added Phillips.

Entwistle continued. 'Ardent is quite the talk of the business community in Manchester at the moment, and considered ones-to-watch in the construction industry. Bailey herself has featured in a number of trade articles, talking about taking over a stagnant business in 2008 and expanding at a rapid rate since then.'

'So why not mention it in our meeting this morning?'

'Maybe she didn't want you to know?' Entwistle said.

Jones folded his arms across his chest. 'So, how much does she stand to make if they go public?'

Entwistle shrugged. 'I'm not a hundred percent sure just yet, but in one of the articles she talks about being the majority shareholder, so on a half a billion listing, hundreds of millions, I'm guessing.'

Phillips nodded slowly. 'That kind of money really would be motive to kill, wouldn't it?'

'Big time,' said Bovalino, nodding.

'Keep digging, see what you can find on share structures and how much of the half-billion each of the directors is in line for.'

'Sure thing, Guv' said Entwistle.

At that moment, Phillips's phone began to vibrate in her pocket. Fishing it out, she answered it. 'DCI Phillips.' She listened intently for a moment. 'Oh God, really? I see...ok... right, well, thanks for letting me know.'

Jones, Bov and Entwistle looked at her with wide, expectant eyes as she placed the phone down slowly on the table on front of her.

'Everything all right, Guv?' asked Jones.

'That was the hospital. Cherie Howard died of her injuries an hour ago.'

8

The next day, Phillips pulled her car into one of the available spaces on the fifth floor of the multi-storey car park situated adjacent to the Manchester Royal Infirmary. It was just after 9 a.m. and the hospital would soon come to life as outpatients and visitors began descending on the city-centre hospital in their droves. Phillips's reason for visiting this morning was to attend the post mortem of Matthew Rice, scheduled for 9.30 a.m. in the mortuary, overseen by chief pathologist, Dr Tanvi Chakrabortty. Phillips had worked with Tan on many cases together over the last five years, and they shared a mutual respect for each other, as well as a strong friendship.

In preparation for the next couple of hours, Phillips followed her usual ritual as she reset her dark ponytail and cleaned her glasses before closing her eyes and taking a few deep breaths, exhaling loudly as she released them. Feeling psyched and as prepared as she could be for watching a human body being dissected, she exited the car.

The walk from the car park to the main building took only five minutes, and she soon found herself striding along the basement corridor towards the mortuary. A few minutes later, after being buzzed through the security door, she stepped inside and waited to be collected.

Chakrabortty was known for her efficiency, and it wasn't long before she appeared, dressed in immaculately pressed green surgical scrubs, her long, dark-skinned legs running into pristine white clogs. 'Morning, Jane.'

'Morning, Tan. How are you today?'

'Busy. I've got three more PMs after yours, and I'm giving a lecture at the university this evening, so we'd better get cracking.'

'Fine by me,' said Phillips.

Chakrabortty handed her a pack containing a plastic apron, gloves and a surgical mask. 'You can leave your coat in my office, if you want.'

Phillips nodded, and followed as the doctor turned on her heels and made her away along the corridor.

Five minutes later, they stood on either side of a mortuary table that supported Matthew Rice's body, which was covered from feet to collar bone by a blue sheet. His face and shoulders were almost grey in colour. As ever, the room was cloaked with the pervasive odour of disinfectant and embalming fluid, every surface gleaming and spotlessly clean.

Chakrabortty grabbed the sheet covering Rice in her gloved hands, then locked eyes with Phillips. 'Are you ready for this?'

'As I'll ever be.'

Chakrabortty pulled back the sheet and folded it around Rice's middle, revealing a cluster of large knife wounds to the chest and abdomen. 'Looks like the killer was aiming for the heart, doesn't it?'

Phillips gazed at the multitude of dark, open wounds,

which strangely resembled a group of slugs stuck to the mottled skin. 'What a mess,' she said.

'Let's find out what caused these, shall we?' said Chakrabortty, then grabbed a scalpel without waiting for an answer.

Over the next ninety minutes, Chakrabortty methodically worked her way through the post mortem with Phillips's gaze locked on her every move as she carried out her duties with grace and deference for the person Matthew Rice once was. By the time the process was all but complete, they were in no doubt a knife wound, which had partially severed the aortic valve, had delivered the killing blow.

'How long would he have taken to bleed out?' asked Phillips.

'About ten minutes, I'd say.'

'Would he have been conscious?'

'Most likely, for about five minutes at a guess,' Chakrabortty said, 'but once his blood pressure dropped due to the massive blood loss, he would have passed out. Probably a few minutes before death.'

Phillips nodded. 'So, in summary, we're saying he was stabbed ten times, three times to the stomach and seven to the chest, with a curved or tapered blade of some kind.'

'Yes. All the evidence points to that.'

Phillips picked up her notepad and pen from the table behind her. 'Just to make sure I brief the guys correctly when I get back, we know it was a curved or tapered blade because the wounds on the surface of the skin are close to an inch in diameter, but the ends of the cavities caused by the blade within the body are much thinner.'

'That's correct.'

'And it was about six inches long?'

'Yes.'

Phillips scribbled in her pad.

'It'll all be in my report.'

Phillips stared down at Rice's body for a moment. 'The poor guy didn't stand a chance, did he?'

'No. And even though he did try to defend himself, the fact there are only a few lacerations to his wrists, hands and fingers suggests he was incapacitated quite quickly and stopped fighting back.'

'Ok. That all makes sense. So, how long before I can have the full report?'

'One of the team will write it up this afternoon, so once I've approved it, I can email it over to you tomorrow morning.'

'Great. Thanks, Tan.'

'My pleasure.' Chakrabortty began to pull off her surgical cloves as she wandered over to the yellow pedal bin next to the sink and dropped them in.

Phillips followed suit, removing her apron, gloves and mask before discarding them in the same bin. 'I'd better let you get on. Sounds like you've got a busy day ahead.'

Chakrabortty let out an ironic chuckle. 'Same as every day, Jane. This is a dangerous city.'

Phillips headed for the door and yanked it open. Stopping in her tracks, she turned back. 'One more thing, Tan. When is Cherie Howard's PM scheduled for?'

Chakrabortty's brow furrowed for a long moment as she appeared deep in thought. 'The hit and run that came in last night?'

'That's the one.'

'I think it's scheduled for early next week. Why do you ask?'

Phillips nodded in the direction of Rice's body. 'Because she and Rice worked together and were attacked within two days of each other.'

Chakrabortty's eyes widened. 'Wow, that's some coincidence.'

'Yeah. It is, *isn't it?*' said Phillips, then left the room.

———

A COUPLE OF HOURS LATER, Phillips returned to her office from the Ashton House canteen, a sandwich in one hand and a cup of coffee in the other.

Entwistle followed her inside. 'Sorry to interrupt your lunch, Guv.'

Phillips chuckled as she placed her quarry on her desk before dropping down into her leather chair. 'It's only a cheese sandwich, Whistler.'

'I've been digging into Ardent and, in particular, the share structure of the founding partners.'

'Oh yeah?' said Phillips taking a bite.

'The stock is divided in such a way that Bailey has a fifty-one percent stake in the business. Nelson has a nineteen percent stake, and Rice and Howard both had fifteen, but the shares are – or were, in *their* case – incentive-based against a future IPO, and only redeemable if the directors were actively part of the company at the time of any share offering.'

Phillips swallowed and took a slug of coffee. 'Which means exactly *what*, in English?'

'Well, that basically, because the IPO hasn't happened yet and Rice and Howard are both dead, their shares are not transferable to their heirs. Instead, their combined thirty percent stake in the company returns to the remaining shareholders, Bailey and Nelson.'

Phillips sat forwards. 'Which means those two stand to make *a lot more* money through the IPO compared to when Rice and Howard were both still alive.'

'Yeah. Around seventy million more each, in fact.'

'Which makes a great motive for murder.'

Entwistle produced a wide grin. 'Money is always a great motivator for murder, Guv, no matter how much is at stake.'

Phillips took a moment to process the information before finally speaking. 'Do Jones and Bov know about this yet?'

'Not yet. I wanted to speak to you first.'

'Well, let's get them in here and bring them up to speed, shall we?'

'I'll go get 'em, Guv,' said Entwistle, moving towards the door.

'Excellent work, Whistler,' said Phillips after him.

Entwistle turned and flashed a smile, then headed out into the office to fetch Jones and Bovalino.

9

Having tasked Entwistle with researching what type of knife could have been used in the attack on Rice, Phillips once again enlisted Jones's help as they headed to Ardent for the third time in four days. As they drove through another period of silence, Phillips checked her phone, hoping in vain to find a WhatsApp message from Adam. She hadn't heard from him since Wednesday night, and hoped he hadn't gone cold on her because of her lack of response the other night. She hadn't meant to ignore his message for as long as she had. It was just that Cherie Howard's hit and run attack had needed her full attention. Surely, as an A&E doctor, he of all people understood the pressured nature of her job and how quickly situations could escalate? He'd virtually said as much when they'd first met at the dinner party.

'You all right, Guv?' asked Jones, glancing to his left.

Phillips nodded, then placed the phone back in her pocket. 'Yeah, fine.'

'You seem a little distracted today.'

'Do I?'

'Yeah. Bloke trouble, is it?' asked Jones.

'I wouldn't call it trouble. In fact, I wouldn't call it anything at the moment. Maybe that's the problem,' she sighed.

'Anything I can help with?'

'Unless you can stop people killing each other outside of the nine-to-five so I can have a life, probably not.'

'Ah, a *real* life.' Jones flashed a crooked smile and shook his head. 'The impossible dream for a murder detective.'

Phillips smiled softly. Jones knew better than most how hard it was to work in Major Crimes and maintain a happy, healthy relationship outside of work.

She decided it was time to change the subject. 'So, here's what I'm thinking when we get to Ardent.' She had Jones's full attention now. 'Let's see them one at a time. That way, we can compare notes, and it'll give us a better chance of spotting any obvious discrepancies in their stories as to where they were when Rice and Howard were attacked.'

'Sounds like a plan, boss.'

'Good. That's settled then,' replied Phillips, as she turned her gaze to the world passing by her window.

Half an hour later, when Phillips and Jones took seats in Bailey's office, the CEO once again appeared cold and impatient, staring at them both from behind her desk, arms folded tightly across her chest. 'Why do you want to know where I was when Matthew and Cherie were killed? Am I suspect?'

'It simply helps us eliminate you from our enquiries,' said Phillips.

Bailey took a moment to answer. 'Well, if you must know, I was working from home the morning Matthew died, and having dinner at home the night Cherie was killed.'

'Can anyone verify that for each of those occasions?'

'My husband, Fred. He's retired now, so was at home with

me on the Tuesday morning and he cooked dinner for me on Wednesday evening.'

'Anyone else?'

'Why? Is he not good enough?' Bailey spat back.

Phillips forced a thin smile. 'The more information we have from different sources, the more help it is to our enquires.'

'Well, there was no one else. Just Fred.'

Jones made a note in his pad.

'Can you explain why you didn't mention the fact your business is about to be floated on the stock market?'

Bailey recoiled slightly. 'I don't see how that's any of your business, actually.'

Phillips continued. 'As we understand it, you and your partners stand to make hundreds of millions from the IPO.'

'So?'

'So, with two of the partners dead, I'm guessing you and Mr Nelson will make even more money.'

Bailey's eyes narrowed. 'Are you suggesting I *wanted* Matthew and Cherie to die?'

'Did you?' Phillips shot back.

'Don't be absurd. I'm a businesswoman, not a bloody murderer.'

Phillips said nothing for a long moment.

Bailey opened her desk drawer, pulled out a card and threw it across the table towards Phillips. 'That's Fred's golf club. You'll find him there most days at lunch time. He can vouch for me. And if there's nothing else, I really must be getting on.'

Phillips picked up the card and studied it for a moment, before signalling to Jones it was time to leave.

Next, they headed straight across the hall to the office of Ardent's managing director, David Nelson. As had been the case on their previous visit, Nelson was dressed like a country gent in spite of the warm weather. As his assistant showed them into his office, he paced the floor behind his desk, barking into his mobile phone. Silently acknowledging them for a brief moment, he indicated they should sit down in the chairs placed opposite his desk while he continued his conversation. They followed his suggestion before sitting in silence for the next few minutes as he continued to pace and growl.

Finally, with the recipient on the other end of the phone suitably chastised for whatever offence they had committed, he ended the call and turned his attention to Phillips and Jones. 'Back so soon?' His tone was sarcastic.

Phillips produced a thin smile. 'We're investigating the double homicide of two of your close colleagues, Mr Nelson. I thought you'd be glad we're taking it seriously.'

Nelson dropped into his high-backed leather seat. 'Of course I'm pleased about that, but as neither Matthew or Cherie were killed at the factory, I can't understand why you keep showing up here day after day.'

Phillips's patience was wearing thin, so she got straight to the point. 'Can you tell us where you were when Matthew Rice was murdered?'

Nelson's eyes narrowed as he reclined in his chair and crossed his arms across his chest. 'Why? Do you think *I* killed him?'

Phillips continued with her no-nonsense approach. 'Did you?'

'Don't be absurd,' Nelson scoffed. 'Why would I want to murder Matthew?'

'The IPO.'

'And what has that got to do with anything?'

'Well, with Matthew out of the way, his shares go back into the business, which means more money for *you* when

Ardent goes public, doesn't it? And by all accounts, the public offering stands to raise half a billion pounds.'

A snarl formed on Nelson lips as he sat forward and locked eyes with Phillips. 'My, my, you have done your research, haven't you? When Matthew was killed, I was at home all day on annual leave.'

'Which is where?'

'I have a farmhouse with a bit of land near Blackden Heath.'

'That's Macclesfield Way, isn't it?' said Jones.

'That's correct.'

'And can anyone vouch for you that day?' Phillips asked.

'I doubt it. I live alone and prefer my own company. I have enough inane conversations at work every day without having them on my day off as well.'

Phillips continued. 'So, what were you doing when you were at home?'

'Shooting,' replied Nelson flatly.

The answer caught Phillips somewhat off-guard, and she felt herself recoil momentarily. 'Shooting? Shooting what, exactly?'

'Muntjac deer. My neighbour's a farmer and I was culling some of the herd as a favour to him. Well, I say it's a favour; more of a quid pro quo, actually. He's given me the shooting rights to his land in return for some herd management.'

'That sounds like a big job for a busy man like you,' Phillips prodded.

'Not really. He only needs me to kill about three or four animals a year, and I enjoy it. Plus, I love venison, so it works out just fine. Plenty of juicy steaks for both our freezers,' he said gleefully.

'And will your neighbour vouch for you?'

'He has a large farm and I didn't see him, so unless he heard the shots, he's probably not much use.'

Phillips nodded. 'And what about the night Cherie was attacked? Were you at home then too?'

'Yes,' he replied emphatically. 'Eating one of those steaks, as it happens, medium-rare, with a nice bottle of Chateauneuf-du-Pape. I had a lovely evening, if you must know.'

'Alone?'

'Yes, Inspector. *Alone*. As I said, I like my own company.' Nelson fixed Phillips with a steely gaze. 'And with that in mind, it feels to me like I've answered all your questions, so if there's nothing else, I'd like to get back to work.'

Phillips held his gaze and her thin smile returned. 'Absolutely,' she said, standing.

Jones slipped his notepad into his pocket and stood.

Nelson, remaining seated, moved his gaze to his laptop screen. 'You'll forgive me if I don't see you out,' he said absentmindedly.

Phillips could feel her blood boiling. She couldn't abide arrogance or rudeness, both traits Nelson had in spades. She was tempted to hit back with a sharp reply, but felt it better to keep her powder dry for the moment. Instead, she turned in silence and headed for the door with Jones in tow.

Striding side by side across the car park a few minutes later, Phillips was careful to speak in a low voice. It was another hot day and, from her own bitter experience, she was aware that open windows allowed words to carry a long way. 'For once I think you were wrong, Jonesy,' she said under her breath. 'He's not a *bit* of a knob...*he's a massive knob!*'

Jones burst out laughing as they approached the car, and deactivated the central locking. 'Hard to like, isn't he, Guv?'

Phillips yanked open the passenger door and stood for a moment. 'I truly hope he's bloody guilty so I can wipe that smug fucking grin off his face.'

Jones chortled.

'"A juicy venison steak and a bottle of Chateauneuf-du-Pape",' Phillips mimicked Nelson as she dropped into the passenger seat. 'What a pretentious wanker.'

Jones jumped in behind the wheel and closed his door.

'They say like attracts like,' said Phillips. 'Well, Lesley Bailey and David Nelson are a perfect match. Arrogant, insensitive, and totally self-serving.'

'They remind me of Fox and Brown,' said Jones, referring to two of their former bosses who, for a long period of time, had made life in MCU very difficult for the team to navigate. The latter was now known as Chief Constable Fox of the Greater Manchester Police, and widely regarded as functioning sociopath, whereas Brown was a superintendent working for West Yorkshire Police, stationed just across the Pennines in the city of Leeds.

'There's definitely something not right with this picture,' ventured Phillips. 'Those two are hiding something. I'm sure of it.'

'But what, Guv? Do you really think either of them could be the killer?'

Phillips blew her lips. 'I don't know, but I'm convinced they're connected to the murders in some way – or hiding information that is. I can feel it in my bones. And I'll tell you this now: I'm not going to stop until I find whatever it is, and shove it right up Nelson's arrogant arse.'

10

E arly Monday morning, Phillips joined the rest of the core team for an update in a huddle at their desks. Entwistle was keen to share the results of the research he'd been doing into the different types of blades that could have been used in the Matthew Rice murder. Having listened intently for fifteen minutes as he had worked his way through a multitude of options, Phillips was beginning to feel a little downhearted. It seemed that any number of different knives – each available in a host of high-street stores – could have been the murder weapon. Narrowing them down to the exact one could take weeks of painstaking research and testing by the forensic team. In this investigation – as in every murder she'd worked on since joining MCU – time was not something they had in abundance. Quite the opposite, in fact.

Just as she was losing all hope of getting a quick result, Entwistle brought up yet another option on his laptop screen. 'This blade is classed as a boning knife, and commonly used by butchers and hunters to separate the meat from the bone of an animal. According to the product information on this one, it has "a long, thin, flexible blade with a sharp tip to make piercing meat easier and safer. The blade is designed to cut through ligaments and connective tissue to remove raw meat from the bone".'

Phillips sat to attention. 'Say that again.'

'Which bit, Guv?'

'The bit that describes the blade.'

Entwistle read aloud from the screen once more. '"It has a long, thin, flexible blade with a sharp tip to make piercing meat easier and safer. The blade is designed to cut through ligaments and connective tissue to remove raw meat from the bone."'

Phillips swivelled in her chair to face Jones. 'David Nelson said he was shooting deer the day Rice was attacked, right?'

'Yeah, that's right.'

'And that he and the farmer split the animals between them, for venison steaks.'

Jones nodded.

'So, which of them is the butcher?' mused Phillips.

'Well, if it's Nelson, it would put him in the frame for Rice's murder,' Bovalino chimed in.

'Yeah, but how do we prove it?' asked Jones.

Phillips drummed her fingers on the desk absentmindedly. 'At the moment, I don't think we can. We'd need to find the knife in his possession, and we can't do that without a search warrant. There's not a magistrate in Manchester who would sign off on that with the little that we have on him so far.'

The team fell silent as each of them considered the possible next steps.

Phillips was the first to speak a minute or so later. 'But maybe there's another way to get a warrant to search his house.'

Each of the team looked at her with wide, expectant eyes.

She continued. 'It's common knowledge that Bailey and Nelson stand to make a lot more money from the IPO now Rice and Howard are dead, right?'

Each of the team nodded.

'Which goes to motive for murder. So, I think it's about time we checked their financials.'

'For what, Guv?' asked Entwistle. 'We're not allowed to go on a fishing expedition.'

'And we won't be. For all intents and purposes, we'll be looking for any financial irregularities associated with either of them. Large debts, gambling problems, failed investments, that type of thing.'

Entwistle's brow furrowed. 'But how much debt can either of them really be in? They both stand to make millions from the IPO as it is, without needing to kill Rice and Howard.'

'I know that, but within the confines of the law, that doesn't matter to us.'

'So, what are we *really* looking for?' asked Jones.

Phillips shrugged her shoulders. 'Well, *if* in the process of our searches we find any purchases related to butchery or knives, that would certainly help us get a warrant.'

Jones produced a wide grin. 'Smart move, Guv.'

'Pragmatic,' replied Phillips with a wink.

'I'll take Nelson, if you want,' said Bovalino.

'And I'll take Bailey,' offered Entwistle.

'Great,' said Phillips. 'Let's see if our remaining partners are as innocent in all this as they claim to be.'

Each of the men nodded.

'Right, I'd better go and brief the chief super, let him know what we've got so far, and give him a heads-up on the financials.' With that, Phillips left the office and headed up to see Carter.

She took the stairs from MCU's third-floor offices. A few

minutes later, as she reached the fifth-floor landing, her phone pinged. Fishing her phone from her pocket, her pulse quickened as she scanned the message on the home screen.

Hi Jane. Fancy grabbing some food in the next few weeks? I'm still on nights at the mo but could do lunch next week. Let me know if you fancy it? A xxx

Adam hadn't gone cold on her after all. Phillips found herself grinning like a Cheshire Cat, butterflies turning in her stomach as she stood alone in the silence of the landing. For a moment she allowed her mind to wander, imagining herself and Adam out on a proper date, away from work, away from the foul stench of murder, crime statistics and police politics. It seemed like heaven to her, but the moment was short-lived as the door connecting the stairs to the offices opened and a couple of plain-clothes officers she recognised from the Fraud Squad walked through.

'Ma'am,' they said in unison as they passed her.

She squirrelled away her phone and replied with a nod, then moved through to the main corridor of the fifth floor, where she headed towards the office of her boss, Chief Superintendent Harry Carter.

As with every visit to see Carter, she was met by his diminutive executive assistant, Diana Cook, sharply dressed as ever, her cream blouse and charcoal pencil skirt matching her immaculately maintained dark brown bob. 'Morning, Jane. How are you today?' she said with her customary warm smile.

An image of Adam's sparkling blue eyes flashed across her mind, and she found herself returning Cook's smile. 'I'm good thanks, Di. *Very* good, in fact.'

'Very good? The boss will be pleased.'

'Is he free for a catch-up?'

Cook nodded. 'Yeah, he's got a call in twenty minutes, but he's all yours 'til then. Go straight in.'

Phillips knocked once before opening the door to the adjoining office and stepping inside.

Chief Superintendent Carter, who was sitting reading a document behind his desk, looked up as she entered. 'Jane. I wasn't expecting you. Have I forgotten a meeting?'

'No, sir. I took a chance that you might be free,' she said as she crossed the room and dropped into the chair opposite. 'I wanted to give you an update on the Matthew Rice and Cherie Howard murders.'

Carter smiled as he removed his reading glasses and placed the file on his desk. 'What have you got for me?' His soft Newcastle accent perfectly matched his gentle face, framed by a shock of dark wavy hair, greying slightly at the temples.

Over the next ten minutes, she brought Carter up to speed on Bailey's and Nelson's less than sympathetic reactions to their partners' deaths, the impending Ardent IPO, and the company share structure, as well as the fact that, since Rice and Howard's deaths, the values of the remaining directors' shares had increased exponentially.

'I agree money can often provide a clear motive for murder,' said Carter when she was finished, 'but you know better than anyone, Jane, that we're going to need a lot more than an increase in share value to get the CPS to sanction any kind of case against either Nelson or Bailey.'

'Yes, sir, and that's why, out of the two, Nelson looks the most likely to give us that at the moment.'

'What makes you say that?'

'Well, he has no alibi for either murder,' said Phillips. 'He claims he was home alone, shooting deer on his neighbour's land.'

'Can the neighbour verify that?'

'He seems to think not.'

Carter curled his bottom lip.

Phillips continued. 'Chakrabortty believes the weapon used to kill Rice was a curved or tapered blade, about six inches long. Entwistle has been researching what types of knives would be a match for those dimensions, and we believe it could be a boning knife.'

'Like a butcher would use?'

'Yes, sir, and a *hunter*. Nelson told us he eats the deer after he shoots them, and to do that, the animals need to be butchered first. As part of the financial search, the guys are looking for any purchases that might be connected to knives or butchery.'

Carter frowned. 'A fishing trip?'

'I prefer to call it a specified search within the confines of the law, sir.'

'Be very careful, Jane. You're walking a very fine line here.'

Phillips nodded. 'I know, and we will be. But like you say, we need more than just the potential financial gain to get a warrant.'

Carter said nothing for a moment and appeared deep in thought. 'Well, let's hope the guys come through,' he said eventually, 'because at the minute, without the knife, it would seem we can't touch him.'

Much to her frustration, she knew he was right, but all her senses were telling her that Nelson was as dodgy as hell. Whether he was capable of murder, only time would tell, but right now she was sure of one thing: the more they dug into him and his cohort Bailey, the more shit they were going to find.

Just then, Carter's phone rang. Glancing at the digital display, he let out a loud sigh and his shoulders sagged. 'My next call: a two-hour review of our half-year-one budget.'

'Lucky you, sir,' said Phillips with a smirk as she got up from the chair. 'I'll leave you to it.'

He gave her a silent thumbs-up as he picked up the phone. 'This is Carter.'

Soon after, Phillips found herself back on the stairs heading down to the MCU offices on the third floor. Suddenly remembering the message from Adam, she stopped, pulled out her phone and typed her reply.

Hi Adam. Lunch would be lovely. Is there a time we can talk on the phone to arrange? Jx

After pressing send, she watched as the message status changed to delivered, smiled to herself, and carried on down the stairs with a spring in her step.

11

The following day, Phillips spent the morning studying the threatening letters. While the forensic team analysed the originals, Phillips had been issued with photographic copies. With the photos spread out across her desk in neat rows, she'd been poring over every detail of them for the last few hours, searching for any clues that might help identify the person behind them. Frustratingly, she'd found nothing of note so far. The handwriting was some of the worst she'd ever witnessed – an angular, scrawling style that oddly resembled some of the Cantonese lettering that had surrounded her as a child, growing up in Hong Kong. The spelling too was awful; so bad, in fact, she wondered if it had been written that way intentionally, a ploy to throw off the reader, making them think the author was uneducated when, perhaps, the opposite was true? Either way, the sentiment running through each of the letters was the same: *Bailey was a bitch and she deserved to die.*

A knock at the door drew her gaze to Bovalino, his huge frame almost filling the doorway. 'I've think we've caught a fish, Guv.'

Phillips raised an eyebrow. 'The financials?'

Bov nodded and moved towards her, holding a logoed document in his outstretched hand.

Taking it from him, she scanned down the page.

'It's copy of David Nelson's credit card statement from last month. Look at the highlighted transaction.'

Phillips's eyes locked on the yellowed-out transaction description. 'Macclesfield Hunting, Game and Fishing – £96.47' she read aloud.

Bov continued. 'It caught my eye yesterday afternoon, so I called the store and asked what it was for. It took the guy a couple of hours to come back to me, but he eventually emailed me a copy of the sales invoice.' He handed her another document.

Phillips's eyes landed on the product description and her pulse quickened as she read aloud. '"One Hiscok Classic Boning Knife – 6-inch carbon steel blade with pakkawood handle, £96.47". Jesus, Bov. That sounds like an exact match.'

'It pretty much is. I called Chakrabortty's assistant over at pathology this morning and sent him the product dimensions. He checked it against the PM report for Rice and confirmed there's a high chance that type of blade was used in the attack.'

'This is brilliant work, Bov, brilliant. And more than enough for a warrant to search Nelson's home.'

'Do you want me to speak to the Magistrates' Court and get one sorted?'

Phillips slapped the sheet of paper with the back of her hand. 'Too bloody right I do.'

'I'll get right onto it,' said Bov as he headed back to his desk.

Phillips followed him out to the main office, where she addressed the core team. 'Right, guys. Bov's come up trumps with a potential match for the murder weapon, purchased recently by David Nelson.'

'You want me to sort out the warrant, Guv?' Entwistle asked.

'Already on it, Whistler,' said Bovalino, his chest puffed up with pride.

Phillips turned her attention to Entwistle. 'As Nelson's a hunter, we can assume he owns at least one firearm, so we'll need support from the TFU. Can you sort that?'

He picked up his desk phone. 'I'll call them now.'

'Great!' Phillips felt a spike of adrenaline rush through her body as she headed back to her office with renewed energy. Stopping at the door, she turned back to look at Jones and Bovalino. 'Don't forget to set your alarms, guys. We'll be going in at dawn.'

IT HAD BEEN another long day in the office, but a very rewarding one. She was so proud of the team, and especially Bovalino. He really had come up trumps with Nelson's financial searches, and thanks to having a friend in the Magistrates' Court, he'd managed to expedite the search warrant with little fuss.

After arriving home, she had poured herself a large glass of ice-cold Pinot Grigio and settled down in front of the TV with Floss curled up in her lap. She couldn't help feeling satisfied with her own work, too. It had been her idea to check the financials, after all.

A little after 10.30 p.m., she headed upstairs to try and sleep, but despite the prospect of a 3 a.m. start, Phillips was still awake when her phone rang on the bedside table just before 11. Her heart sank. Calls at this time of night were never good news.

She reluctantly grabbed it from the nightstand, but her frustration was replaced by a rush of excitement as she realised it was Adam, his name flashing across her phone screen. 'Hello, stranger,' she said through a beaming smile.

'*Hi, Jane. Sorry to call so late. Did I wake you up?*'

'Not at all. I am in bed, but I can't sleep. My mind's racing around of a couple of cases I'm working on.'

'*I'm not officially on a break at the moment, so I can't speak for long, but I just wanted to say hi.*'

'Hi,' she replied coyly.

'*How you doing?*'

'Ok, work's crazy busy at the moment, but then what's new? How about you?'

'*The same. In one way I quite like the night shift because I see such a variety of patients, but it really messes with my body clock. I mean, I do my best to sleep during the day, but I must only be getting three or four hours max.*'

'Three or four hours? I don't know what you're complaining about,' she teased.

Adam chuckled. '*So how are you fixed for lunch on Saturday?*'

Phillips felt like a teenager again as butterflies danced in her stomach. 'Sounds great.'

'*Shall I come to you?*'

'Yeah. I can book us a table somewhere. What do you fancy?'

'*After eating my own body weight in vending machine sandwiches for a couple of weeks, I'll eat anything. So, surprise me.*'

Phillips loved his easy-going nature, which was a stark contrast to the high-intensity energy she was surrounded by in MCU. 'Well, this is Chorlton, so we're spoilt for choice. But there's one place I think you'll love. Shall we say 2 p.m.? Give you time to wake up?'

'*Sounds perfect.*'

Suddenly Phillips could hear raised voices at his end. 'Is everything ok?'

'Yeah, looks like we've got an urgent RTE on the way. I've gotta go. Sleep well.'

The phone went dead before she could reply, and for a long moment she stared at her reflection on the screen. The Cheshire Cat grin had returned, and she felt wonderful: her bed was suddenly more comfy than she remembered, her pillows plump and unctuous. Placing the phone back on the nightstand, she switched off the light and allowed herself to imagine Adam sitting opposite her on Saturday, his broad smile, strong jaw and sparkling eyes staring into hers.

'Night, night,' she whispered softly, before curling up and drifting off to sleep.

12

The time was approaching 5 a.m. when Bovalino steered the squad car off the main road and onto the rough track that led to Nelson's farmhouse. Phillips was next to him, with Jones in the rear. Entwistle was back at Ashton House, ready and waiting to organise any additional operational support as needed. Twenty yards in front of them was a BMW X5 that contained the Tactical Firearms Unit, made up of four officers led by Sergeant Roy Matthews. They passed through the open gates and pulled the car up in the middle of an L-shaped courtyard, next to an old blue Land Rover Discovery. The TFU had already parked behind it, purposely blocking it in. Protocols dictated that all officers attending a raid on potentially armed suspects should be fitted with a stab vest, and, considering the nature of their search, Phillips was grateful for the protection they offered, as well as the support of Matthews and his team.

A moment later, Phillips stepped out of the car, along with Jones and Bovalino. The early morning air felt fresh against her cheeks and the horizon glowed, hinting at another scorching day ahead.

Ninety minutes earlier, huddled around the large table in the MCU's conference room, they'd run through the operational plan. As usual, the TFU would go in first. There had been some debate as to which approach they would take: knock and demand access to search the property, or the shock and awe option of breaking down the door and taking Nelson by surprise. Given that he had no record and no known history of violence, the former would normally have been adopted, but based on the fact he owned at least one firearm and a knife capable of butchering large animals, Phillips had decided to take no chances. So, as the display on Phillips's wristwatch clicked from 04:59 to 05:00, she instructed Matthews and his team to go in using force.

The ancient farmhouse door offered little resistance to the hand-held metal battering ram, and a couple of seconds after the first contact, Matthews's team rushed inside shouting "Armed police!", their MP5 semi-automatic machine guns ready, the extended stocks pulled hard into their shoulders, ready to repel an attack. Phillips and the team followed them in and waited in the large, empty kitchen as they swept the house, continuous shouts of "Armed police!" following their movements.

A few minutes later, Matthews strode back into the kitchen flanked by his team. 'It's empty, Ma'am.'

Phillips frowned. 'Where the hell could he be?'

Suddenly, the sound of a shot being fired came from outside.

Matthews and his men instinctively took a knee and pivoted in the direction of the shot. Phillips and her team stood motionless. It was clear the TFU was prepared for such a situation, and Phillips watched on as each of them looked to Matthews for their orders.

'On me,' he said, getting to his feet before leading them back out into the courtyard.

Staying low, Phillips, Jones and Bov followed them out. Another shot rang out. This time it was clear it had come from the land on the opposite side of the house.

Matthews's men moved across the courtyard in formation, staying close to the building for protection. Holding their weapons firmly, they stopped when they reached the end of the farmhouse. Phillips couldn't hear what was being said, but could clearly see Matthews giving instructions to his team. A second later, one man got down on his belly and crawled along the ground, moving into a firing position perpendicular to the end of the farmhouse, but still out of sight. Another of the team peeled away about twenty yards back from his position, whilst Matthews and the fourth member remained with their backs to the farmhouse. Matthews signalled once again, and the man on the ground rolled out at speed into the open, so half his body was exposed.

Phillips held her breath.

The man on the ground released his left hand and stuck up a thumb. The officer behind him stepped out, took in the scene for a long moment, then dropped his weapon, saying something to the rest of the team. Matthews turned and signalled for Phillips to join them as he moved into the open.

By the time Phillips, Jones and Bovalino reached them, the four officers were staring out across the farmland behind the house. Matthews turned to face them as they approached, then pointed up the hill. 'Looks like someone shooting pheasants, Ma'am.'

Phillips followed his line of sight and spotted a man standing next to a quad bike about five hundred yards up the hill, just a few feet from the tree line. From this distance, she couldn't say for sure, but it looked like Nelson. He appeared to be reloading a shotgun.

'He shouldn't be shooting pheasants in May,' said Bovalino. 'The season finished at the end of last month.'

Phillips turned to face the big Italian. 'How do you know this stuff, Bov?' she asked.

He shrugged. 'I just do, I guess.'

'Well, illegal hunting is the least of his worries right now,' said Phillips.

The man on the hill snapped the gun shut and waited. A second later, a pair of pheasants flew out of the trees, and he lifted the gun to his shoulder and took aim.

A single shot rang out across the landscape, louder this time than those they'd heard a few minutes ago. The powerful noise caused crows to flee the trees that surrounded the farmhouse, drawing Phillips's attention. Turning back to face the hill, her mouth fell open as she realised the pheasant hunter now lay face down in the mud. 'Shit!'

Despite Matthews insisting they should secure the area, Phillips set off running in his direction, Jones and Bovalino on her heels. Thanks to the recent heat wave, the soil was mercifully dry, but the terrain was challenging. It took them almost five minutes to ascend the hill and reach the man. As they drew closer, there was no doubt it was Nelson. He was dead, a bullet wound visible in the middle of his back.

'Jesus, Guv,' said Bovalino as he joined her at the summit.

Jones arrived a moment later, struggling for breath. 'I'm getting too old for this kind of stuff.'

They each gazed down at Nelson's lifeless body as blood pooled under his chest and shoulders.

'Who the hell took the shot?' said Phillips, turning back towards the farmhouse. 'And where the fuck is Matthews?'

'Over there, Guv,' said Bovalino, pointing to the tree line in an adjacent field.

'What in God's name is going on, guys? Another director of Ardent dead?'

Jones rubbed the back of his neck. 'This makes no sense.'

'None of it does,' growled Phillips. 'Our prime suspect has just become our latest victim. Carter's gonna love this.'

At that moment, Phillips's radio crackled into life.

'Ma'am. You're gonna want to take a look at this,' said Matthews.

'What have you found?'

'Looks like a sniper's den.'

Phillips closed her eyes for a long moment as the words sank in. A sniper's den in the middle of the Cheshire country-side? 'We're on our way.'

In order to preserve the scene as best they could, Jones and Bovalino stayed at the end of the tree line along with the remaining TFU officers as Phillips followed Matthews back into the woods. About thirty yards in, he stopped by a fallen tree and pointed to the ground. 'This looks like where the shot was fired from, Ma'am.'

Phillips took a careful step closer and stared down at the flattened grass behind the log, then turned back to face the location of Nelson's body. There was indeed a clear line of sight up to the quad bike and the crest of the hill.

'Whoever took it must be one helluva marksman,' said Matthews. 'Taking into account the elevation of the land and the distance, very few people would be capable of hitting the target from here. I'd probably struggle myself, to be honest.'

'How did you know to look here?'

'After the shot rang out, one of the boys heard something over this way. When we came to check it out, we came across this.'

'Did you see anything?'

'No, Ma'am, sorry.'

'Damn it.'

'We did hear what sounded like a motorbike over the

other side of the trees, but by the time we got over there, there was no-one around.'

Phillips let out a frustrated sigh and shook her head. 'Ok. Well, we need to preserve the scene—'

'My team can help with that.'

'Thank you.' Phillips pulled out her phone and began walking back in the direction of Jones and Bovalino. 'Time to call Forensics,' she added as she searched for Senior CSI, Andy Evans's number.

13

L ater that morning, Phillips was sitting in her office with her back to the door, staring blankly at the rich blue sky through the window. There was a knock on her open door. Spinning round, she found Chief Superintendent Carter standing in the doorway, shoulders sagging, expression grave.

'Is everything all right, sir?'

Carter shook his head and stepped inside. 'In a word, Jane, no.'

Phillips sat to attention. 'What's the matter?'

'Fox,' he said with a heavy sigh as he dropped into the chair opposite.

'Let me guess; she's not happy with the way the Ardent case is being handled.'

Carter raised his eyebrows. 'You must be psychic?'

'No, but I do know how Fox operates, and she only ever likes good news. Sadly, when it comes to murder, that's a rarity. So, what's she said?'

'Oh, you know. The usual stick she beats me with ... that when she was head of MCU, she delivered the best arrest numbers in the GMP, but since I've taken over, we seem to be going backwards.'

'That's bollocks!' Phillips protested. 'Utter bollocks. And I should know, seeing as how they were all my cases. Yes, we had some big wins when she was in charge, but we've also got a filing cabinet full of open cases out there that date back to her time in charge that are still no closer to being solved.'

'Well, the way she sees it, I'm not pulling my weight and she's made it abundantly clear that MCU needs to improve our conviction rate in the second half of the year or I'll be transferred out.'

Phillips removed her glasses and rubbed her hand down her face. 'She's a piece of work, that woman. Does she really think threatening your job is the best way to motivate you? She's living in the bloody dark ages of management.'

Carter nodded sagely. 'I have to say, Jane, I really don't know how you worked with her for as long as you did. I mean, I knew of her reputation before I got the job, but now I'm working for her, well, it's far harder than I could have imagined.'

'I think I developed a very thick skin. I had to, or I'd have gone nuts.'

Carter flashed a wry grin. 'So, with Fox's words ringing in my ears, I have to ask. How are you getting on with the Ardent murders?'

Phillips replaced her glasses and exhaled loudly. 'I'm not going to lie, sir. It's not good. Nelson was our prime suspect in the Matthew Rice stabbing, and now he's dead, we're back to square one. Bailey appears to have the most to gain from the three partners' deaths, as she's now the sole shareholder in a company valued at half a billion quid.'

'Can she account for where she was this morning when Nelson was shot?'

Phillips nodded. 'Yup. Jones and Bov paid her a visit when

we'd finished up at the farmhouse, and she claims she was having an early breakfast with her husband before heading straight into the office.'

'So, she has alibis for all three murders?'

'Looks that way. But again, it's her husband vouching for her. Hardly cast-iron.'

'No,' said Carter.

'That said, though, Matthews from the TFU reckons whoever took the shot that killed Nelson was an expert marksman. There's no evidence of Bailey owning a gun, let alone knowing how to fire a rifle from distance.'

Carter pursed his lips for a moment before speaking. 'So, if she's not the killer, could she be a potential next victim?'

'It crossed my mind, and Jones said she seemed quite shaken when he told her about Nelson's death.'

'So, do we need to organise some uniform teams to keep an eye on her?'

'I would certainly think that's a good idea, sir, given what's happened to her partners, but it'll mean overtime and more strain on the budget.'

Carter remained silent for a long moment, appearing deep in thought. 'Sod the budget. If there's a chance she could be next, we need to protect her.'

Phillips nodded. 'I'll get Entwistle to sort it with Control.'

At that moment, there was another knock at the door.

'Sorry to interrupt, Guv,' said Entwistle as he stepped through the doorway holding a printed file in his hand.

'Whistler, just the man,' Phillips said.

Carter's brow furrowed. '*Whistler?*'

'It's his new nickname,' Phillips explained. 'Bovalino thought calling him Entwistle was too formal, that now he's a bona fide member of the team, he should have a nickname. So, he got *Whistler*.'

'Whistler? I like it,' said Carter.

Entwistle smiled.

'Anyway, what did you want?' asked Phillips.

He handed over the file. 'I've been digging into Ardent and found a historical lawsuit against the company that I thought you should be aware of.'

Phillips read the name of the suit from the front sheet aloud, for Carter's benefit. 'Joseph Meyer vs Ardent Technologies Ltd, in the matter of copyright infringement and the illegal patent of product IT67843—'

'IT67843 is the industrial foam they make, Guv. Joseph Meyer was, at the time of the lawsuit, an ex-employee who claimed he came up with the formula for the foam and should have been registered on the patent and, as such, received an equal share of the profits. He sued for two million quid.'

Phillips's eyes widened. 'Bloody hell, two million?'

'So, what happened?' asked Carter.

'Looks like it was settled out of court for a fraction of that amount.'

Phillips's mind was suddenly awash with theories. Could Meyer be involved? 'So, where is his now?'

'He's dead, Guv. Shot himself a year after the case was closed.'

Phillips groaned. 'Bugger. I thought we were onto something then.'

Entwistle handed over another printed sheet, this time of a local newspaper. 'His suicide made the local papers. It seems his wife had died of lung cancer a couple of months before, and he left a note saying he couldn't go on without her.'

Phillips scanned the old article. 'It says here he had two teenaged children. Any ideas where they are now?'

'His daughter Meghan lives in Broadbottom. I got her address from the council tax register. She runs her own business as a virtual assistant, from what I can see. The son, Daniel, disappeared off the grid eight years ago, just after Joseph's death.'

'Did he really?' Phillips's interest was piqued.

'Yep. His dad died in July 2013, and after September of the same year, there's no record of Daniel on the electoral role. The balances of his bank accounts have remained exactly the same since October 2013.'

'Could he be dead, too?' offered Carter.

'There's no record of it, sir,' Entwistle replied.

Phillips placed the printout on the desk, along with the copy of the writ. 'A two-million-quid lawsuit and a son that suddenly disappeared? That's gotta be worth a closer look.'

'I thought so, boss,' said Entwistle.

Phillips stood. 'Will you excuse me, sir?'

'Of course,' said Carter, following her lead. 'Don't let me keep you.'

'Thank you,' she said before striding out into the office, where she threw her car keys at Jones, who caught them in his right hand. 'We're heading out to Broadbottom and you're driving.'

14

Jones parked the car on the steep road directly outside Meghan Meyer's tiny end-of-terrace house, located in the leafy village of Broadbottom. Once home to mill-workers and their families, the area had been gentrified over the last twenty years. With its direct rail links to central Manchester, as well as the host of good schools, it had become very desirable to young families.

As Phillips stepped out of the car, her eyes were drawn to the vibrant pink and blue flowers bursting out from the blooming pot plants positioned under the small window at the front of the house. A moment later, she walked up the short path and rapped her knuckles on the door, Jones at her back. With no immediate answer, she knocked again, this time louder, and waited once more.

Finally, after another minute, she heard footsteps from inside and the door opened tentatively. A diminutive brown-haired woman – Phillips guessed she was in her late twenties or early thirties – peered out. 'Yes?'

'Meghan Meyer?' asked Phillips.

The woman's brow furrowed. 'It's Meghan Butler now. Meyer's my maiden name.'

Phillips flashed her credentials. 'DCI Phillips and DS Jones. We're from the Major Crimes Unit. We'd like to speak to you about your father, if you have a moment?'

Butler's face twisted. 'Dad? He's been dead eight years.'

'We know. That's what we'd like to talk to you about. May we come in?'

Butler glanced back over her shoulder. 'Erm, the place is a bit of mess.'

'It won't take long,' Phillips assured her.

'Ok. You'd better come in, then.' Butler opened the door wider and ushered them inside.

The construction of the house was a classic example of a millworker's cottage, which meant Phillips and Jones stepped straight from the front step into the modern living room – which seemed anything but a mess. The walls were painted a rich blue, complemented by a grey suede sofa and a tan leather armchair sitting on stripped wooden floorboards. A child's toolbox was positioned in the corner of the room with a cluster of teddy bears sitting on top. Framed pictures of Butler's young family adorned the walls. It was small, but perfectly formed.

'I'd hate to see it when it's tidy,' joked Jones as he surveyed the room.

Butler stood at about five foot two, and was casually dressed in jeans and a baggy pink sweatshirt that had the word LOVE emblazoned in red across the chest. Having positioned herself with her back to the cast-iron fireplace, she frowned and appeared distracted. 'What's that?'

'You said it was a bit of mess in here. I just said I'd hate to see it when it's tidy.' He smiled.

'Oh yeah,' replied Butler absentmindedly. 'So, why do you want to talk to me about my dad?'

'Do you mind if we sit down?' asked Phillips.

Butler shook her head. 'Sorry. Where are my manners?' She gestured to the sofa to her right. 'Please, go ahead.'

Phillips and Jones took a seat next to each other, while Butler remained standing by the fireplace.

'We understand your dad used to work for Ardent Technologies,' said Phillips.

Butler's lip curled into a snarl as she nodded. 'I lost both my parents because of those parasites.'

'What makes you say that?'

'Because they robbed my dad of his rightful claim to his patent, and when he stood up for himself, they ruined his reputation and bloody bankrupted him. I've no doubt the stress of all that brought about Mum's cancer.'

'Would you mind telling us what happened?' asked Jones.

Butler exhaled loudly, then dropped lightly into the leather armchair opposite them. 'It's still very painful to talk about, even after all these years.'

Phillips nodded and sat forward. 'We understand, but it would really help.'

'Why?'

Nelson's name had not yet been released to the press, so Phillips decided to stick to the Rice and Howard murders. 'We're investigating the deaths of two of Ardent's directors, Matthew Rice and Cherie Howard.'

Butler recoiled. 'What?' She seemed genuinely shocked.

'You haven't heard?' asked Jones.

'No, I haven't.'

'I'm surprised about that. It's been all over the news.' Phillips studied her face to gauge her reaction.

Butler forced a thin smile. 'I'm not much of a TV watcher. I prefer books.'

'I see,' said Phillips.

'So, what has any of this got to do with my dad?'

'We can't really share any specific information just now,' Phillips replied, 'but like I said, if you could tell us what happened between your dad and Ardent, it'd really help.'

Butler folded her arms across her chest and blew her lips. 'Where do I start?'

'How did your dad end up suing Ardent?' asked Jones, pulling out his pad to make notes.

'Dad worked in the research and development team there for ten years. He had an idea to develop a lightweight alternative to concrete, and came up with the formula they use now for the industrial foam. It was simple, but brilliant, and had the potential to save millions of pounds in production, as well as on-site installation costs. He presented it to the board, and they loved it.'

'When you say the board, who was that?'

'The four partners.'

'Rice, Howard, Nelson and Bailey?' asked Jones.

'Yep. That's them.'

'Then what happened?' Phillips said.

'They all agreed it could revolutionise the business and they should patent it. Dad said it was his idea so he would register it, but Bailey argued that the idea had been developed with Ardent's funding, and so it belonged to them. After a few weeks of back and forth, both sides reached a compromise and Nelson agreed my dad would receive a forty percent share of the patent, with Ardent taking sixty.'

'Seems quite fair,' said Phillips.

'That's what my dad thought, until out of the blue he found himself accused of sexual misconduct by Bailey.'

Phillips did a double-take. 'Sorry? What happened to him?'

'A couple of days before the patent contracts were due to be signed, Bailey made an official complaint and accused my dad of making lewd comments about her.'

'Bailey?'

Butler nodded. 'Yeah. She said he'd talked to her about buying a new car with his share of the patent – or, as she put it, "he wanted a big, shiny sports car that would reflect the size of his manhood".'

Jones scribbled in his notepad.

'Was that the kind of language your dad would use?' asked Phillips.

'No way! That's what made it all the more ridiculous. Dad was a sweet soul and a total gentleman; old-school. I don't even remember him swearing as a kid, never mind making comments about his sex life.'

'So, then what happened?'

'He was suspended without pay, marched out of the building by security that day, and blocked from accessing any files or emails.'

'Surely that's not legal,' said Phillips.

'Not it's not, but Bailey doesn't care about HR policies. She's a law unto herself. Dad fought it as best he could, but when witnesses came forward and backed up Bailey's claims, he was dismissed and Ardent registered the patent as theirs, meaning Dad got nothing.'

'Who were the witnesses?' asked Jones.

'I don't know their names, just that they were women from the office who backed up what Bailey had said. They had to be lying. That just wasn't my dad.'

'Why would they lie?' asked Jones.

'Because Bailey was a psycho. She probably threatened to get rid of them too, if they didn't.'

Jones made another note in his pad.

Butler continued. 'Anyway, Dad being Dad, there was no way he was about to walk away without a fight. He'd seen first-hand the bullying culture within Ardent, and wanted to make a stand. I heard him talk to my mum about how badly the staff were treated, all the time. Plus, he wanted his share of the patent. Bailey and her cronies stood to make tens of millions from his idea, so that's when he sued for damages.'

'We understand the case was settled out of court,' said Phillips.

Butler scoffed. 'Yeah, for a measly hundred thousand.'

'That's a big drop from a two-million suit.'

'Bailey's lawyers dragged the case out for as long as they could, knowing the legal costs were racking up with every day that passed. At one point, Mum and Dad had to remortgage the house to keep the action going. The stress became unbearable. Then Mum was diagnosed with stage-four lung cancer and given twelve months to live. Dad just wanted it to be over, so decided to settle. Ardent gave him a hundred grand to walk away, but by the time the money landed, Mum had already died. She was everything to Dad, and he just couldn't live without her.' Butler swallowed hard as her gaze dropped to the floor. 'A month to the day after her funeral, he shot himself with his hunting rifle.'

The room fell silent for a long moment.

Phillips could feel Butler's grief. 'I'm sorry, Meghan. I can't imagine how hard that must have been for you.'

'It was horrific. Like a bad dream you can't wake up from. If it wasn't for Daniel, I don't know how I would have got through the funeral and the weeks that followed. I was in a complete daze.'

'Daniel. Is that your brother?' asked Phillips.

Butler nodded, and pointed to a framed picture on the wall of herself and a man, hugging and smiling for the camera. Based on the quality of the print, the haircuts and clothes worn in the photograph, it had been taken some years earlier. 'That's me and Daniel on our eighteenth birthday. We're twins.'

Jones cut in. 'And where is he now?'

Butler cleared her throat. 'He's in prison, in Bali.'

Phillips felt herself recoil slightly. 'Bali? Do you mind telling us how he ended up there?'

'After Mum and Dad died so close together, it rocked us both. We were devastated, and after the funeral and the reading of the will, Daniel just wanted to get away. He decided to go travelling, and ended up in India for a month, then Asia for a few weeks, before heading to Bali. Everything was going well, and he seemed to be enjoying the trip, when he got into a bar fight one night, and a man was killed. Daniel was arrested and convicted of manslaughter. He got ten years.'

Phillips nodded softly. Daniel disappearing from the grid now made sense. 'Do you still have contact with him?'

'Yes. We write to each other once a month. I did fly over there to see him a couple of times before we had the kids, but it's too expensive now. With both my little ones in private nursery, I simply can't afford to fly halfway round the world each year.'

'So, when did you last see Daniel in the flesh?'

Butler took a moment to think. 'It was the year before my eldest, Sam, was born, so it'd be four years ago, now.'

'And when is he due to be released?' asked Phillips.

'In just over eighteen months.'

'I see. When was the last time you had a letter from him?'

'It'd probably be a couple of weeks ago, now.'

'And how was he?'

'The usual. Longing for home and looking forward to the day he can meet his niece and nephew.'

Phillips offered a soft smile. 'It must be very hard for you.'

Butler nodded. 'Our lives were ruined by bloody Ardent Technologies. Even the name's a joke. It's not *their* technology; it was my dad's.'

'You're still seem very angry at them,' said Jones.

'Wouldn't *you* be? In one year, I effectively lost *everyone* that mattered to me because of their actions. I tell you, whatever your investigation is about, I hope it ruins them like it ruined my family.'

Phillips studied Butler's face. The anger was etched in every line. 'Well, we should be going,' she said, standing. 'Thank you, Meghan. You've been very helpful.'

Butler nodded, but remained silent as Phillips and Jones took their leave.

Once back in the car, they took a moment to debrief.

'At least we now know why there's no trace of Daniel Meyer for the last eight years,' said Jones.

'True,' said Phillips as she fished out her phone and dialled Entwistle.

He answered a few moments later. '*Guv?*'

'Whistler. It looks like Daniel Meyer is serving time in a Bali prison.'

'*Oh, wow! Well, I wasn't expecting that.*'

'No, neither were we. Look, I want you to get onto the British Embassy and find out which prison he's in and when he's due for release. If we can, I'd like to get his version of his father's death.'

'*Sure thing. I'll start the ball rolling straight away, but I gotta warn you, it's gonna take time. Overseas bureaucrats aren't known for their efficiency. Least of all in South East Asia.*'

'Well, do what you do best and find a way to expedite it. Ok?'

'*Of course, boss.*'

'Can you put me on to Bov?'

There was a moment's silence as Entwistle passed over the phone to the big Italian.

'*Guv?*'

'Bov. I need you to see if you can find any historical workplace complaint cases against Ardent.'

'*Anything in particular I'm looking for?*'

'Bullying, harassment, wrongful dismissal, that kind of thing.'

'*No worries. I'll get straight onto it.*'

'Thanks,' said Phillips, and rang off. 'There's something about Meyer's lawsuit that isn't sitting right with me. I can't say why just yet, but I'm sure it's connected to the murders somehow.'

'But how? Joseph's dead, Daniel's locked up in Bali, and I'm not seeing Meghan as our sniper. Are you?'

Phillips shook her head. 'No. Looking at her, I think she'd struggle to hold a rifle, let alone fire one, but my guts are telling me we're not seeing the full picture here either. I don't know what it is, but I'm sure we're missing something that can help us find our killer.'

Jones nodded as he slipped the car into gear, then pulled away and headed back to headquarters.

15

The next morning, as Phillips returned from the Ashton House canteen with a black coffee, she wandered over to the bank of desks where Jones, Bovalino and Entwistle sat. A chorus of 'Morning, Guv' greeted her. Taking her place at the spare desk next to Entwistle, she took a sip of the steaming hot drink. 'Any news from the British Embassy in Bali?'

Entwistle nodded. 'I finally managed to get through to them late last night.'

'And?'

'Good news and bad news, boss.'

'What's the good news?'

'Right, so I spoke to a guy at the embassy called Martin Anders and asked him about Meyer. He explained it wasn't information they had access to, but that he would look into it for me.' Entwistle opened an email on his laptop. 'I got this from him about ten minutes ago. It confirms Daniel Meyer was indeed convicted of manslaughter, and sentenced to ten years imprisonment. However, as yet, he hasn't been able to find out where he's currently serving his sentence. He said he'd need to speak to the Balinese prison service to get me those specifics.'

'So, what's the bad news?'

'Anders says tracking down that kind of information will take time.'

'How much time?'

Entwistle winced. 'A week. Maybe longer.'

'A *week*? Do they know we're investigating a triple homicide here?'

'I explained all that to Anders, Guv, but he said the wheels turn slowly in the Balinese prison system. There's no way to expedite the search without being on the ground and paying for the information.'

'Bribes, you mean?'

'He didn't call it that specifically, but essentially, yes, bribes.'

'Well, seeing as we don't even have the budget to buy a new photocopier, I think it's fair to say we can rule out flying you to the other side of the planet just so you can grease the wheels of the Bali prison system.'

Entwistle flashed a lopsided grin. 'I didn't think you'd go for that. Shame. I quite fancied a trip to Bali.'

'Did Anders know if there was any chance Meyer could have secured an early release?'

'He didn't say, but then I didn't ask him,' replied Entwistle.

'Well, do that, then get onto immigration and see if Daniel Meyer has re-entered the country since he left in 2013. It's a long shot, but you never know.'

Entwistle made a note on his pad.

Phillips took a moment to think. 'Ok. So, what about the sister?'

'As the killer?' asked Bov.

'Yeah,' Phillips replied.

Jones shook his head. 'Not for me, Guv. In my opinion she's too petite to be able to handle a high-powered rifle, and I can't see her getting the upper hand on Rice either. She can't be more than seven stone, wet through.'

'You're probably right.' Phillips sighed, and turned her attention to Bovalino. 'What about Ardent? Did you find anything about historical workplace complaints?'

The big man shook his head and let out a frustrated sigh. 'I'm still waiting for Ardent's HR manager to send me the files. She's being less than helpful.'

'Well, why don't you remind her that, if need be, we can get a warrant to secure the documents, and we'll send a bunch of uniformed officers to pick them up with the sirens blaring.'

Bovalino frowned. 'But we don't have enough evidence to do that, Guv.'

'*I* know that, and *you* know that, but she doesn't.'

A wide grin spread across Bov's face. 'I'll call her now.'

'Good,' said Phillips. She then turned her attention to Jones. 'What are you doing for lunch?'

Jones's eyes narrowed. 'My usual – ham and cheese butties. Why?'

'Put them in the fridge and save them for tomorrow. I'll buy you a burger instead.'

Bovalino feigned being upset. 'Oh yeah, and why's Jonesy so special?'

Phillips pulled the card Lesley Bailey had given her from her pocket. 'I think it's time we met Mr Bailey and, according to his wife, Lesley, he's always at his golf club at lunchtime.'

Jones smiled. 'Count me in.'

Phillips checked her watch; 9.45 a.m. 'It'll take about half an hour from here, so let's aim to leave at half eleven.'

'Roger that,' said Jones.

Phillips stood, patting Bovalino on the shoulder as she did. 'And don't worry, big man. I promise we'll bring you back a doggy bag.' With that, she picked up her coffee and headed for her office.

16

B ramall Golf and Country Club was typical of many of the courses dotted in and around the Cheshire countryside. It certainly wasn't the most exclusive establishment in the area, but neither was it the cheapest. Memberships were relatively expensive, and required approval from the central committee, who would consider age, profession, and ability to contribute to the members' community and the club's charitable events calendar.

Phillips and Jones had arrived just after midday and discovered that Frederick Bailey – or Fred, as the club professional had referred to him – was competing in that morning's competition and was expected back in the club house sometime around 1 p.m. So, with time to kill, Phillips fulfilled her promise to Jones and bought him a bacon double cheeseburger, and a club sandwich for herself. Sitting in a comfortable corner booth facing the entrance to the bar, they tucked into their food with relish. It might not have been Michelin-starred fare, but it certainly was very tasty, and there was plenty of it. When they'd finished their meals, they sat in silence and waited for Bailey to arrive.

Phillips picked up her phone and pulled up the image of Fred Bailey she'd found on his Facebook page. He appeared older than his wife, but clearly took care of himself. His profile was littered with pictures of him road racing in France and Spain, as well as lots of golfing holidays in the sun. Notably, nearly all his holiday snaps showed him having fun with his mates, as opposed to with his wife.

Right on time, Bailey sauntered into the bar. He was dressed in expensive-looking golf attire and chatting with a friend. He appeared much taller in the flesh than in his photos, and had an athletic build with wavy grey hair and a handsome face. He was clearly well liked, nodding and saying hello to virtually everyone in the room.

'Time for a little chat,' said Phillips, stepping out of the booth and making her way across the room.

Jones followed suit.

Bailey was standing with his back to her as she stepped behind him at the bar. 'Mr Bailey. Can we have a word?' she asked.

Bailey turned, a puzzled look on his face.

Phillips presented her credentials. 'Detective Chief Inspector Phillips, and this is DS Jones.'

Jones flashed his badge.

'We'd like to ask you a few questions about your wife.'

Bailey's eyes darted around the room for a moment before he flashed an easy smile. 'Been racking up more parking tickets, has she?' he said, loudly, with forced joviality.

Phillips and Jones followed him to a table in the farthest, quietest corner of the bar, and took their seats opposite him. Jones retrieved his notepad from his pocket.

Bailey took a sip of what looked like a large gin and tonic. 'Is this about the murders?' he asked in a low voice, his expression suddenly grave.

'Yes. Specifically, where you were when Matthew Rice,

Cherie Howard and David Nelson were killed.'

Bailey recoiled. 'Me? What? You think I killed them?'

Phillips stared him dead in the eye. 'No. But you are your wife's alibi for all three deaths.'

Bailey stumbled slightly before answering. 'Er, yes, of course. I see what you mean.'

'So, for the record, can you tell us exactly where you were on the morning of Tuesday 11th May, around 10 p.m. on Wednesday 12th of May, and at 5 a.m. on Wednesday 19th of May?'

'Didn't Lesley already tell you all this?'

Phillips flashed a thin smile. 'We'd like to hear it from you, if you don't mind?'

Bailey appeared to gather his thoughts. 'Er, well, on the 11th, I was at home with Lesley. I wasn't playing golf that day, so I was doing some stuff in the garden.'

Jones began to scribble down the details.

'On the Wednesday, Lesley and I had dinner at the house. I cooked a meal—'

'What did you have?' Phillips cut in.

'Erm, steak. I cooked steak on the barbecue. She was working, so we didn't eat until about half-nine. Then we watched a movie.'

'Which movie?'

'Everest, you know, the one with Josh Brolin in it?'

Phillips nodded. 'And what about on the 19th of May. Where were you then?'

'What time?'

'5 a.m.'

Bailey scoffed. 'In bed. I rarely see that time of day, I'm afraid. Early mornings aren't my thing.'

Phillips cast her eyes around the well-maintained bar. 'Your wife says you spend a lot of time here. Is that true?'

'Yes. Most days.'

'So, she mentioned you're retired.'

Bailey flashed a coy grin. 'You could say that, but I think she may have been playing with you. You see, I'm more of a kept man.'

Phillips frowned. 'What do you mean by that?'

'Lesley has always been very successful, so we decided a long time ago that I would stay at home and look after our son, Greg, and she would earn the money. Well, Greg's twenty-five now, so I don't have to look after him quite as much as before. Well, until he needs money for another one of his business ventures.'

'And what does Greg do for a living?'

Bailey blew his lips. 'Whatever the latest craze or fad is, he's usually trying to make money from it. Not that he ever does.' He took a long drink from his glass. 'I think it's fair to say, Greg doesn't have his mother's flair for economics.'

Nor do you, thought Phillips.

'Is there anything else I can help you with?' asked Bailey.

Phillips changed tack. 'You must be looking forward to the launch of the IPO, Mr Bailey. I mean, now it's just Lesley in charge, it looks like she's about to make half a billion quid.'

The faintest of smiles appeared in the corner of Bailey's mouth before he caught himself, but Phillips spotted it. 'It really is tragic what happened to Matthew, Cherie and David,' he said sombrely.

'Yes, it is.' Phillips locked eyes with him. 'But it's all looking quite rosy in the Bailey house now, isn't it?'

Bailey sat upright and appeared affronted. 'Look, we can't take back what happened to those guys, but equally, Lesley made that company what it is. It's not her fault they're dead. She deserves whatever she gets from floating the business.'

'And what do *you* get when it floats, Mr Bailey?'

'Me?'

'Yes. Like you said, you're a kept man. So, what will Lesley be giving you when the cash comes in.'

Bailey drained his glass, and as he placed it back on the table, he forced a thin smile. 'I already have everything I need, Chief Inspector.'

Phillips eyed him for a long moment. 'It certainly seems that way, doesn't it? Right, well, don't let us keep you from your lunch,' she said, and stepped up from the table with Jones close behind.

Bailey offered a faint smile.

'Maybe we'll talk again, Mr Bailey,' said Phillips.

Bailey nodded, but didn't reply.

'And you make sure you look after that wife of yours. It seems she's very valuable.'

'I'll do that,' said Bailey flatly.

Phillips nodded to Jones, then headed for the exit.

As they walked back to the car, Jones was the first so speak. 'Pleased with his lot, isn't he, Guv?'

'Yeah, he is. The smarmy bugger. And no wonder; he gets to play golf every day and lives off his wife.'

'Sounds ideal,' joked Jones.

'Let's see if we can find out who gets Lesley Bailey's shares if *she* dies.'

'I'm guessing the husband?'

'And the son?' added Phillips as they reached the car.

'What? Are you thinking the two of them could be involved?'

'Maybe,' said Phillips opening the passenger door. 'Kill off your wife and mother's partners so she becomes the sole beneficiary of half a billion quid? If they're in her will, what's to stop them bumping her off and sharing the spoils between them?'

'That's messed up, boss.'

'Yeah, but we've seen worse, haven't we?' replied Phillips as she jumped into the passenger seat. 'A lot worse.'

17

B ack at Ashton House, Jones headed back upstairs to MCU, while Phillips took a slight detour via the canteen. On the ride back from the golf club, she'd recalled her promise to bring Bovalino back a doggy bag. Looking at the time as she arrived, it was almost 3 p.m. She was pretty sure he'd already have eaten, but a promise was a promise, and besides, the big Italian could always find space for more food. So, after picking up a pastrami sub with extra pickle, she headed back to the office.

By the time she reached their desks, Jones had filled the rest of the team in on their meeting with Fred Bailey.

'Sorry I forgot your doggy bag,' said Phillips as she offered Bov the sub. 'So, I got you this.'

Bovalino's eyes widened as he took the sandwich from her, grinning. 'That'll do nicely.'

'Sounds like we have two more potential suspects, Guv,' ventured Entwistle.

Phillips nodded as she dropped into the spare chair next to Jones. 'Maybe. It's at least worth taking a closer look at Bailey's husband and son.'

'I can do that,' said Entwistle. 'Oh, and I heard back from immigration. They have no record of Daniel Meyer coming into the country since he left in 2013.'

'Another avenue closed, then,' sighed Phillips, her frustration building. She turned to Bovalino now, just as he took an enormous bite of his sandwich. 'Any joy with the Ardent HR team?'

Bov nodded, his mouth full as he chewed.

It's all right. I'll wait,' said Phillips sarcastically.

'Sorry, Guv,' replied Bovalino, when he eventually swallowed his mouthful, and placed the sandwich on the desk in front of him. 'Your idea worked a treat. As soon as I mentioned sending in a load of uniformed officers, they agreed to send me everything they had on workplace complaints.'

'And?'

'And there's a *lot.*'

Phillips raised her eyebrows. 'Go on.'

'Well, having read through some of the complaints, either many very sensitive people have worked at Ardent in the last five years and made unsubstantiated complaints, or there's a culture of bullying and harassment. So far, I've found six cases of bullying and three of racism, all of them settled out of court. Apart from *one*, that is.'

'And what happened in that case?' asked Phillips.

'A guy named Omar Aziz took Ardent to a tribunal, specifically Lesley Bailey and David Nelson, for racist remarks in the workplace, but Ardent won.'

'How?'

'Bailey and Nelson produced witnesses who said Aziz had made up the claims and that he'd admitted to them that he wanted to leave, and was after a large pay-out.'

Phillips glanced across at Jones. 'More internal witnesses, just like the Meyer case.'

Jones stuck out his bottom lip and nodded. 'Lucky for them, hey?'

'Do you have an address for Aziz?' asked Phillips.

'Yep. He lives in Harpurhey.'

Phillips checked her watch. 'It's almost three-thirty. If he has a job, he might be at work.'

'Already thought of that. He works for Speedy-Bee's Delivery Services. I've got their address, too.'

'Great. I want you and Jones to pay him a visit. Get his version of what happened.'

Bovalino nodded and grabbed a set of car keys from his desk, along with what was left of his sandwich. 'I'll drive,' he said with a wide grin.

Jones chuckled as he looked across at Phillips and Entwistle. 'I knew I should have brought some spare under-pants today.'

18

As luck would have it, Omar Aziz was at home when Jones and Bovalino arrived at his dilapidated council house located in the relatively deprived suburb of Harpurhey. The red-brick mid-terrace was typical of Manchester's less salubrious streets, and the front door positioned adjacent to the pavement. Aziz was quick to answer their knock, and begrudgingly invited them in when pressed by Jones. Sitting opposite them at the small kitchen table to the rear of the house, he glared with cold, dark eyes that matched his thick black hair and beard.

'We understand you used to work for Ardent Technologies,' said Jones.

Aziz frowned. 'Yeah. What's that got to do with you?'

'We're investigating the deaths of three of the partners at Ardent—'

'Are you being serious?'

Jones nodded.

'So, which ones are dead?'

'Matthew Rice, Cherie Howard and David Nelson.'

'Bloody hell.' Aziz sat back and blew his lips. 'How did they die?'

'We were hoping you might be able to tell us,' Bov cut in.

'What? You think *I* did it?'

'Did you?' asked Bovalino, his glaze unflinching.

Aziz locked eyes with the big Italian. 'No, I didn't. But I'd like to shake the hand of whoever it was that did.'

'And why is that?' Jones cut back in.

'Because they did the world a favour by getting rid of those arseholes. I'm just sorry Bailey wasn't one of them that copped it.'

'Can you tell us why you took Ardent to court, Omar?' asked Jones.

Aziz shifted in his seat. 'Read the court report. It's all in there.'

'We'd really like to hear your side of things.'

Aziz's eyes narrowed and he said nothing for a long moment. 'Bollocks to it,' he said finally. 'I don't owe them anything.'

Bovalino took out his notepad and pen.

Aziz continued. 'I worked at Ardent for the best part of five years in the planning team, managing projects through the Gulf states. Not the most exciting job in the world, but because it was specialist work, the money was good. Anyway, it was well known that Lesley Bailey had a vicious, hair-trigger temper and would fly off the handle at any given moment. In fact, it happened *so* often it became the norm, and she usually had someone in tears most days. Anyway, on one particular day she turned on my mate Estelle, calling her a stupid bitch and tearing strips off her in front of everyone. I don't know why, but that was it for me. I'd had as much of her as I could stomach, and I flipped. I pulled Estelle out of the way and told Bailey what I thought of her.'

'How did she take that?' asked Jones.

'She told me to shut my Paki mouth and that if I didn't like it, I could piss off back where I came from. Bloody ignorant bitch. I'm from Iran, not Pakistan, and I've lived in England since I was two years old.'

'So, what happened after she said that to you?'

'I told her she could stick her job up her fat arse, and I walked out.'

'And that's when you took them to court?'

Aziz nodded. 'Yeah. A few weeks later. I wasn't going to, and I'd never thought about it, to be honest, but I saw an advert for a solicitor on the TV that said I could get thousands of pounds in compensation. Wendells and Co. – no win, no fee.'

'I've seen those ads,' said Bovalino.

'Anyway. I told them what had happened, and they said I had a great case and took me on.'

'So, what happened then?' asked Jones.

'Then we got it double barrels from Ardent's solicitors, Freeman and Cross. Jesus. If I thought Bailey was a bully, she's got nothing on them. The threats they made were terrifying.'

Jones sat forward on his chair. 'Such as?'

'That they were confident their client would win, and they were prepared to fight the case in court for as long as it took. They even went to the bother of listing their projected costs, which my solicitors would've had to cover if we lost the case. My solicitor bottled it and told me we should try and settle, but I wanted to fight. So, we went to court. Biggest mistake of my life.'

'Why was that?'

'Because, out of nowhere, they produced two female witnesses who said I'd been threatening and aggressive towards Bailey on a number of occasions, and that I was a volatile character who they were frightened of. I didn't stand a chance after that. The court sided with Ardent. Thank God I didn't have to pay the legal fees, or I'd have been fucked.'

'Have you had contact with any of the directors since then?' Jones asked.

'No, but I'm pretty sure Bailey ruined my name in the construction industry. I've not been able to get one single interview since I left two years ago, which is why I'm driving a van and living in this dump.'

Jones took in the room around him fully, for the first time. He noted the wallpaper coming away where it connected to the ceiling, an issue commonly associated with damp. The space was dark and dingy, and felt depressing. As he looked around, his eyes were drawn to a framed photo behind Aziz, on top of a small cabinet in the corner of the room. He squinted to get a better look. 'Are you holding *a gun* in that picture?'

Aziz turned towards the photo. 'Yeah. I was on national service in Iran.'

Jones frowned. 'I thought you said you'd lived here since you were two years old?'

Aziz faced them again. 'I have. Apart from a couple of years when I was eighteen and went back to Iran to serve my time in the army. My two older brothers did the same. It was our way of honouring our family and our roots.'

'You chose to do military service when you didn't have to?' asked Bovalino.

'That's right.'

Jones's eyes narrowed. 'So, I'm guessing you know how to fire a rifle?'

'Of course. Not that I have done so for a long time. I'd had enough of them by the time I got out.'

Jones scrutinised Aziz's face as he asked his next question. 'Where were you yesterday morning, at around 5 a.m.?'

Aziz didn't flinch. 'At work, driving.'

'At 5 a.m.?' Jones scoffed.

'Yeah. I was on the early shift, and I have to be at the depot for 4.30.'

'And someone will vouch for you, will they?' said Jones.

Aziz remained stoic. 'Yes. My boss...and about *four* other drivers.'

Jones held his gaze for a long moment. 'What about last Tuesday morning, about eleven? Where were you then?'

'Working.'

'Are you sure? Don't your shifts change?'

'Not much, no.'

Jones nodded slowly. 'How about Wednesday night, around ten o'clock?'

Aziz shrugged his shoulders. 'I was probably here, watching TV.'

'Alone?'

'Yeah. I don't have a girlfriend and I've never invited any of my friends round to this shit-hole. Why would I?'

'So, you haven't always lived here, then?'

'No. I used to rent in the Northern Quarter, but since I now earn about a quarter of what I used to, I can't afford a place like that anymore.'

'Harpurhey is quite a change from the Northern Quarter, isn't it?' said Bovalino.

'You think?' Aziz said, his voice laced with sarcasm.

Jones pointed towards the photo of Aziz holding the rifle. 'Would you mind if I took a copy of that?'

'I would, actually. That's private. If you want it, you'll have to get a warrant for it.'

Jones recoiled slightly, glancing first at Bovalino, and then back at Aziz. 'You're clearly a man who knows his legal rights.'

Aziz glared at Jones now. 'Yeah, I do. So, if there's nothing else?'

'Ok.' Jones nodded. 'I can see we've outstayed our welcome.'

Bovalino took his cue and stepped up from the chair.

Jones followed suit, slowly and deliberately, his eyes locked on Aziz's. 'You do know we'll be checking those alibis, Omar, don't you?'

'You do that. I've got nothing to hide.'

Jones held his gaze in silence for a long, uncomfortable moment. Then flashed a thin smile. 'I'm sure we'll talk again, soon.'

'You can see yourselves out,' Aziz said without emotion.

A few minutes later, safely back in the car with Bovalino at the wheel once more, Jones called Phillips through the in-car system. When she answered, her voice boomed out through the stereo speakers.

'Jonesy. What have you got for me?'

'One super-pissed-off ex-Ardent employee with an axe to grind and military-level weapons training.'

'You're kidding?'

'I'm not, Guv. Aziz did national service in the Iranian military and knows how to handle a rifle.'

'Which means he has to be a suspect, right?'

'Potentially. But he has alibis for two of the murders. Reckons he was working and has four or five people who can back him up.'

'Well, alibis can be broken. We know that better than most.'

'That's what we're thinking, too.'

'Who did you say he worked for again, Bov?'

'Speedy-Bee's Delivery Services in Monsall, Guv.'

'Right. I'll get Entwistle onto it straight away. Great work, guys.'

'Thanks, boss,' said Jones.

'See you when you get back to the office,' said Phillips as she rung off.

Jones glanced left out of the window in silence as he considered Aziz as a suspect in the three murders, then felt himself being pushed back into the seat as Bovalino moved out into the outside lane and the car accelerated rapidly.

'Let's open her up!' said the big man from the driver's seat.

Here we go again, thought Jones, glancing at his partner – an amateur rally driver in his spare time – in his happy place, racing at high speed back to the office.

Early the next morning, Phillips made the twenty-minute journey from her Chorlton home to Ardent's offices in Stockport. Having made so many visits, the receptionist recognised her and alerted Lesley Bailey to her presence. Five minutes after walking through the doors of reception, she found herself once again sitting across the desk from Bailey in her large, no-frills office.

Bailey, who wasn't managing to hide her irritation at yet another intrusion, crossed her arms in front of her chest and exhaled loudly. 'Am I the only person you're speaking to about these murders?'

Phillips ignored the jibe and got straight to the point. 'What can you tell me about Omar Aziz?'

'Aziz? Well, he was lazy and incompetent, and we had to let him go,' said Bailey without missing a beat.

'He says you called him a Paki, along with other racial slurs.'

'He's also a liar.'

'Aziz told my officers you were well-known for being a bully in the office. That you have a hair-trigger temper—'

'Chief Inspector. I've built a multi-million-pound business from nothing, and I demand the best from my team. Some people can't handle that. Aziz was one of them. We pay well at Ardent – well above the market rate – but also, we expect our employees to earn that money. I'm not running a bloody social club, and if I see people messing about when they should be working, I let them know about it. But I'm no bully. You can ask anyone of my team. They'll tell you what it's *really* like to work here.'

Phillips decided to change tack. 'How are you coping without your partners? You must be finding it very difficult.'

'I'm getting on with the job in hand, like I always do.'

Phillips tilted her head to the side slightly as she studied Bailey's face. 'You do seem to be handling their sudden deaths very well.'

Bailey shrugged. 'How else am I supposed to react? When you grow up in a large Irish family – the youngest and only girl of six children – there's no time for sentiment or emotions. You learn very quickly to get on with the cards you're dealt, and that's what I'm doing here. I have a business to run and an IPO to negotiate. I've worked too damn hard to see it collapse now.'

Phillips stared into Bailey's cold, dark eyes and was reminded once again of Chief Constable Fox. Perhaps, like Fox, she too was a sociopath? After all, statistics showed that one in four company CEOs displayed sociopathic tendencies, which are often cited as the driving force behind their success; ensuring they triumphed *whatever the cost to others*. Phillips continued. 'Do you think Aziz could have sent you the threatening letters?'

'Possibly. As was proven in the tribunal, he was a very volatile character. But I've been thinking a lot about those letters since I gave them to you, and there is someone else who fits the bill.'

'Oh? Who?'

Bailey uncrossed her arms and sat forward in her chair, linking her fingers on the desk. 'Liam Bush. Worked for us about five years ago, but, like Aziz, we got rid of him. I read in the papers he was convicted of assault back in 2018 and served a couple of years. Turned up at my house when he got out last year. He was drunk, calling me a bitch and telling me I'd ruined his life. As soon as I threatened to call the police, he ran off. The letters started arriving not long after that.'

Phillips's eyes narrowed as she shook her head. 'And you're only telling me this *now*? You didn't think this kind of information would be useful to us earlier?'

'I've had a lot on my mind,' Bailey said nonchalantly.

Phillips took a deep silent breath as she attempted to hide her contempt for the woman. 'Has he been back since that visit?'

'No, which is another reason why he didn't jump to the top of the list when we were talking about the letters. Plus, if I'm being honest, I wasn't mad on raking up the past when the future direction of the company is so delicately poised around the IPO.'

Bailey really was like Fox, thought Phillips: nothing would get in the way of her success. 'Are there any other disgruntled employees I need to be aware of?' she asked, giving way to her mounting frustration.

'Not that I can think of, no. But it's fair to say I've made a few enemies in my time, Chief Inspector. As they often say, success comes at a price.'

'Well, that was certainly true in the case of your three partners,' said Phillips sardonically as she stood up from the chair. 'Right. Well, I won't take up any more of your time. I'm pretty sure I know the way out by now.'

Stepping outside into the sunshine a few minutes later, Phillips's frustration was almost at boiling point. Bailey was typical of so many people she had met in her career: selfish, self-involved and economical with the truth. Rather than doing everything she could to help the investigation, she seemed determined to throw curveballs into the mix as and when it suited her. Was that because she was somehow involved in the murders and playing a game? Or was she so self-serving, she really did think of little else besides her company's impending stock-flotation? Experience told Phillips all would be revealed in the fulness of time, but time was not something she had the luxury of just then. Unless they solved these murders soon, Fox would remove Carter as the boss of MCU. And, based on bitter experience, God only knew who would take his place.

As she reached her car, she fished out her phone and dialled Jones's number. They needed to track down Liam Bush, *and quickly.*

20

Phillips parked the car in her designated spot at Ashton House and switched off the engine. The inside of the car was lovely and cool thanks to the air-conditioning, which had been blasting cold air throughout the journey back from Ardent. She hoped the team would already have updates on the case. Her mind wandered to Jones's revelations that Omar Aziz was a trained soldier.

At that moment, her phone pinged, signalling the arrival of a new WhatsApp message. Picking the handset out of the central console, she smiled as her eyes fell on the message on screen. It was from Adam.

Can't wait to see you tomorrow. It's been so long, I've forgotten what you look like. So, I'll just have to introduce myself to the sexiest woman in the restaurant! A xxx

Opening the message fully, she replied.

I bet you say that to all the women. Jxx

A second later, another message appeared.

Rumbled, Detective! Did it work? A xxx

Phillips chuckled.

Yes. And you're right, it does feel like ages. Come to mine for 1.45. We can walk to the restaurant from there. Jxx

His response landed almost instantly.

Counting the hours! A xx

Grinning, she stepped out of the car and slipped the phone into her pocket before setting off towards the building with renewed vigour.

A few minutes later, as she opened the door to MCU, Jones spotted her and beckoned her over.

'What's up?' she said as she arrived at his desk.

Entwistle and Bovalino gave her their full attention too.

'I've found our man, Bush, Guv.'

'That was quick,' she replied.

'Well, he's not been out of prison very long, meaning he's still registered with the Probation Service, who were very helpful, actually. He's living in Longsight in a council flat, and at the moment he's registered as unemployed.'

'Good work. Let's pay him visit,' said Phillips.

Jones nodded and reached for his car keys.

'Before you go, Guv, I have an update for you Omar Aziz's alibis,' Entwistle cut in.

'Go on.'

'I spoke to his boss at Speedy-Bees, and he confirmed he was driving for them when both Rice and Nelson were killed.'

'And he's *sure* about that?'

Entwistle nodded. 'They use GPS-monitoring devices on all deliveries so customers can track the parcels. He's pulling the data off for me as we speak, but from what he could see in Aziz's reports, our man was nowhere near the murder scenes.'

Phillips shook her head in frustration. 'Make sure you go through that data with a fine-toothed comb. And find out if the tracker is connected to the van or to a handset. Because if it's a handset, it could easily have been passed to someone else to give him an alibi.'

'Will do, Guv.'

Jones was on his feet now.

Phillips turned her attention to Bovalino. 'I'm still not convinced Lesley Bailey isn't somehow involved in this. She seems completely unfazed despite the fact three of her partners have been murdered. She should be terrified and panicking that she could be next, but it seems like it's just business as usual for her. Take another look at her background and see if you can find anything – anything at all – that could connect her to the murders. I don't care how small the link may be, ok?'

'You got it,' said Bov.

Phillips turned to Jones now. 'Right. Let's get over to Liam Bush's place. You can debrief me on what the probation team had to say about him on the way.'

21

By the time they arrived at Liam Bush's address, Jones had fully briefed Phillips on his previous conviction for assault, which had seen him serve two years of a four-year sentence in Hawk Green – Manchester's maximum-security prison. By all accounts, Bush had inflicted a vicious and sustained attack on a fellow motorist as the result of a road-rage incident in the city centre. Released just over twelve months ago, he now lived in a small flat in Longsight, one of Manchester's most crime-ridden suburbs.

As Bush opened his front door, the stench of cannabis was pervasive. 'What do you want?' he said as he peered out from the darkened hallway through bloodshot eyes that were recessed in his gaunt features. He had the unmistakable look of a man who had served hard time.

Phillips and Jones identified themselves and suggested they speak inside, knowing that as a probationer, he had little grounds to refuse them entry.

A minute later, Bush took a seat on the only chair in the small living room where the curtains remained drawn. The only light came from the small TV in the corner, which was showing an ancient quiz show of some kind. A small coffee table in front of him was covered in the various paraphernalia needed to roll joints. Phillips and Jones had no choice but to remain standing.

'Seeing as you're on probation, aren't you supposed to be drug-free?' said Phillips.

Bush shrugged his shoulders. 'It's for medicinal purposes.'

Phillips shook her head. She had more important things to worry about than a *proby* breaking the conditions of his bail. 'What can you tell us about Ardent Technologies, Liam?'

'Nothing,' Bush shot back.

'Really? Well, let me be more specific. What can you tell me about a visit you paid to Ardent's CEO, Lesley Bailey?'

'Has she put you up to this? That snide bitch!' His accent was pure Mancunian.

'Why did you go round to her house and threaten her, Liam?' asked Phillips.

'I didn't threaten her. I was just walking by, and we got into an exchange.'

'Oh, so you just happened to be walking past her house in Bramall, did you?' Phillips shot back sarcastically. '*You*, an ex-con living in Longsight, went for a walk *ten miles*, and at least *two* train journeys, away from home? Do you think we're bloody stupid, Liam?'

Bush pulled a cigarette from the packet of red Marlboros on the table front of him, lit it and inhaled deeply. As he spoke, smoke billowed from his nostrils. 'All right. So, I did go round there that day, but I didn't do anything. I was just pissed, and angry, and wanted to tell her what I thought of her.'

'How on earth did you know where she lived?' Jones chimed in.

'I'd given her a lift home once when I worked at Ardent. I

remembered it was close to the train station, so I started there and just walked around and eventually recognised the house. One of the benefits of being unemployed, you see: nothing else to do all day.'

'And once you had her address, did you start sending Lesley Bailey threatening letters?' asked Phillips.

Bush took another drag before responding. 'I don't know anything about any letters.'

'Really?' said Phillips. 'Because not long after your little day trip, Lesley Bailey started receiving threatening letters written by someone calling her a bitch and telling her she'd get what was coming to her.'

'They've got nowt to do with me.'

'I don't believe you,' said Phillips flatly.

'Believe what you want. I don't care. And I didn't stab Matthew Rice, either.'

'Oh, so you heard about that?'

'Saw it on the news. Shame that whoever did it didn't get Bailey, too.'

Phillips scrutinised Bush's face for a long moment, then cast her gaze around the small room. It was riddled with used food cartons, empty bottles of cheap cider and overflowing ash trays. 'What did you do when you worked for Ardent?'

'Why does it matter?'

'Just answer the question,' Jones cut in firmly.

Bush glared at him for a long moment before answering. 'I was in the planning team.'

'Did you work with Omar Aziz?' Jones asked.

'Yeah, for about a year, and then I left.'

'Why did you leave?' said Phillips.

'I was fired. For calling out Bailey in the office for being a bully. She was laying into me because I was behind schedule on a project in the US, but it wasn't my fault we were running over. We'd taken on too many jobs and she refused to hire more staff because it would eat into her precious profits. I stood up to her and she called me a pathetic, useless little man and told me to get the job done or not to bother coming back the next day. I saw red and told her she was a bitch and a bully. She fired me on the spot. I'd had enough of her by then, so I said she could go fuck herself and walked out. As I reached the lift, she caught up with me. That was when she told me I'd messed with the wrong person, and she'd make sure I never worked in construction again.'

'Surely no one has that kind of influence?' asked Jones.

Bush exhaled a large cloud of cigarette smoke. 'When you supply pretty much every major construction company in the UK, you do. And whatever she said about me in the industry worked. After leaving Ardent, I couldn't get a job in construction anywhere.'

'So, what did you do?' Phillips said.

'That was the problem. What I did at Ardent was specialist work related specifically to the industrial foam, so it wasn't like I could switch to another industry. With no severance pay and no job, I was up shit creek. I had no money, and a wife and kids to support, not to mention a bloody big mortgage. I ended up working all hours as a taxi driver to try and pay the bills, which meant I never got to see my family. I got depressed and started drinking, and just spiralled out of control, drinking more and more. My wife eventually had enough and left me. Took my kids away too. Not long after that, the assault happened. I was in a state of permanent rage. One day, when this guy cut me up in the taxi, we got into it and I lost control. There isn't a day goes by I don't wish I'd kept my bloody mouth shut at Ardent. Standing up to Bailey was the biggest mistake of my life.'

'Sounds like you did what you thought was right at the time,' said Phillips.

'Yeah, and look where that got me,' Bush opened his arms

out wide, 'living alone in this dump with no job, no partner and, thanks to my ex-wife's lawyer, no chance of seeing my kids.'

Phillips could feel Bush's anger brimming under the surface. 'Where were you on the morning of Tuesday, the 11th of May?'

'Why do you wanna know?' Bush's eyes widened suddenly. 'Wait a minute? Is that when Rice was murdered?'

'You tell us.' said Jones.

'Listen, I'll admit I hate that bitch and what she did to me, but I never had anything against Matthew Rice. I mean, he was bit flash and if he was chocolate, he'd have eaten himself, but I had no reason to kill him. My beef was always with Bailey, not him.'

'What about Cherie Howard?' asked Phillips. 'What did you think of her?'

'She was all right. Nice enough, I guess. Why?'

Phillips ignored the question. 'And David Nelson?'

Bush exhaled loudly. 'That fella? He was a right prick. Cut from the same cloth as Bailey. Another one fond of throwing his weight around.'

'Can you remember where you were around ten p.m. on May twelfth?' Phillips asked.

Bush shrugged. 'Where I always am – here.'

'And what about Wednesday just gone at 6 a.m.?'

Bush recoiled. 'Are you kidding me? I've not seen that time of day since I got out of prison. I'm a night owl. I usually go to bed about three and don't get up until midday, so I'd have been fast asleep in my pit at that time.'

Phillips scrutinised his face for any signs he was lying, but saw nothing to suggest it. Glancing at Jones, she nodded towards the door. It was time to go.

Once outside, they walked back to the car at pace.

'Well, he definitely has motive,' said Phillips. 'I mean, it sounds as if Bailey ruined his life like she did with Aziz.'

'Yeah. Their stories are almost identical, Guv. But if that's the case, why kill the other three and leave Bailey alive?'

'I dunno. Maybe he's saving the best 'til last?'

'Maybe,' said Jones.

'At this moment in time, I don't really care about the why's and what's. I just wanna know if he was involved. So, get a warrant to search his flat for anything that could tie him to the murders.'

Jones checked his watch as they approached the car. 'It's almost four o'clock on a Friday, Guv. I don't think we'll get one until Monday morning, now.'

Phillips stopped and let out a low, frustrated growl. 'I'll never understand why the courts shut down on weekends. It's not as if villains take time off, is it?'

Jones laughed. 'Be good if they would. I might see more of Sarah and the girls that way. Look, I'll ring the magistrates now and see what they can do. You never know, we might get lucky.'

'Well, if not, get Bov to ring his mate and push it through,' said Phillips as she opened the car door and jumped inside.

22

A s expected, Jones was unable to secure a warrant that late on a Friday afternoon, and with Bovalino's friend in the magistrates' office on annual leave for the next week, they were at the mercy of the judicial system and its protracted timescales. The one silver lining in all of this was that Phillips did at least have Saturday to herself. As desperate as she was to make progress on the case, she could enjoy her date with Adam without fear of interruption.

So, after a very rare lazy morning enjoying a light break-fast, followed by a long soak in the tub, she began to get ready for their lunch together. Feeling unusually nervous, she laid out several outfit choices on the bed before opting for a white shirt, light blue skinny jeans and, for the first time in over a year, a pair of blue heels with open toes to show off her freshly painted toenails. She'd even decided to wear her hair down for the occasion, something almost as rare as the heels. After looping large silver hoops into her ears, she applied a delicate layer of makeup, in stark contrast to the bright red lipstick that covered her lips.

Checking her reflection in the mirror one last time, she smiled at the sight of weekend Jane, who was almost unrecognisable when compared to weekday DCI Phillips. At that moment, the doorbell rang. She checked her watch; 1.45 p.m. exactly. She was impressed. She loved punctuality. Pulling her short black jacket from the wardrobe, she headed downstairs and felt butterflies turning in her stomach as she approached the frosted glass front door, through which she could see Adam's silhouette as he stood on the front step. Taking a deep breath, she grabbed the handle and yanked it open.

'Did someone call for a doctor?' he said with a wide grin as he passed across a large bouquet of flowers.

Phillips chuckled as she took them. 'They're beautiful.'

'Yeah, I found them by one of the patient's beds last night,' he joked.

Phillips grinned as she opened the door wide and motioned for him to follow her. 'Come in. I'll stick them in some water.'

'Wow, what a lovely kitchen,' said Adam as he wandered in behind her.

'Thanks. I had it done a couple of years ago when I put the extension on.'

As she filled a vase with water, he wandered over to the bi-folding glass wall that covered the back of the house. 'Cute little garden, too.'

Phillips followed his gaze. 'Yeah, south-facing, so a proper sun trap in the summer. On the rare occasions we get sun, of course. Like this week for example.'

He turned to face her. 'Well, it wouldn't be Manchester if it wasn't raining, would it?'

She chuckled again. 'Exactly.' Placing the vase of flowers in the middle of the dining table, she checked her watch.

'Our table's booked for two, and it's ten-minute walk from here, so we'd better get going or we'll be late.'

'What are we having?' he asked.

'Tapas at one of my favourite restaurants in the village, Bar San Juan. It's amazing.'

'Sounds perfect,' said Adam.

'Come on, then. Let's go,' she said, and took him by the hand and led him towards the front door.

The short walk from her terraced home to Chorlton village seemed to fly by as they walked hand in hand, catching up on the last few weeks. WhatsApp messages and short calls were all well and good, but nothing compared to the easy conversation that flowed between them when they were face to face. Before she knew it, Phillips took her seat outside the restaurant, a high stool placed next to the large barrel that was their table. Adam did the same opposite her. The sun was shining, and the surrounding tables were filled with people, chatting and laughing. Soft Spanish music wafted on the breeze as she gazed across at the handsome doctor, who seemed even more rugged than she remembered.

For the next couple of hours, they shared small plates of sizzling gambas pil-pil, juicy chorizo, lashings of potatas-bravas, as well as Spanish omelette and paella, washed down with ice-cold beers, followed by a bottle of delicious red. Each drink allowed Phillips to relax further, forget her other life as a murder detective. By the time they'd finished the meal, it felt like they'd known each other forever, and were both keen for the date to continue.

So, as Adam stepped inside to settle the bill – despite Phillips's insistence they go Dutch – she took a moment to consider their next destination. 'How about Horse and Jockey?' she asked when he returned.

'Can we sit outside?'

'Yeah. There's a huge village green in front of it. Most people just sit down on the grass.'

'Count me in,' he said as he wrapped a thick arm around her shoulder. 'Lead the way, my lady,' he said in a mock English gentleman's voice.

Ten minutes later, drinks in hand, they weaved their way through the throng of people who had all had the same idea on this blazing hot Saturday afternoon. Eventually they found a small patch of grass where they sat down, leaning against the trunk of a large oak tree. From their position, they were able to take in the whole of the green and the pretty tree-lined streets that surrounded it. 'I love it here in the sunshine,' said Phillips, wistfully.

'I'd love anywhere with you,' replied Adam, glancing sideways at her.

Matching his gaze, his bright blue eyes seemed to sparkle, his chiselled jaw accentuated by his broad smile. Her stomach flipped as he moved his head towards her. Instinctively, she leaned in and closed her eyes as their lips met. Every fibre in her body exploded with desire. As his soft lips caressed hers delicately, his strong arm wrapped around her middle and he pulled her closer as her senses danced around her body.

Eventually, after what seemed like forever – but was probably less than a minute – he pulled away. 'I've been wanting to do that since the moment I met you,' he smiled.

Phillips swallowed hard. 'Me too,' she whispered.

'I think I'll try that again,' he said, and leaned in and kissed her once more.

The rest of the afternoon passed by in a blur, and Phillips felt a sense of elation she had never thought possible, sitting against a tree, drinking, chatting and kissing.

She liked being *Jane* for once, as opposed to DCI Phillips, and she *loved* being with Adam. He made her feel safe and protected, yet at the same time, excited and more alive than she had felt in a very long time.

As the sun began to set, they decided it was time to call it a night. After a slow, fifteen-minute meander back, they reached her front door. Phillips unlocked it and stepped inside, leaving it open behind her as she moved along the hallway, then turned to face him. 'You can stay if you like.'

Adam's wide grin appeared once again as he nodded, stepped inside and closed the door behind him. A split second later, he rushed towards her and kissed her passionately, his arms wrapping around her tightly, their mouths grabbing at each other greedily as she moved backwards, dragging him into the lounge, where they fell onto the large sofa. In a frenzy of movement, they began unbuttoning each other's clothes, desperate for the feeling of skin against skin.

Phillips heard Floss's faint meow somewhere in the distance, but paid her no mind. All she wanted in this moment was to make mad, passionate love to Adam, and nothing was going to stop that from happening, right here, right now.

THE NEXT MORNING, as the sun filtered through the blinds in her bedroom, Phillips smiled as she opened her eyes and came face to face with Adam, lying asleep next to her. She took a deep breath and savoured his unique scent as she gazed at him in silence, tracing the creases on his rugged face with her eyes. In that moment, he really was the most gorgeous man she'd ever seen. Leaning across, she kissed him gently on the lips, causing him to stir. He opened his eyes a few seconds later, followed by a broad smile.

'Morning,' she said, her smile matching his.

'Morning,' he replied as he stretched out his arms and yawned. 'What time is it?'

'Just after nine.'

Adam closed his eyes again, allowing his head to be enveloped by the pillow. 'That's the best night's sleep I've had in months.'

'I'm not surprised,' she giggled. 'That was quite a workout last night.'

'*Workouts*, I think you'll find.'

A Cheshire Cat-like grin hijacked her face. 'Do you want some coffee?'

'I'd love some.'

With that, Phillips jumped out of bed, unashamedly naked, and padded over to the bedroom door, where she pulled her robe from the hook before wrapping it around herself. She turned to face him, still smiling. 'I won't be long.'

Returning ten minutes later, she nudged open the bedroom door with her toes as she carried a tray through and placed it on the bed between them. On it was a cafetiere of fresh coffee, as well as a couple of freshly warmed croissants.

Adam sat up on one elbow as he took in the breakfast spread. 'Quite the hostess, aren't you? I could get used to this.'

'So could I,' said Phillips as she poured two cups of steaming hot coffee before passing one over.

Adam sat up as he took it from her, and for the next few minutes they sat in a comfortable silence as they tucked into the pastries.

Eventually Phillips was the first to speak, placing her cup on the tray in readiness. 'I just wanted to say that last night wasn't normal for me—'

'Don't tell me you like weird shit with masks and nipple clamps,' he teased.

She punched him softly on the shoulder and chuckled. 'That's not what I meant.'

Adam flashed a boyish grin. 'Look, I know what you're getting at, and for what it's worth, I'm not in the habit of throwing myself at women on the first date myself. But last night felt totally different. It was as if I'd known you for years rather than just a few weeks. What happened between us felt right.'

Phillips blushed. 'Yeah, it did.'

'And I'm really hoping we can do it again.'

'The sex or the date?'

'Both,' said Adam firmly.

'I'd like that.'

'The bummer in all this is that I'm on nights for the next month and my shifts land mostly on weekends, so I might not be able to see you for a few weeks.'

Phillips took another gulp of coffee. 'To be honest, with my current caseload, that might not be a bad thing. I've got so much going on at the moment with the Ardent murders, I'm not sure I'll have much free time either.'

Adam took the cup from her grip and put it on the tray before placing everything carefully on the floor. 'Well, in that case, we'd better make the most of the time we do have,' he said, drawing her into a passionate kiss before pulling her down onto the bed.

PHILLIPS AND ADAM had made the most of the time they had left on Sunday before he had to leave and get ready for his first nightshift of the week. In the hours after he left, she lay on the couch cuddled up with Floss, listening to Elvis Presley's Greatest Hits album. She'd dug out the record earlier that afternoon after realising both she and Adam loved his music, mainly thanks to their fathers' obsession with The King.

As 'Are You Lonesome Tonight?' echoed around the lounge, she felt like a love-sick teenager, missing her handsome doctor already. How on earth was she going to get through the next couple of weeks without seeing his beautiful face and kissing his luscious lips?

23

———

By the time Monday morning came around, she could not get 'Are You Lonesome Tonight?' out of her head, and found herself humming it as she unlocked the door to her office at Ashton House just after 8 a.m.

A minute later, as she was hanging up her coat, Jones appeared in the doorway. 'You sound unusually chipper for a Monday morning, Guv.'

'Do I?' she replied with a broad smile.

'Good weekend?'

'It was, actually.' She dropped into her chair and switched on her laptop. 'How about you?'

'Oh, the usual. Sarah provided me with a list of jobs as long as my arm, and the girls grunted occasionally as they stared at their iPads all weekend.' Jones stepped inside. 'So, come on. What's his name?'

Phillips feigned shock. 'I'm sure I don't know what you mean, DS Jones.'

Jones chuckled.

At that moment, and much to Phillips's relief, Entwistle appeared. 'The ballistics report has just come back on the

Nelson shooting, Guv. I thought you'd want to see it right away.' He strode across the room and handed her the file.

Phillips opened the folder on her desk and began scanning the pages in silence as Entwistle and Jones looked on.

After a minute or so, she found what she was looking for. 'It says the bullet that killed him was a 308-calibre, fired from a high-powered bolt-action rifle.'

Jones nodded. 'Makes sense, given the distance the bullet had to travel from the shooter's position in the trees.'

Phillips's eyes narrowed as she reclined in her chair for a long moment, before sitting forward and drumming her fingers on the desk. 'I seem to remember Meghan Butler saying her father shot himself with his hunting rifle. Do we have the details of that gun on file?'

Entwistle shook his head. 'No, but it shouldn't be too difficult to get them from the coroner's office.'

'Do that, Whistler. As quickly as you can.'

'On it, boss,' said Entwistle, leaving the room.

Phillips turned her attention to Jones. 'Where are we at with the warrant for Bush's flat?'

'I'm just about to call the Magistrates' Court now for an update.'

'Ok. You do that and let's regroup in an hour.' She tapped the open file on her desk. 'In the meantime, I'm gonna read the rest of this report. See if there's anything else in it that might help us.'

As the time approached, 9.30 a.m. Entwistle reappeared at her office door.

'Anything from the coroner?' she asked.

'Yes, Guv. Turns out Joseph Meyer shot himself with a 308-calibre bolt-action rifle.'

'Bingo!' said Phillips. 'That can't be a coincidence, can it?'

Entwistle shook his head. 'I'm sorry, Guv, but I think it

could. It's a very popular hunting rifle with potentially thousands registered in the UK.'

That wasn't the news Phillips wanted to hear. 'Have you heard anything back from Bali about the whereabouts of Daniel Meyer?'

'Not yet, no. I've been chasing the Embassy since last Friday, but they just keep saying they're waiting to hear back from the Balinese authorities.'

'Well, ring them again. We need to know if he's still in prison, because if not, that means he could be back here, and firmly in the frame for the three murders.'

Entwistle frowned. 'But immigration were clear, he's not been back into the country since he left in 2013.'

'Have you ever been to Asia, Whistler?' asked Phillips.

'No, I haven't, actually.'

'Well, trust me. The fake passport trade is rife over there. Immigration may have no record of *Daniel Meyer* coming into the UK, but that doesn't mean he's not here under another name.'

At that moment, Jones walked past her door.

Phillips beckoned him in.

'What's up, Guv?' asked Jones.

'Anything from the Magistrates'?'

Jones shoulders sagged as he shook his head. 'No, Guv. Apparently they're short-staffed and have a full schedule of cases across the day. They're saying it may be tomorrow before they can get the paperwork in front of a magistrate to authorise the warrant.'

'They really are fucking useless in that office,' growled Phillips. 'It's bad enough they shut down for the weekend, but when they are at work, they may as well not bother showing up.'

'I know, boss. It's hard enough just getting them to answer

the phone. I must have been ringing for at least half an hour before I got through.'

'And all the time they're messing about, Bush could be clearing his flat of any evidence we have against him.' Phillips's frustration was in danger of boiling over. She took a deep breath and exhaled loudly before continuing. 'Right, Whistler. I want you to double your efforts with the British Embassy in Bali. Do whatever you can to get that information on Daniel Meyer.'

'Yes, Guv.'

'Jonesy, pull whatever strings you can to see if we can get that warrant approved today.'

'Of course.'

Phillips got up from her chair and plucked her coat from the hook on the wall. 'I'm gonna go for a ride with Bov, see if Meghan Meyer can shed any light on the location of her father's gun.' With that, she strode out into the main office. 'Bov. Get the car keys, you're driving me to Broadbottom.'

The big Italian looked up from his computer and grinned. 'You got it, boss.'

24

Once again, Meghan Butler took her time answering the door. When she did finally open it on the chain, she frowned. 'What do you want now?' she said curtly.

'Can we come in, Meghan?' asked Phillips.

'It's not convenient.'

'It'll only take a minute.'

'Sorry, but I'm very busy with work.' Butler began to close the door.

Bovalino held it open with his thick left hand.

'Please, Meghan. We need your help,' Phillips said.

Butler swallowed hard, then nodded as she closed the door and released the chain, opening it again a moment later and ushering them inside. 'I have a client call in ten minutes, so I haven't got long.' She moved across the room and took a seat on the armchair.

With Bovalino at her side, Phillips remained standing opposite her. 'We need to ask you a couple of questions about your father's rifle.'

Butler recoiled slightly. 'Dad's gun? Why?'

Phillips ignored the question. 'Do you know what happened to it after your dad died?'

'No. Can't say I do.'

'Are you sure? It's very important.'

Butler's eyes switched focus over to the door to the stairs before she answered. 'I have no idea. Shooting was always Dad and Dan's thing. Plus, Dad used the rifle to kill himself. Why would I want anything to do with it after the police were finished with it?'

Phillips's interest was piqued. 'I thought you said you had no interest in shooting?'

'I don't.'

'But you knew he used a *rifle,* specifically?'

'What else would he use for hunting?'

Phillips pursed her lips. 'Well, a shotgun maybe?'

Butler shrugged. 'Same difference. It was long and he used it to shoot animals from a distance, so I just assumed it was a rifle. Truth be told, I really couldn't say what it was, for sure.'

'Could your brother have put it somewhere for safe-keeping at the time of your father's death?' asked Phillips.

'Possibly, Inspector, but it was eight years ago, and a lot has happened since then. If Dan did claim it, then he never mentioned it to me.'

Before Phillips could respond, her attention was drawn to the sound of footsteps upstairs. Instinctively she looked to where she thought she had heard them, just above her head, then back to Butler, who shifted in her seat uncomfortably.

'Is there someone up there?' Phillips asked.

'No. I'm home alone,' Butler shot back.

'Are you sure? It certainly sounded like there was.'

Butler appeared jumpy. 'It's an old house. It creaks and moans all the time.' She glanced at her watch and stood. 'Look, I really need to be getting on that client call.'

Phillips's guts told her Butler was hiding something from them. Without a warrant, she couldn't officially search the house, so she feigned concern for Butler's safety. 'I definitely heard someone up there, and I couldn't live with myself if something happened to you after we'd gone. Bov, go make sure the house is safe, will you?'

The big Italian had worked with Phillips long enough to know what she was doing, and without hesitation he set off towards the stairs.

Butler forced a smile. 'Honestly. There's no need.'

WHILE PHILLIPS REMAINED DOWNSTAIRS, Bovalino made his way up the narrow staircase to the first floor, and found himself facing three doors leading off the long, narrow landing. Nudging open the first door, positioned immediately at the top of the stairs, he stepped into what was obviously the bedroom belonging to Butler's children; Pokemon wallpaper covered the wall next to the beds. It appeared empty, but he dropped to his knees and checked under both beds just to be sure. Content the space was clear, he stepped back out onto the landing and moved into the next room: the master bedroom, replete with a king-sized bed and stylishly decorated in green and grey furnishings. After checking the wardrobes and under the bed once more, he was satisfied the room was also empty.

A few moments later, he approached the third and final door, which was slightly ajar. A few white floor-tiles visible through the gap in the door indicated it was the family bathroom. Bov stepped up, pushed the door open and stepped inside. There was a rush of movement to his right, and something heavy struck him hard against his temple. He fell forwards. A hand then grabbed at the back of his head and smashed his face with immense force onto the edge of the roll-top bathtub. He cried out in agony and hit the ground heavily. His assailant leapt over him and rushed along the landing towards the stairs.

———

PHILLIPS HEARD THE COMMOTION ABOVE, then the rare, yet unmistakable, sound of Bovalino crying out in pain. 'Who the hell's up there, Meghan?' she shouted.

Butler opened her mouth to speak, but Phillips didn't wait for a reply. Instead, she rushed to the bottom of the stairs. Opening the door at the bottom, she turned left to go up, but was immediately forced backwards as a man charged at her, carrying something in his hands. He knocked her back against the wall, and she hit her head. Momentarily dazed, she dropped to her knees and placed a hand against the wall as she attempted to steady herself.

The sound of heavy footsteps descending the stairs roused her once more, and she jumped to her feet as a bloodied Bovalino reached her. 'Are you ok, Guv?'

'I'm fine,' she said, as she rushed towards the front door to give chase. 'Let's just get the bastard!'

Jumping out onto the street a second later, they scanned the surrounding area but could see no sign of the man.

'Shit!' growled Phillips.

Bovalino wiped his bloody nose with the back of his right hand. 'He jumped me in the bathroom. I think he must have been waiting for me in the bath.'

'Did you get a look at him?' asked Phillips.

Bov shook his head. 'Sorry, Guv. He blindsided me.'

'Well, I got a quick glimpse, and I'm pretty sure I know who he is and what he hit you with,' she said, then marched back towards the front step, where Meghan Butler now stood, arms folded against her chest, eyes wide.

'So, how long has your brother been back in Manchester, Meghan?'

'Look. I can explain—'

'Save it,' Phillips cut her off. 'Meghan Butler, I'm arresting you for perverting the course of justice. Namely, withholding information relating to three homicides. You do not have to say anything, but it may harm your defence if you do not mention, when questioned, something which you later rely on in court. Anything you do say may be given in evidence.'

25

Phillips called Carter on the way back from Meghan Butler's house to brief him on the encounter with Daniel Meyer. Her boss was waiting for her when she returned to her office.

He wasted no time. 'So, you're sure it was Daniel Meyer that attacked Bovalino?'

'It was him all right. I got a good look at him just as he slammed my head into the wall. He's lost weight since the photo we have was taken, but it was definitely Meyer.'

'But how did he get past immigration without showing up on their system?'

'Probably a fake passport, sir. I understand they're not that difficult to get hold of in South East Asia.'

'So, he must be our number one suspect now, surely?'

'After beating up Bovalino and making a run for it, he's right in the frame.'

'And how is Bov?' asked Carter.

'Just a scratch, really. Meyer caught him off guard.'

'And where's the sister now?'

'In the custody suite, being processed as we speak. She's

asked for a lawyer, so we won't be able to talk to her until they show up.'

'Who's on the call list today?' asked Carter.

'The custody sergeant mentioned Erica Newsolme.'

'Is she any good?'

Phillips shrugged. 'I've come up against her a couple of times. She's by the book and efficient, but nothing we need to worry about.'

'Good. Keep me posted with any updates, ok?'

'Of course, sir.'

With that, Carter left.

Because of a delay in sourcing the duty solicitor, it was almost four hours after the initial arrest by the time Phillips took her seat opposite Meghan, seated alongside her court-appointed legal representative, Erica Newsolme, in Interview Room Three at Ashton House. Having had his superficial facial wounds attended to by one of the force's first aiders, Bovalino took the seat to Phillips's left.

After explaining the interview protocols, Phillips switched on the DIR – digital interview recorder. As soon as the long tone that signalled it was working had sounded, she got straight to the point.

'How long has Daniel been back in the UK, Meghan?'

Butler shifted in her seat and glanced nervously up at the video camera positioned on the wall behind Phillips's head before answering. 'I'm not sure of the exact date he got back—'

'Oh, come off it, Meghan. Surely you don't expect us to believe that?' Phillips cut in.

'I swear it's true. I didn't know he was coming back. He just turned up at my door a few weeks ago, unannounced. Gave me the shock of my life.'

Phillips scrutinised Butler's face to assess if she was lying. She sensed she was probably telling the truth – in this instance, at least. She continued. 'So why did you lie to us when we first asked about Daniel? Why say he was still in Bali when he was actually in Broadbottom?'

'I didn't want to get him into trouble.'

'Trouble for what?'

'Well, you know, coming into the country illegally.'

'Are you saying he used a fake passport?' asked Phillips.

Butler nodded.

'For the tape, the suspect nodded,' Phillips said. 'So where is he now?'

'I don't know.'

'I don't believe you, Meghan, and you're not helping him by covering for him. Your brother is a potential suspect in three homicides. You need to know that if he's eventually found guilty of those murders, *you* could be charged as an accessory.'

Butler's mouth fell open. 'Dan's not a murderer.'

'So why did he hide in the bathroom, then attack Detective Bovalino and make a run for it?'

'Because of the fake passport. He was frightened you'd send him back to Bali.'

'Do you think we're idiots, Meghan?' Phillips growled. 'The UK does not deport British citizens to other countries, even if they *have* used a fake passport to get into the country. No. I believe Daniel ran because he stabbed Matthew Rice to death, and was responsible for the deaths of Cherie Howard and David Nelson.'

Butler's brow furrowed. 'You think Dan killed Dad's old bosses?'

Phillips locked eyes with Butler and nodded. 'Yes, I do.'

Butler recoiled. 'That's insane.'

'Is it? You yourself said Ardent destroyed your family. That the stress of the court case brought about your mum's terminal cancer, which is why your dad killed himself. You and your brother both lost everything, thanks to the Ardent board. And eight years in a stinking Bali prison is a long time for Daniel to stew on what happened to his parents. That gives him plenty of motive to want to see them dead.'

Butler shook her head. 'No, that's not Dan. He wouldn't hurt anybody. He's a gentle soul, just like Dad was.'

'Prison time changes people, Meghan. Especially in the kind of prisons he'll have served his time in.'

'Look. I'm telling you; he ran because he thought he'd get into trouble for using a false passport. He opened up to me about it after I told him about your first visit. He said he couldn't risk going back to Bali, that he wanted to stay off the radar in case immigration found out he'd come back illegally. He just wants to recover from what happened to him in prison.'

'Which is what?'

'Violence, mainly, from the guards and other inmates. Because the man who died in the fight with Dan was Balinese, everyone gave him a hard time. When he turned up at my house, I hardly recognised him. He looked awful.'

Once more, Phillips scrutinised Butler's face. Again, she appeared genuine enough. She decided to change tack. 'When your brother rushed past me at your house, he looked to be carrying a laptop with him. Do you know where he got that from?'

Butler shrugged. 'He said he got it cheap from a guy he met in the local pub.'

'So, it's stolen?'

'He never said.'

'Why was that laptop so important to him that he'd hide in the bathroom with it?'

'I really don't know,' said Butler.

Phillips stared directly into her eyes. 'You see, Meghan, the person who killed Matthew Rice also stole his laptop. I think Daniel was responsible for both those crimes, and that's why he carried it with him when he made a run for it. Because if we found it, it would link him to the murder.'

Butler opened her mouth to speak, then seemed to think better of it.

Phillips continued, but again changed tack. 'Back at the house, you said you didn't know where your dad's rifle was. Were you lying?'

Butler again said nothing for a long moment.

'And remember, Meghan, if you don't tell us the truth and we find out Dan *was* involved in all three murders, you could be charged as an accessory to the fact, which brings a long prison sentence. By the time you get out, your two babies will be all grown up.'

Butler stared wide-eyed at Phillips, then glanced at Newsholme.

Phillips continued. 'So, I'll ask you again. Were you lying when you said you didn't know where your dad's rifle was?'

Newsholme nodded in silence as she made a note in her legal pad.

'Yes,' said Butler, finally.

'Good,' Phillips smiled thinly. 'So where is it?'

'In storage with a lot of Mum and Dad's stuff. Dan and I always planned to go through it when he came back from his trip overseas, and it's been there ever since.'

'Where?'

'The Big Blue Storage centre in Stockport. Just off the M60, near the pyramid.'

'And who has keys for the storage unit?'

Butler shifted in her seat. 'I do. I keep them in a drawer under the cooker in my kitchen.'

'Does Daniel know you keep them there?'

'Yes. He asked me about it last week. Said he wanted to

have a look at what was in the unit. It'd been so long since we put everything in there, he couldn't remember.'

'Do you know if he's visited the unit since you last talked about it?' asked Phillips.

'I honestly don't know. He's out of the house most days, and he doesn't really speak much when he comes home. Just sits in the back garden, smoking and staring into space. That prison really messed him up.'

'And when was the last time *you* visited the storage unit?'

'To be honest, I haven't been there since after Christmas,' said Butler. 'I keep my artificial tree and decorations in there, and packed them all away in January.'

'So, you have no idea whether the rifle is still in there or not?'

Butler shook her head.

'Once again, for the tape, the suspect is shaking her head. So, if you're not sure if it's there or not, that means Daniel could have taken it without you knowing, doesn't it?'

There was a long pause before Butler answered. 'Yes.'

'Do you have a recent picture of your brother?'

'No. Just the one of us together that you saw at the house. He hasn't let me take one since he came home.'

'You wouldn't happen to have a copy of that on your phone, would you?' Phillips said.

'Yes, I do, actually.'

'Good. I'm gonna need a copy myself. What's the passcode to your handset?'

'Why do you want that?'

'Because I'm going to need to look through your phone.'

Butler glanced again at her solicitor, who nodded once more. 'Erm, it's 280594. Our birthday.'

Phillips made a note of it on her pad, then spoke loudly for the benefit of the tape. 'I'm suspending this interview at 5.48 p.m.' She signalled to Bovalino that it was time to leave.

The big Italian followed her out of the room. When the door closed and they were out of earshot, she turned to face him. 'Get a couple of uniform teams to patrol the roads around Ardent's offices and Bailey's home.' She ripped the sheet with Butler's passcode from her notepad and handed it to him. 'Also, speak to the custody sergeant and pull off a copy of that photo of Daniel Meyer from Meghan's phone. Send it to the patrols and tell them to keep an eye out for him. There's more than a strong possibility he could be our shooter. If that's the case, and he does plan to go after her – now that he knows we're onto him – he could be heading there as we speak. We just can't let that happen, Bov. Ok?'

'Leave it to me, Guv,'

'And organise a warrant to search that storage locker. I want to know where that bloody rifle is.'

'On it,' said Bovalino, then turned on his heels and headed in the direction of the custody suite.

Phillips pulled out her phone and opened the web browser, taking a moment to find what she was looking for. Clicking on the phone number, she put it to her ear just as it connected.

'*Ardent Technologies, Louise speaking. How may I direct your call today?*'

'Lesley Bailey, please.'

'*Can I ask who's calling?*'

'Detective Chief Inspector Phillips from the Major Crimes team. It's urgent.'

'*Please hold.*'

The phone went silent for a long moment before the receptionist returned. '*Putting you through now.*'

A second later, Bailey appeared on the line. '*Chief Inspector. I'm beginning to think you're stalking me,*' she said sardonically.

26

The sun was setting as Lesley Bailey turned her convertible C-class Mercedes into her street. Another long day at the office meant she was arriving home just after 9 p.m. However, the extra hours would all be worth it once the company floated. Soon she would finally have the kind of wealth she had dreamed of all her life.

The May heatwave showed no signs of letting up, and with the car's top down, she was enjoying the evening breeze in her hair, the throaty hum of the V8 engine under the hood. A few moments later, she pulled the car right onto her sweeping, pebbled driveway and stopped just in front of the large double garage. After activating the automatic roof, which began to arch over her head from behind her, she took a minute to gather her phone and house keys as it closed shut and locked into place.

DCI Phillips had explained she had instructed a number of uniformed teams to patrol the areas around her office and home, for the next few days at least. Purely a precautionary measure, the inspector had assured her. Yet, between leaving the office and arriving home, she had failed to see any sign of her police protection. 'Typical bloody police,' she muttered as she climbed out of the car and closed the door behind her. Activating the central locking, which beeped behind her, she set off towards the front door of the house, stopping in her tracks as she reached the front step. The security light had failed to come on. An icy shiver ran down the length of her spine and her adrenaline spiked as she recalled Phillips's instructions to be extra vigilant. 'Come on, come on,' she whispered to herself as she fumbled to find the correct key in the fading light.

It was at that moment she heard noisy footsteps racing towards her across the gravel. On instinct, she spun round, raising her arms in self-defence, but it was too late. A split second later, something heavy hit the side of her head. The hard gravel underfoot stabbed into her body as she dropped like a stone onto it. In that moment, as she lay helpless on the ground, everything seemed to slow down. Someone stood above her, shouting her name, his voice distorted by the fuzziness of her brain. Oddly, she thought she could smell something sweet. She wanted to cry out, to ask for help, or mercy, or forgiveness, but her mouth remained unresponsive as the world around her began to fade to black. A moment later, there was nothing but silence.

27

P hillips switched off the TV and sat in silence on the sofa stroking Floss, who was curled up, purring loudly in her lap. Picking up her phone, she clicked on the photo album icon and grinned as the selfie she had taken of herself and Adam on Saturday afternoon filled the screen. Captured smiling in the sunshine, leaning against the tree outside the Horse and Jockey. It had only been a day since she had kissed him goodbye on her doorstep as he headed back to Liverpool and another spate of nightshifts, and once again she wondered how she would get through the next few weeks without seeing him. Gazing at the handsome face staring back at her, butterflies fluttered in her stomach. She had fallen hard and fast for Adam. He was like no one else she had ever been with. How on earth had she let that happen?

Suddenly, a withheld number filled the phone screen. Clicking the green phone icon, she answered it. 'DCI Phillips.' She listened intently for about thirty seconds. 'Thank you, Sergeant. I'll be there in twenty minutes.'

Jumping up from the sofa, much to Floss's displeasure,

she rushed into the kitchen and grabbed her car keys, then headed for the front door.

Once in the car, she pulled up Jones's number on the touch-screen console and pressed dial. As she pulled out into the road, he answered.

'*Evening, Guv. Everything ok?*'

'Looks like someone's attacked Bailey at her home in the last hour'

'*Shit.*'

'What the fuck happened to the extra police patrols?'

'*Bov definitely booked them, I heard him do it. Do you think it's Meyer?*'

'Could be. The uniform team said Bailey didn't get a look at her attacker, but her husband thinks he did, so I'm heading over to speak to them both now. I know it's late, but can you meet me there?'

'*Of course. I can be there in about thirty minutes.*'

'Great. Thanks Jonesy,' she ended the call.

Twenty minutes later, as Phillips approached Bailey's Bramall home, she could see the alternating blue and red lights of the police patrol car that had set down on the street in front of the driveway. Next to it was a yellow and green ambulance. Parking a few feet away, she got out and made her way over to speak to the uniformed team standing next to the patrol car.

'Ma'am,' they said in unison as she flashed her credentials.

'Are you the extra patrol I asked for?'

'Yes, Ma'am,' said one of the officers, identified as Sergeant Merchant on the name badge velcroed to his stab-vest – the one who'd called her at home half an hour ago.

'So, what the hell happened here tonight? I thought you were supposed to be watching Bailey?'

'We were, Ma'am. We spotted someone heading down the

back of the house so went to look, but we couldn't see anyone. By the time we got back to the front, the attack had just happened.'

'Jesus,' muttered Phillips, barely able to hide her irritation. 'Where's the victim?'.

'In the back of the ambulance. The paramedics are giving her the once-over.'

'Was she badly hurt?'

'Looks like a single blow to the head,' said Merchant.

'Did she get a look at her attacker?'

'No, Ma'am. She said he came up from behind her. But her husband reckons he got a good look at him. Apparently he arrived just as the attack was taking place and disturbed things.'

'You mentioned her husband on the phone earlier. Where is he now?'

'He's inside the house, Ma'am. His name's Fred.'

'I know. I've already met him.'

At that moment, Phillips spotted Jones's car moving slowly towards them. A minute later, after parking up in front of her car, he jumped out and walked quickly over to their position.

'This is DS Jones,' said Phillips as he reached them.

Jones nodded at both officers, then turned his attention to Phillips. 'What have I missed, Guv?'

'Sergeant Merchant says Bailey didn't see her attacker, but her husband did. He's in the house. I was just about to head in and speak to him.'

Jones frowned as he scanned the area. 'Where's Bailey?'

'Back of the ambulance. Being looked over by the medics.' Phillips nodded in the direction of the house. 'Shall we go in?' she said, then set off without waiting for an answer.

Fred Bailey was standing next to the large cooking island in the middle of the kitchen as Phillips and Jones walked in, cradling what looked like a large brandy. Once again, he wore golfing attire. He looked up as they walked in, his expression grave. 'Is Lesley going to be ok, Chief Inspector?'

'I haven't had chance to speak to the paramedics yet, I'm afraid.'

Fred Bailey dropped his head down and stared into his glass. 'I don't know what I'd do without her,' he said. His shoulders shook as he began to weep.

Phillips studied him closely for a long moment, but couldn't tell if his candid show of emotions was real or just for show. Either way, he had some questions to answer.

'We believe you saw your wife's attacker tonight?'

Bailey looked up, took a gulp of brandy, and nodded. 'Yeah. I saw him in my headlights as I pulled into the drive. He was standing over Lesley with a baseball bat in his hand, but as soon as he saw my car, he legged it.'

Phillips stepped forward and pulled out her phone. Taking a moment to find what she was looking for, she presented him with a digital copy of Meghan Butler's photo of Daniel Meyer. 'Was it this guy?'

Bailey's eyes narrowed as he scrutinised the image for a long moment, then shook his head. 'No. I don't think it was him.'

'Are you sure? This is an old photo. He might look a bit different now.'

Bailey took the phone from Phillips and had another long look. 'I'm pretty sure it wasn't him. This guy has quite a round face, whereas the man who attacked Lesley looked really skeletal, although to be fair he was wearing a black hoodie at the time.' He passed the phone back.

'Are you sure it wasn't him? The man we're looking for may have lost significant weight since that was taken.'

'I'm sure.'

Phillips put the phone in her coat pocket and sighed,

barely able to hide her frustration. 'Ok. Why don't you tell us what happened from the beginning?'

Bailey drained his glass, then perched on one of the tall chairs next to the island. 'Like I said, I came home from the golf club at about nine. I pulled into the driveway and parked up behind Lesley's car as normal. That's when my headlights landed on the guy standing over her, shouting and waving a bat around in the air. He took one look at me and set off running. I jumped out of my car to go after him, but I then saw Lesley wasn't moving and rushed over to her. She was bleeding badly from the head, so I called for an ambulance.'

'You said Lesley's attacker had a skeletal face. Would you recognise him if you saw him again?' asked Jones.

'Oh yeah. He stared right into my headlights for a split second, just before he ran off.'

Jones continued. 'In that case, would you be up for working with our photofit team to work up a likeness for our guy?'

'Sure. Whatever I can do to help catch the bastard.'

'Great. We can get that set up in the morning. Would you mind coming into the station?'

'Not at all.'

'Once I've organised the photofit team, I'll call you first thing tomorrow and make the arrangements.'

Bailey nodded emphatically. 'I'll give you my number.'

Jones made a note of it, then returned his notepad to his pocket.

'Right, well, we'd better go and check on your wife,' said Phillips, then turned and made her way outside, Jones on her heels.

As they reached the ambulance, Phillips stepped forward and rapped her knuckles lightly on the large side door.

A second later, it opened, and a female paramedic dressed in the distinctive green uniform peered out.

Phillips presented her ID. 'Is the patient ok to talk?'

'Yes, I bloody am!' Bailey bellowed from inside the vehicle. 'No thanks to you lot!'.

Stepping backwards, the paramedic beckoned them inside.

Phillips moved in first, with Jones falling in behind.

Bailey lay on the gurney, the back support positioned at a forty-five-degree angle. The top and right side of her head was wrapped in a large bandage, but other than that, she appeared her usual unimpressed self. 'I thought you were supposed to be protecting me,' she snapped.

Phillips ignored the jibe. 'Can you tell us what happened?'

Bailey shifted her position on the gurney and winced with pain, before eventually replying. 'I arrived home just after nine, and as I reached the front door, I spotted the security light hadn't come on. After speaking to you this afternoon about added protection, I panicked. As I was messing on trying to find the front door key, he came at me from behind. I turned to face him, and he hit me on the side of my head with something heavy. I fell to the ground and passed out a few seconds later.'

'Did he say anything to you?' asked Phillips.

'He was shouting something at me, but I couldn't make it out. My head wasn't working right.'

'And you never saw his face?'

'No. Like I say, he hit me as I was turning and I went straight down, but that doesn't matter. I know who did it.'

Phillips felt her eyebrows raise. 'Oh? Really?'

Bailey nodded. 'When I was lying on the ground, I swear I could smell something sweet, and I've just realised what it was.'

'Which was what?' asked Phillips.

'Cannabis. The last time I smelt that was when Liam Bush came here spoiling for a fight.'

'You think *Bush* attacked you?'

'Don't you?' spat Bailey.

Before Phillips could respond, the paramedic cut in. 'I'm sorry guys, but we really must be heading off to A&E. Mrs Bailey needs an urgent MRI scan.'

'I've told them I don't want to go,' said Bailey gruffly.

'We can't take any chances with a head injury,' replied the paramedic.

Phillips nodded. 'One more thing before we go. We believe Matthew Rice's killer stole his laptop after he murdered him. Do you know if there's anything on there that might be of value to anyone?'

Bailey remained stoic, staring Phillips straight in the eye. 'No, I don't.'

'Ok,' said Phillips with a forced smile, before signalling to Jones it was time to leave. As he stepped outside, she turned her attention back to Bailey. 'I'm very sorry you had to go through this tonight, Mrs Bailey, and I want to assure you, we'll be upping the police patrols, both here and at your work, to help us catch whoever did this.'

'Pah!' scoffed Bailey in return. 'You can do what the hell you like, but I'm not taking any chances. First thing tomorrow morning, I'm hiring my own personal bodyguards to protect me, because you lot clearly don't know what you're doing.'

Phillips opened her mouth to respond but thought better of it and instead followed Jones out of the ambulance.

'Charming as ever,' Jones said in a low voice as the ambulance prepared to leave.

'Where are we at with the warrant for Bush's place?' asked Phillips.

'Still waiting on the Magistrates'. I chased them again this afternoon, just before they finished, and they promised me I'd have it first thing in the morning.'

'Well, they'd better, or I'll head over to the court myself and force one of the lazy bastards to sign it in person!'

Jones chuckled.

'As soon as it comes through, we need to get over there and go through his place with a fine-toothed comb. We really need a result of some kind, or it won't be long before Fox will be looking for someone to hang.'

'I'll call them as soon as the office opens in the morning, Guv.'

Phillips tapped him on the shoulder. 'Thanks Jonesy.' She checked her watch. It was approaching midnight. 'It's late. We should both get to bed.'

Jones nodded. 'Your place or mine?' he joked.

Phillips laughed out loud. 'You should be so lucky.'

28

The warrant to search Bush's flat arrived in Jones's inbox at 9.10 a.m., and by 10 a.m., he and Phillips found themselves standing alongside a uniformed search team at Bush's front door in Longsight, made up of PCs Carole Lawford and Mo Devi, each of them wearing purple latex gloves.

After knocking repeatedly for a number of minutes, Bush finally answered. As per their previous visit, he peered out of the half-open door through sunken, bloodshot eyes. The sickly smell of cannabis hung thick in the air.

Before he had time to speak, Phillips explained the reason for the visit. 'Liam Bush, we have a warrant to search these premises under Code B of the Police and Criminal Evidence Act 1984, as well as search of your person under Code A of the same act.' She handed him the warrant. 'It's all in there if you want to read it.'

Bush stared at the piece of paper in his hands for a moment as Phillips stepped past him, followed by Jones and the two uniformed officers. It was a small one-bedroom flat, so Phillips took the bedroom whilst Jones and Lawford searched the lounge and kitchen respectively. Devi searched Bush himself.

A few minutes later, chaperoned by Devi, Bush appeared in the doorway to his bedroom. 'What's this all about?' he said, his voice cracking nervously.

Phillips turned away from the chest of drawers she was searching to face him. 'Where were you at nine o'clock last night, Liam?'

Bush rubbed the back of his neck and smiled nervously. 'Why do you wanna know?'

'Just answer the question, please.'

'I was here, watching TV.'

'Can anyone vouch for you?'

'I was on my own. Like I always am.'

'Really?' said Phillips, 'Because we have two witnesses who put you at the scene of a vicious attack in Bramall.'

Bush swallowed hard and forced a weak smile. 'That wasn't me. Despite what people think, I'm not violent and I rarely get out of Longsight these days.'

Phillips stared at him in silence, a deliberate ploy to unnerve him. It obviously worked, as he cleared his throat and looked away. Seizing her advantage, she moved across the room to stand next to him. 'Liam, you must know that this city has CCTV cameras on almost *every* corner, bus, train and taxi driving around the streets. If you're lying to us, it's only a matter of time before we'll find out, and with your record, that'll mean going back to Hawk Green for a very, very long time. Is that what you want?'

Bush stared at her with wide, red eyes as he bit his bottom lip.

'Tell us the truth and I'll make sure the CPS takes it into account.' Phillips continued to stare at him. 'Come on. Let me help you get out of this mess you've got yourself in.'

At that moment, PC Lawford appeared from behind Bush and PC Devi. 'Ma'am, I think you'll want to see this.'

Phillips ordered Devi to take Bush through to the lounge, then followed Lawford into the kitchen, where the back door was wide open

'It's outside in the alley,' said Lawford as she stepped out into the small yard.

Phillips followed her out and through the metal gate at the end of yard, into the alley running adjacent to the flat. They stopped next to a black wheelie bin.

'Seeing all the bins on the street when we arrived, it occurred to me it was bin collection day today. If it's anything like where I live, the trucks could arrive at any minute, so I figured I'd better check Bush's wheelie bin before it was emptied, just in case he'd thrown anything away. I found this.' She opened the lid to reveal a heavy-duty black refuse sack, open at the top.

Using a gloved finger, Phillips pulled back the neck of the bag to reveal a large black sweater secreted inside. Fishing it out, she held it up and inspected it.

'A black hoodie, Ma'am, just as Fred Bailey described. I guess Bush was either too lazy or too stoned to dispose of it properly.'

Phillips nodded, and scanned her surroundings for a long moment. 'Or he's smart enough to know there are no CCTV cameras along here.' Placing it back in the bin bag, she headed inside to where Bush sat smoking a cigarette, staring at the TV. 'Care to tell me what this was doing in your bin?'

'It's not mine,' he said without looking up.

'So how did it get in your bin?' asked Phillips.

He shrugged. 'That bin's been out there since last night. Anyone could have dropped it in there.'

Phillips turned back to Lawford. 'Bag this and get it into evidence.'

'Yes, Ma'am,' she said, and grabbed the hoodie before leaving the room.

Just then, Jones appeared, holding a piece of paper in his hand. He passed it to Phillips. 'I found this old shopping list under his bed, Guv.'

Phillips inspected it closely.

'Recognise the handwriting?'

'Looks like the handwriting from the threatening letters sent to Bailey,' replied Phillips.

'A perfect match, I'd say.'

Phillips turned back to face Bush and held up the list. 'I suppose this isn't yours either?'

Bush took a long drag from his cigarette before letting the smoke billow from his nostrils, but remained silent.

'I see. You're the strong, silent type all of a sudden, are you? Well, we'll see what you have to say back at the nick. Jonesy, cuff and caution Mr Bush, will you?'

'With pleasure, Guv,' said Jones, and pulled out his handcuffs as he moved next to him. 'Liam Bush, I am arresting you on suspicion of assaulting Lesley Bailey and causing grievous bodily harm. You do not have to say anything...'

29

One of the great frustrations of any detective is that, from the moment a suspect is arrested, British law only allows them to be held in custody for a maximum of twenty-four hours before being either charged or released. So, unless the investigating officers can find enough evidence within that time to charge them – or further crimes in order to hold the suspect for an additional twenty-four hours – the suspect must be released. Added to that, if there is a delay in sourcing legal representation for them, then the time is further shortened.

With a growing sense of frustration, Phillips and Jones finally took their seats across the table from Bush and his solicitor, Paul Freeman, with just under twenty hours left on the clock. Freeman was a portly man nearing retirement, with a shock of white hair and a permanently sweaty appearance, probably due to his ill-fitting off-the-rack suit and his tight shirt collar and tie.

Under the stark strip light of Interview Room Four, Bush's face appeared gaunter than ever, his bony face and sunken eyes a perfect match for Fred Bailey's description of his wife's 'skeletal' attacker.

With the formalities of the interview process out of the way and the DIR running, Phillips was ready to start firing questions at him.

However, she was stopped in her tracks by Freeman. 'Before we start the interview, my client has asked me to read a short statement he has prepared, after which he will not be answering any further questions.'

Phillips clenched her jaw in frustration. Bush was about stonewall them to avoid incriminating himself, a common tactic of many a guilty man.

Freeman began reading the handwritten notes from his legal pad. '"Last night, at around 7.30 p.m. I decided to take a walk. It was a warm night and my flat felt oppressive, so I went outside. I walked around for an hour or so, then returned home to find my moped had been stolen from my back yard. I considered calling the police, but because of my prison record and poor relationship with the police, I decided against it as I believed I could somehow be implicated in the theft. Instead, I reluctantly accepted the theft, and hoped it might yet be returned by whoever took it. I proceeded to put my wheelie bin out in the alley behind my house ahead of today's refuse collection, then went back inside my flat, where I stayed all evening watching television alone."' Freeman looked up from his notes. 'That concludes Mr Bush's statement.'

Phillips could barely hide her contempt for both Bush and Freeman. 'So, your moped was stolen just last night, but you never thought to mention it *this morning*?'

'No comment,' replied Bush.

Phillips smiled thinly. 'So, you're saying you were in Longsight at nine o'clock last night, and *not* Bramall?'

'No comment.'

'And I'm guessing you're also claiming your moped was stolen, because if we look at the ANPR cameras, we're likely to find evidence it was near Lesley Bailey's home last night. Is that right?'

'No comment.'

Phillips glanced at Jones. She could tell from his dead-eyed stare that he was as frustrated by these tactics as she was. Opening a Manila folder, she pulled out the photofit likeness that had been created, with Fred Bailey's help, earlier that morning. She turned it around, so that it faced Bush and Freeman, and slid it across the table. 'Our witness says this was the man he saw standing over the victim of last night's attack. Do you recognise him, Liam?'

Bush kept his eyes locked on Phillips. 'No comment.'

'You must admit, it looks a lot like you, doesn't it?' She tapped her index finger on the image for effect. 'I mean, this guy could be your double.'

'No comment.'

Phillips was fully aware of the fact Bush would continue to answer no comment to each and every question she put to him, but she also knew that if the Crown Prosecution Service wanted to pose the same questions to him at a later date in court, she had no option but to present every piece of evidence, follow every potential line of enquiry, during the interview. So, with mounting frustration, she pulled out two clear evidence bags. One contained the shopping list found at his flat, the other the threatening letters Bailey had received. She held up the bag of letters in both hands. 'Do you know what these are, Liam?'

'No comment.'

'These are abusive and threatening letters sent to Lesley Bailey over the last nine months. Whoever wrote them calls her a "fucking bitch", "a bully" and "a whore", as well as saying "you'll get what's coming to you, bitch!" Did you write them?'

Bush continued to stare back at Phillips, contempt oozing from his bony features. 'No comment.'

'You see, I think you did.' Next, Phillips held up the bag containing the shopping list. 'Because this is a handwritten shopping list that we found at your home this morning. As you can see, the writing is identical to that in the letters. One of our handwriting experts will easily be able to establish, in court, that they were written by the same person. That person being *you*.' Phillips glared at Bush in silence for a moment, hoping to unnerve him. 'Plus, once we check the DNA on the shopping list with the samples we took from the letters, I am one hundred percent certain we'll find they're also a match to *you*. So, why don't you do yourself a favour, stop this charade, and tell us what really happened last night at Lesley Bailey's house?'

Bush paused for a moment, his mouth moving slightly as he appeared to consider his options, before finally replying. 'No comment.'

For the next thirty minutes, again for the purpose of future cross-examination in court, Phillips probed Bush as to his whereabouts at the times of the Rice, Howard and Nelson murders respectively. All questions received the same response. Finally, with every legal box ticked and every avenue explored, Phillips drew the interview to a close and Bush and Freeman – as was their legal right – were escorted to a side room for further discussions. Once those discussions had been concluded, Bush would be sent back to the custody suite.

By the time the interview was complete, they had just eighteen hours to convince the CPS to charge him for the attack on Bailey, based on the evidence gathered so far, or find further evidence to get it over the line.

Back in her office, Phillips and Jones took seats on either side of her desk and debriefed.

'Well. Freeman's not as daft as he looks,' said Jones. 'He knows that, at this stage, all we've really got are the letters. Everything else is circumstantial, or explainable, which gives him a fifty-fifty chance of getting Bush off. *If* we can convince the CPS to charge him, that is.'

Phillips clasped her hands together under her nose as if in prayer, and nodded gently. 'He definitely wrote the letters and attacked Bailey last night. I have no doubt about that. But I'm really not convinced he's our killer. Not by a long way. He's an angry stoner who hates Bailey, sure, but he has little motive to kill the others.'

'So, you think him attacking Bailey is merely a coincidence, Guv?'

Phillips smiled wryly. 'I know, I know. I don't believe in them. But I'll admit, they can occasionally happen.'

Jones blew his lips dramatically. 'Bloody hell. I'd better make a note of the time and date. This is a historic day!' he teased.

Phillips sat forward. 'Personally, with the letters, the likely DNA match and eyewitness, and the discarded hoodie, I think we have enough to convince the CPS to charge him. But for completeness, I'll ask Entwistle to check ANPR cameras for Bush's moped, as well as his mobile phone activity.'

'Sounds good,' said Jones.

At that moment, Bovalino appeared in the doorway. 'The warrant's just come through for the Meyers' storage unit, Guv.'

Phillips slammed her hand down on the desk triumphantly. 'Bov, you're a legend!' She turned to Jones and grinned. 'If only everyone was as quick getting their warrants approved.'

Jones held up his hands in mock defence. 'Hey, no fair. I put mine in at four o'clock on a Friday. What do you expect?'

Jumping up from her chair, Phillips felt a surge of energy. 'Come on, guys, let's see if this storage unit contains Joseph Meyer's rifle, or can at least shed some light on Meyer's whereabouts.' With that, she made her way out into the office, stopped to brief Entwistle on his latest tasks, then led Jones and Bovalino out of MCU and down to the car park.

30

T he Big Blue Storage centre was a purpose-built unit housed on redeveloped industrial land just outside Stockport town centre. It had been constructed roughly fifteen years prior. Spaces like this had become more and more popular in recent times as families outgrew their homes, but not their possessions. Older facilities, such as this one, had once been adopted by members of the criminal fraternity, but with wall-to-wall CCTV at every turn, it was now rare to find anything untoward being stored in the more modern versions. Still, Phillips was hopeful they might find something within the Meyer unit to help accelerate the stalling investigation.

After presenting their credentials to the receptionist, along with the search warrant, Ross, an über-cheerful member of Big Blue's team, led them through a network of corridors to the Meyers' unit on the second floor. Keying in the passcode held on file, Ross opened the door and suggested they use the intercom connected to the wall in the corridor if they needed any further help during their visit. A moment later, he was gone, lost once more in the maze of corridors.

Taking in the packed room in front of them, Phillips's stomach churned in anticipation as she handed out latex gloves and assigned tasks. It wasn't long before each of them was opening cardboard storage boxes, duffle bags and old suitcases as they threw themselves into their search with gusto.

As expected, the unit was overflowing with the contents of Meghan and Daniel's parents' home, likely packed away shortly after their untimely deaths. An old sofa and matching armchair took up much of the space, packed in alongside box after box of figurines, clocks, ornamental plates, and the kinds of trinkets that were once so fashionable and popular with the previous generation. It was the type of stuff Phillips's mother kept at home on her mahogany cabinets and small marble-topped tables.

For well over an hour, the three of them carefully unpacked and repacked boxes, but to no avail. They could find nothing untoward, nor anything to suggest Daniel Meyer was involved in the three murders.

Growing increasingly frustrated, Phillips took a break, sitting down on an old traveller's chest that had already been searched and which she now knew contained a large selection of old and feathered cookery books, all written and published in the eighties. She exhaled loudly and rubbed the back of her neck as she attempted to ease the tension headache building in her temples. 'Jesus, it's as if the kids literally emptied the entire house and just chucked the contents in here.'

Jones stopped searching for a moment. 'They probably did, Guv. I mean, grief makes it hard to let go of stuff, doesn't it? Losing both parents in quick succession, they probably weren't ready to part with any of it.'

'I guess you're right, but it doesn't make our job any easier, does it?' Phillips vented.

Bovalino appeared lost in the task and continued without them, pulling down an old cardboard box with the words *Certificates and Medals* daubed on the side in black marker. Laying it on a small side-table in front of him, he opened it up and peered inside for a moment, before his eyes darted towards Phillips. 'I think you'll want to see this, Guv.'

He had Phillips's full attention as she moved across the room. 'What is it?'

Bovalino reached inside and pulled out a framed certificate, which he handed across.

She took it from him and read aloud. '"This is to certify that Daniel Meyer has achieved Deer Stalking Certificate Level 2, recognising excellence in stalking, marksmanship and butchery".' Phillips looked at Bovalino and Jones in turn. 'Daniel Meyer's an expert marksman?'

Bovalino tapped the framed certificate with his large index finger. 'And he knows how to use a boning knife, Guv.'

Phillips felt a rush of excitement. 'Right. We need to get Meyer's picture circulated across the force. I want *every* copper in Manchester looking for him.'

'I'll call Entwistle and get that sorted,' said Jones, pulling out his phone as he walked out of the storage unit.

Phillips turned back to Bovalino. 'Let's keep looking. We need to know if that rifle is still in here somewhere, or if Meyer already has it.'

Ten minutes later, Bovalino dragged an old wooden wardrobe away from the wall and peered into the space behind it. 'Bingo!' he said loudly.

'What have you found?' asked Phillips.

Bovalino pushed the wardrobe farther away from the wall to reveal a long metal box, fitted with an open padlock. 'Looks like a gun case,' he said. Reaching down, he picked it up and carried it over to the centre of the room, where he placed it on the floor. He and Phillips got down on their haunches for a closer inspection. 'Looks big enough for a rifle,' he said, opening it up.

Phillips peered inside. 'Shit! It's empty.'

'Apart from this,' added Bovalino, pulling out a box of cartridges. He read the product info from the side. '"Winchester 308 calibre high velocity centre fire cartridge".'

Phillips grinned. 'Which is the same calibre used to shoot Nelson. Bov, I could kiss you.'

The big Italian beamed and blushed at the same time.

'Bag that so Ballistics can check it against the bullet that killed Nelson.'

'You got it, Guv.'

She patted him on the back. 'If they match, we've got our killer.'

31

Late the following morning, Phillips returned from the staff canteen with a tray of coffees and teas for the team. After carefully placing the cardboard cup holder on the spare desk adjacent the bank of desks that housed Jones, Bov and Entwistle, she handed out hot drinks to each of the guys in turn, then dropped down at the spare desk.

She took a sip of her coffee and turned her attention to Bovalino. 'Any news from Ballistics on the cartridges we found yesterday?'

'Not yet, Guv, but they said they'd have something before the end of the day.'

'Good.' She switched to Entwistle. 'Whistler, what about Bush's phone and moped? Any sign of them on the grid the night Bailey was attacked?'

'His phone pinged off the Levenshulme mobile tower just after 7 p.m. the night she was attacked, then disappeared for *four* hours before reappearing on the same tower at 11.11 p.m.'

'Meaning he likely switched it off,' said Jones.

'To cover his tracks, no doubt,' added Phillips. 'And what about the moped?'

'Nothing specific to his registration on ANPR.' Entwistle swivelled his laptop so Phillips could see his screen. 'But I did find this identical moped with a different plate on the cameras nearest to Bailey's house. The rider was wearing a black hoodie, as well as a full-head crash helmet that covered his face.'

Phillips shook her head. 'It *has* to be Bush.'

'The plates were fake, Guv. That registration doesn't exist in the system. I also checked the data for Omar Aziz's GPS. It is connected to the van, as opposed to a handheld terminal, so it looks like he was where he said he was when the three murders took place.'

'So, he's not our killer.' Phillips exhaled loudly.

'Doesn't look like it.'

Phillips turned to Jones now. 'Going back to the Bailey attack, how are the lab boys getting on with DNA on the letters and the shopping list we found at Bush's flat?'

'They said it's in the queue, but not a priority. Could be a week before we get the results.'

'And what about the fingerprints?'

'Kelly is looking at them tomorrow morning. She's stacked at the mo,' said Jones.

'Damn it! Why does everything take so long?' Phillips growled.

Jones folded his arms across his chest. 'Budget cuts, Guv. Since Fox got the top job, we've been getting less and less overtime.'

Phillips nodded sagely. 'It does my head in, and it also means we've got no choice but to bail Bush until the results come back.'

'Looks that way,' Jones replied. 'Do you think we should speak to Lesley Bailey to let her know he's being released?'

Phillips closed her eyes and sighed loudly. 'Oh God. I'd almost forgotten about her. I can only imagine her reaction when we tell her that.'

'Do you want me to call her?' asked Jones.

Phillips's eyes shot open, and she sat forward in the chair. 'You're actually *volunteering* to call Bailey?'

'If you want me to.'

'Yes. Yes, I do. That would be brilliant, thank you. The less I have to do with that woman, the better.'

Jones grinned as he grabbed the landline. 'In that case, I'll call her now.'

'Are you sure?'

'Yeah. Piece of cake.'

Phillips clasped her hands together and stood. 'Jonesy, you are an absolute legend,' Then turned on her heels and headed for her office.

Five minutes later, Jones wandered in, eyes wide, lips pursed.

'How did it go?' asked Phillips, sitting behind her desk.

Jones whistled for effect. 'Well. I think it's fair to say that Lesley Bailey is not a happy bunny.'

'I didn't think she would be. What did she say?'

'Oh, you know, we're a bunch of incompetent morons, we don't know what we're doing, we couldn't catch a cold. Stuff like that.'

Phillips chortled as she imagined the call. 'She sounds just like Fox!'

Jones chuckled. 'You know, I thought it sounded familiar.'

'Well, thanks for doing that. I really couldn't face her today.'

'Any time. That's what I'm here for, Guv. I'm your human shield,' replied Jones, before heading back to his desk.

Phillips was still at her desk several hours later when her

landline rang. She answered it by flicking on the speaker function. 'DCI Phillips.'

'*Ma'am, it's Sonia on the front desk. I'm sorry to bother you, but there's a woman in reception demanding to speak to you. She seems very upset.*'

'Really? Did you get her name?'

'*Lesley Bailey, Ma'am.*'

Phillips closed her eyes and placed her head in her hands for a long moment.

Sonia continued. '*She also has two men with her who she claims is her security-team.*'

Lifting her head up, Phillips released a frustrated sigh. 'Right. Tell her I'm coming down.'

'*Thank you, Ma'am.*'

'Bov, you're coming with me,' said Phillips as she strode out into the main office a minute later. 'We have a couple of issues in Reception and I need some muscle.'

The big man was up out of his chair in a flash as Jones and Entwistle gazed at her expectantly.

'Lesley Bailey and her new security team,' explained Phillips.

Jones winced. 'Looks like it's your turn, boss.'

'Lucky me,' she replied as she headed for the door with Bovalino at her side.

Phillips and Bovalino found Lesley Bailey standing in the reception area, her face like thunder, flanked by two burly looking men wearing chinos matched with white shirts under blue sports jackets. One of them had bright ginger hair, and both wore earpieces.

'I want to know what the hell is going on,' demanded Bailey as they approached.

Phillips pointed to the nearest conference room, adjacent to Reception. 'Let's talk in there, shall we?'

Bailey nodded, somewhat reluctantly, and followed as Phillips led the way.

The two men fell in behind her, causing Phillips to stop in her tracks and turn to face them. 'Gentleman. I would ask that you stay out here with DC Bovalino.'

'Our principal's safety is our priority,' said one of the men.

Phillips offered a thin smile. 'This is a police station. She's quite safe, I can assure you.'

AS THE DOOR to the conference room closed behind Phillips, Bovalino moved over to stand next to the two men. He offered his outstretched hand to each of them in turn. 'DC Bovalino.'

'Dexter,' replied the first man.

'Harper,' replied the second.

Bovalino nodded and gestured towards the sofas in one corner of the reception area. 'Would you gentlemen like to sit down?'

Harper shook his head.

'We're good right here,' said Dexter.

Bovalino shot a glance at their identical maroon ties, which carried the paratrooper insignia. 'Which regiment were you in?' he asked.

'2 Para,' replied Dexter.

'Me too,' said Harper.

'Really?' said Bovalino. 'I had a run in with a couple of your lads a while back.'

'I bet I can guess who came off worse,' sniggered Harper.

'*I* did, as it goes. Maybe you know them?'

'I doubt it. It's a big regiment,' Dexter shot back as he scanned the surrounding area with all the intensity and scrutiny of a secret service agent.

Bovalino studied them both closely for a long moment. 'How long were you in for?'

'Long enough,' said Harper.

Dexter ignored the question and continued his surveillance.

'Did you see any active duty?' Bovalino asked.

'Afghanistan,' replied Harper. 'Two tours.'

'Really? What year?'

'That's classified,' said Harper.

Bovalino raised his eyebrows. 'What? Like *Special Forces*, classified?'

'Something like that,' Dexter cut in now.

'Wow,' said Bovalino, pretending to be impressed. In truth, he wasn't buying it. After chasing down a team of ex-paratroopers on the Hollie Hawkins kidnapping case a couple of years ago, he'd developed a fascination with the regiment. His keen interest had seen him connecting into the veteran community. Based on the conversations he'd had, and the type of guys he'd met during those exchanges, his gut was telling him something wasn't quite right with the so-called former paratroopers, Dexter and Harper.

———

DESPITE BEING OFFERED a seat at the conference table, Bailey made it quite clear that she preferred to stand.

Phillips decided it best to follow her lead. 'What can I do for you, Mrs Bailey?'

'You can start by explaining to me how a crack-head junkie who attacked me with a baseball bat has been allowed to walk free?'

'Are you referring to Liam Bush?'

'Of course I bloody am!'

'Mrs Bailey. I know you're upset—'

'What?' Bailey cut her off. 'Because you've released the man who murdered my partners and tried to kill me? Damn right, I'm upset.'

'There is no evidence to suggest Liam Bush had anything to do with any of the murders.'

'Apart from him trying to beat me to death, you mean?'

Phillips raised her arms in defence. 'Look. Strictly speaking, I'm not at liberty to discuss the full details of an open investigation with a victim, but because of what's happened to you and your partners, I'm happy to bend the rules in your case. Please rest assured, we're doing everything we can to bring the man who attacked you to justice. In the coming days, I'm very confident we'll gather sufficient evidence to do just that.'

'And what if Bush comes after me again in the meantime?'

'He won't,' said Phillips. 'He's out on police bail and not allowed to go within one mile of your house or workplace. Plus, since the attack, I've increased the number of uniformed patrols around your home, as well as your factory and offices. He'd have to be an idiot to try anything.'

'So that's it? A few extra coppers riding around is supposed to placate me, is it?'

'I'm not sure what else I can do within the confines of the law.'

Bailey folded her arms across her chest and resembled a petulant teenager as she snorted defiantly through her nose. 'I haven't got time for this crap. I need to get back to work. I'm due in London for the IPO presentation on Monday.'

'I really don't think that's a good idea, Mrs Bailey. Taking that trip would make it very hard for us to protect you from whoever attacked Matthew, Cherie and David.'

'Well, that's as maybe, but I have no choice. If I'm going to float Ardent, I have to be there.'

'Could you do a video link instead?'

Bailey scoffed. 'I built Ardent up from nothing into a multi-million-pound company. *I am* Ardent and my best chance of getting the level of investment I want is to be there, whether I like it or not.'

'It just seems very risky under the circumstances.'

'I stand to make almost half a billion pounds from the IPO, Chief Inspector, so it's a risk I'm willing to take.' With that, Lesley Bailey headed for the door.

Phillips followed her out and watched as she marched across the reception area towards her two bodyguards and Bovalino. One of the guards lifted his wrist to his mouth and spoke into what Phillips assumed must be a two-way radio. A few moments later, a large black Range Rover pulled up outside reception. The two men escorted Bailey out and bundled her in the back before jumping in after her.

Phillips watched them lurch away at speed, then wandered back across Reception to meet Bovalino at the bottom of the stairs. 'That was all a bit dramatic, wasn't it?'

The big man nodded. 'They're a couple of Walts if you ask me.'

Phillips frowned. '*Walts*?'

'Walter Mittys, Guv,' Bov explained. 'Named after the functional character who lived a fake life. It's what military people call fake soldiers: those who claim to be veterans but have never served.'

'I didn't know there was such a thing.'

'Yeah. There is, and more than you'd think. The ex-forces guys I met despise them. And those two seem like Walts to me.'

'What makes you say that?'

'Well, they were both super-cagey about their military backgrounds, and indirectly claimed to be ex-Special Forces.'

'Maybe they were. I guess I'd expect all ex-Special Forces soldiers to be cagey about their exploits,' said Phillips.

Bovalino shook his head. 'There's a saying in Hereford, where the SAS are based, that you can always tell the guys that are actually Special Forces...because they *never* talk about the regiment. That way, there's no need to be evasive. Nah, these two are fakes. I'm convinced of it.'

'Well, fakes or not, they're Bailey's problem, not ours.'

'I'd like to know for sure, Guv.'

'Why, Bov? We've got enough on our plates right now.'

'I know that. But if they aren't who or what they claim to be, Bailey could be at risk. Say it is Meyer who's behind the Ardent murders and he's not finished yet. Those idiots playing at protecting her could end up getting her killed.'

Phillips said nothing for a moment as she considered what Bovalino was saying. 'All right,' she said finally. 'But it's on top of your current workload. It can't slow down the main investigation.'

A wide smile appeared on Bovalino's face. 'It won't, Guv. I promise.'

32

As Phillips and Bovalino walked back into MCU, Jones beckoned them over.

'How was Bailey?' he asked with a wry smile.

'Pleasant as ever,' said Phillips.

Jones chuckled to himself as Bovalino dropped into his seat.

'You're just in time, Guv,' said Entwistle. 'I have a couple of updates for you.'

'Go on.'

'Firstly, Martin Anders at the Embassy in Bali has finally come back to me and confirmed Meyer was released early, due to overcrowding.'

'Better late than never,' Phillips said sarcastically.

'He also sent a copy of his prison record over. It seems Meyer had a tough time in there. There's a number of entries suggesting he was involved in violent altercations with staff as well as inmates, and his inmate notes suggest he became more and more aggressive as his sentence went on. Bit of a troublemaker, by all accounts – which might also be why they released him early, according to Anders.'

'What? They let him out *because* he was violent?'

'Anders thinks it's possible. The Balinese prison governors are well known for liking an easy life, apparently, and they may well have decided he was better off being someone else's problem.'

'You couldn't make it up, could you?'

'Sounds like the bloody Wild West,' Bovalino chimed in.

'So,' said Phillips. 'We now know Meyer's a crack shot, knows how to use knives and has a history of violence. He *has* to be our guy.'

Entwistle's face lit up with excitement. 'I've found something else which I think confirms just that.'

'Really?' said Phillips, eyes wide.

'I've been working my way through security footage from the storage unit, and found this.' He clicked open a window on his laptop screen.

Phillips leaned in to get a better view of the screen. 'Jesus,' she whispered.

Jones was out of his seat in a flash. 'What is it?'

Bovalino followed suit and they all gathered behind Entwistle to view his screen.

Entwistle tapped the image with his pen. 'CCTV footage of Daniel Meyer, leaving the storage facility two days *before* Nelson was shot, carrying what looks like a rifle bag.'

'Bloody hell, guys, we've got him!' said Phillips triumphantly. 'Meyer *has* to be our killer.'

33

As the day drew to a close, Phillips suggested that the team go for impromptu drinks after work; they'd all been working flat out on the Ardent investigations, and she felt it would do them good to let off some steam. Much to her disappointment, Bovalino already had plans that evening to work with his cousin and co-driver, Fabio, on the rally car they raced at weekends, and Entwistle had yet another hot date with someone he'd met on Tinder. Jones was free, but only for an hour or so, as he'd promised to help one of his girls with a school project. It wasn't quite the night she had envisaged, but at least Jonesy offered to drive, meaning she could have a drink and not have to worry about getting home.

Thirty minutes later, they found seats in the sunshine, overlooking the canal outside the ever-popular Dukes 92 pub-cum-restaurant in Castlefield.

'So, how are things with you, Guv?' asked Jones, taking a sip from his Diet Coke.

Phillips took a gulp of her ice-cold Pinot Grigio before answering. 'Fine. Why do you ask?'

Jones's mouth curled up at the corner. 'Oh, you know. Just wondering if your domestic situation has changed at all?'

Phillips eyed him suspiciously. 'And what does that mean?'

'Well, are you maybe seeing anyone at the moment?' he said with a wry grin.

Phillips chuckled. 'Am I being interrogated here, Jonesy?'

Jones laughed along. 'Yes. Yes, you are.'

'And what makes you think I might be seeing someone?'

'The other morning. You looked really happy, glowing, even, and I haven't seen you that way in years.'

'So I'm a miserable cow most of the time, is that what you're saying?' Phillips teased.

'No.' Jones shook his head slowly. 'That's not what I'm saying.'

Phillips took another drink, closed her eyes and turned her face into the sun. 'I did have a date on Saturday as it happens, but I'm not sure how serious it is,' she lied.

'I knew it! So?'

'So, what?' replied Phillips, her eyes still shut.

'Details, boss, details.'

'What do you want to know?'

'Name? Occupation? Prospects?'

Phillips cackled as she opened her eyes and turned her attention back to Jones. 'Prospects? What are you? A Victorian father, or something?'

Jones chortled. 'You know what I mean.'

Phillips took another mouthful of wine, then set her glass down on the table. 'His name's Adam. I met him through my brother. He's a doctor in A&E, and he's got a lovely bum. Will that do you?'

Jones's eyes bulged as a wide grin spread across his face. 'Sounds ideal.'

'We'll see,' said Phillips, now keen to change the subject.

'So how about you and Sarah? How are things at the moment? Better?'

Jones nodded. 'To a degree, yeah.'

'Doesn't sound overly positive.'

'She still thinks I spend too much time at work, and after what happened in the Carpenter case, she worries I could get hurt again. But, that said, we're getting on much better and trying to make time for each other as a couple – which isn't always easy with two teenage girls in the house.'

'I can imagine. How old are they now?'

'Becky's seventeen and Pippa is fourteen,' said Jones.

'They must be quite a handful.'

'Oh yeah. And now Pippa's old enough, and their cycles are in sync with Sarah's, the atmosphere at home can get a bit fractious at times, to say the least.'

'No wonder you spend so much time at work,' joked Phillips.

'Exactly!' chuckled Jones.

For the next hour they basked in the sunshine, chatting about nothing of any real consequence and content to sit in silence from time to time, just watching the world go by. It made a nice change from the stress and intensity of the Major Crimes office.

Eventually, and three glasses of Pinot to the good, Phillips suggested it was time she let Jones go home. As promised, he offered her a lift, which she initially rejected, suggesting that she get the tram back, but he insisted.

So, it was thirty minutes later when Jones pulled the car into a parking space on the street outside her home.

'Thanks for this, Jonesy,' said Phillips, patting him on the wrist from her position in the passenger seat.

'My pleasure, Guv. It was good to catch up. I enjoyed it.'

'Yeah, it really was. Anyway, I've kept you out long

enough. You should be getting home to your girls,' she said, and opened her door.

'Oh, the joys of homework with a moody teenager. Can't wait,' Jones said, his tone sarcastic.

Phillips climbed out, then bent back over so she could see Jones in the driver's seat. 'See you in the morning,'

'Do you want me to pick you up?'

'Would you mind?'

'Not at all. Eight o'clock?'

'Make it eight-thirty. We can head straight over to Ardent to see Bailey,' replied Phillips, before straightening and closing the door.

As she reached her front step, she turned to see Jones pulling out into the road. He tooted his horn as he set off down the street. Turning back, she pushed her key into the lock. But her front door opened of its own accord.

Her adrenaline spiked as she carefully, and quietly, stepped into the hallway. She stood in silence for a long moment. When she heard footsteps, followed by a door closing upstairs, she tried her best not to panic, her heart beating faster. Slowly, she retraced her steps back through the front door, down the path and onto the pavement. Walking up the road out of sight of the house, she pulled out her phone and dialled Jones.

He answered almost immediately. 'Did you forget something, Guv?'

'There's someone in my house!'

'You what?'

'An intruder. My front door was open and I heard them upstairs.'

'Where are you now?'

'Back on the street. I got out of there as quickly as I could.'

'Stay there. I'm coming back.'

A few minutes later, Jones met Phillips on the street and

together they made their way back to the house. Police batons at the ready, Jones led the way inside with Phillips close behind. Silence filled the air, and for a brief moment she wondered if – after three large glasses of wine on an empty stomach – she had simply imagined it.

But then – *there it was again*. The noise of someone moving about upstairs. Adrenaline surged through her.

They both swallowed hard. With Jones taking point, they padded up the staircase as quietly as possible. As they reached the landing, it was clear that whoever it was, was hiding in the bathroom. Phillips was reminded of Meyer's vicious attack on Bovalino at Meghan's house. Creeping along the landing, the noise from the other side of the door grew louder with every step. A few seconds later, they arrived at the bathroom door, which was firmly shut. Jones moved forward and grabbed the handle as Phillips took a step back and raised her baton, ready to repel any attack.

Positioned sideways on to the door, Jones silently mouthed 'One, two, three,' then rammed down the handle and flung the door wide open as they both rushed in, shouting 'Police!' in unison.

'What the fuck!' screamed the naked man in front of them as he spun on his heels to face them.

Phillips stopped in her tracks and dropped her baton to her side. 'Adam? What the hell are you doing here?'

Grabbing a towel from the side of the bath, Adam feverishly wrapped it around his midriff as his cheeks reddened. 'I switched shifts with a mate so I could surprise you.'

Jones coughed nervously. 'I'll, er, leave you guys to it,' he said, and walked out of the room.

Phillips was frowning. 'But how did you get in?'

'I borrowed the spare key you gave to your brother for emergencies. I was just about to have a shower when you burst in. You scared the shit out of me.'

'Ditto,' Phillips spat back. 'It's not the first time I've come home to find someone had snuck into my house. And the last time that happened, I was almost killed.'

Adam's face was incredulous. 'What? Seriously?'

'Yeah. *Seriously.*' Phillips exhaled loudly. 'Look. Just wait there. I need to go and speak to Jonesy.'

Jones was about to jump in his car when Phillips caught up with him. 'Sorry about that Jonesy. I'm so embarrassed.'

'Don't worry about it, Guv.' He opened the driver's door. 'I'm just glad it wasn't anything more serious than your naked boyfriend.'

'He's not my boyfriend,' Phillips protested.

Jones smiled. 'Whatever you say, Guv.'

'Are you still ok to pick me up in the morning?'

'Sure.'

'Thanks, Jonesy. Look, I'd better get back.'

Jones nodded.

Phillips spun on her heels and began making her way back to the house.

'Oh, and boss?' Jones shouted after her, as she reached her path.

She turned to face him. 'Yeah?'

'You were right,' he grinned. 'He really does have a lovely bum.'

Phillips nodded without feeling. 'Night, Jonesy,' she said, then pushed open her gate and headed back inside.

34

Adam was standing in the hallway, dressed and waiting for her, as she walked back through the front door. 'Jane, look, I'm sorry if I embarrassed you in front of your colleague.'

Phillips shook her head as she blew her lips. 'What were you thinking?'

'Like I said, I wanted to surprise you.'

'By breaking into my house?'

Adam rolled his eyes. 'Oh, come on. That's a bit dramatic, isn't it?'

'Is it, Adam? Is it? Have you forgotten what I do for a living?'

'Of course I haven't.'

'Do you know how many nasty bastards I've put away in the last twenty years? Any one of them would love nothing more than to slit my throat as I sleep.'

'Seriously, Jane, I think you're blowing this out of proportion—'

'Oh, I am, am I?' Phillips cut him off. 'When was the last

time one of your patients followed you home and tried to strangle you in your hallway, huh?'

Adam recoiled. 'What the hell are you talking about?'

Phillips pointed to his feet. 'That very spot where you're standing. A couple of years ago, a serial killer I was hunting tried to strangle me right there.'

Adam's eyes widened. 'Oh my God, Jane. I had no idea.'

Phillips let out a low growl as she ran her hand down her face, causing it to redden. 'Why would you?'

Adam stepped forward and attempted to put his arms around her.

Phillips brushed him aside. 'Don't, Adam. Don't.'

'Jane, I'm sorry.'

'So am I.' She let out a long breath. 'Look, I don't think this is going to work out.'

'What?' said, Adam, incredulous.

'I made a mistake. I thought I could handle seeing someone and being a murder detective, but I can't.'

'Come on, Jane. We're great together. Don't do this.'

Phillips looked him dead in the eye. 'I have no choice, Adam. It can't work. Not with everything I've got going on in my life with work.'

Adam raised his arms in defence. 'Look, I get your job is stressful and it takes a lot out of you, but so does *mine*. That's what makes us such a great team. We understand each other and the pressures that come with our lines of work.'

'That's just it, Adam. We obviously don't.'

Adam's shoulders sagged as he stared at her. 'So that's it, then? It's over, just like that?'

'Yeah. It is.'

Adam bit his bottom lip and nodded soberly. 'Well, I'd better go and get my stuff,' he said, and made his way back upstairs.

A few minutes later, Phillips was in the kitchen pouring

herself a glass of wine when she heard the front door close shut behind Adam as he let himself out. The house fell silent. She closed her eyes and took a deep breath. She was better off on her own, she told herself. The job would never allow her to be fully present in a relationship, no matter how hard she tried. Better to get out now before anyone got seriously hurt. Picking up the wine, she wandered through to the living room and dropped down onto the couch. As she stared into her glass, her lips began to tremble. A few moments later, she began to weep, both for the man she'd let go of and the life it seemed she could never have.

35

Meyer had chosen this particular hotel because the owners took cash and asked no questions. In return, he was happy to forego the usual amenities you would expect in a half-decent establishment. His room was cramped and smelt slightly of damp; a tiny en suite bathroom was wedged into the corner of the room. The single bed was fitted with garish flower-print bedding that had seen better days, and the net curtains on the windows ensured the room felt dark and slightly oppressive. Still, compared to the conditions he had become accustomed to over the last eight years in prison, it felt more than comfortable.

Sitting on the edge of the bed, he pulled his Winchester 100 rifle from the soft leather gun case and rested it on his knee. Rubbing it gently with both hands, he was reminded of the times he had spent with his father, who, with his usual approach to most things in life, patiently taught him how to shoot it, and eventually how to stalk, kill and butcher deer in the field. He had loved their times out in the woods, tracking stags together. The happiest times of his life, stolen when his father used the same gun to kill himself. His teeth clenched in his jaw and his stomach churned as he recalled the moment the police knocked on the front door of their family home to tell him and his sister that, just a month after they had buried their mother, their father was dead too. Their world had shattered.

From that moment on, he had blamed the partners of Ardent for his parents' deaths, a belief that had only grown deeper with each day that passed in the Balinese hellhole he'd been forced to call home for almost a decade. His plan for vengeance had been slow to seed, but as each year came and went, his desire to destroy their lives in the same way they had destroyed his had become a living thing within him, consuming every fibre of his being – along with the abject rage that burned in his bones.

Casting his eyes to the old bedside table, his gazed at the faded, dog-eared picture of himself and Meghan, his twin sister, smiling together in happier times on their eighteenth birthday. She had given him the photo the first time she had visited him in prison. Since then, it had never been far from reach. His heart ached as he stared at the smiling face of his beautiful sister, knowing that whatever the outcome of his plan was, he would likely never see her again. He was certain he could never spend another day inside a prison cell, that was for sure. So, if he succeeded, and managed to escape, he would use his fake passport to get out of the country. If he failed, well, he would be dead, either at the hands of the police or his own.

Placing the gun down on the bed, he picked up the laptop he had taken from Matthew Rice's home just over two weeks ago. He hadn't planned to steal it, of course, but when he had heard a woman shouting Rice's name from it, he had instinctively closed it without thinking. Realising it held his finger-prints, he'd picked it up with the intention of dumping it somewhere on the journey back to Broadbottom. However, as he made his way home, he had become increasingly aware of CCTV cameras in various guises on nearly every street. So, instead of ditching it, he'd taken it back to his sister's house and packed it away in his rucksack for a few days. Eventually, though, his curiosity had got the better of him.

Keen to find out what secrets it might contain, he made up a story for Meghan, saying he'd bought it in the local pub, before enlisting her expertise as a virtual assistant to bypass the password and gain access to the main drive. She had also spent some time patiently teaching him how to navigate the machine, which was very different to the computers he'd used all those years ago, before going to prison. Once he had access and a rough idea of what he was doing, he'd searched through every folder and email it contained, looking for proof that the Ardent directors had indeed conned his father out of his patent. After days of intense scrutiny and a growing sense of disappointment, he'd finally hit the jackpot, uncovering an ancient email trail that, amazingly, discussed their plans to register the patent as theirs – and more importantly, to cut his father out. Not only that; he'd also been able to access HR files containing personal info on each of them, including their home addresses, as well as a shared calendar that detailed each of the directors' appointments for the next month. Information that had proved invaluable in stalking Howard and Nelson, as well as leading him here, to his current location.

Inserting a pen-drive, he began copying the relevant files and emails onto it. Once that task was complete, he closed the laptop and placed it back on the bed. Next, he pulled out his phone and spent the following fifteen minutes scanning through a bunch of videos he'd captured earlier that day during a comprehensive recce of the kill zone he intended to use in just a few days.

When he was done with those, he pulled up a web article that featured a stony-faced Lesley Bailey sharing the news of her impending IPO with the business editor of the *Manchester Evening News*, a move that would eventually make her rich beyond her wildest dreams. Money that, by rights, belonged to his father.

His stomach turned once again as he stared at her face. Bailey had stolen everything that mattered to him, and put him and his family through hell. How ironic, he thought, because that was exactly where he was about to *send* her.

36

The following morning, Jones picked Phillips up from home at 8.30 a.m. on the dot.

'Morning,' he said with a lopsided grin as she dropped into the passenger seat.

'Is it?' Phillips shot back.

Jones's face wrinkled. 'Didn't go well last night, then?'

'No. In fact, I think it's fair to say it went about as bad as it could, actually.'

'Oh dear. Do you want to talk about it?'

The look of deep sadness on Adam's face when she had told him it was over flashed into her mind's eye. She shook her head. 'No. I really don't.'

'I'll shut up then,' replied Jones, then slipped the car into gear and pulled away from the kerb as they set off for Ardent's offices.

Lesley Bailey's behaviour was true to form once again as Phillips and Jones found themselves sitting opposite her in her office, thirty minutes later. Her face twisted with irritation as she listened to Phillips's plea to cancel her trip to London.

'We believe the threat to your life is very real now, Mrs Bailey. The man we suspect killed Matthew, Cherie and David is out there somewhere, in possession of a high-powered rifle, and equipped with the skills to use it to deadly effect.'

'Well, you'd better hurry up and catch him then, hadn't you, because I'm not changing my plans. Like I said to you the other day, *I* am Ardent, and the only way I can secure the level of funding, through the IPO, that I believe reflects the true value of the company, is to sell it to the investors in person. So, I'm going to London, whether you think it's a good idea or not.'

Phillips glanced at Jones whose dead-eyed, frustrated expression matched her own. 'Very well. If that's your final decision–'

'It is,' said Bailey firmly.

'In that case, we'd better get back to the office and start preparing for your trip.'

Bailey recoiled and looked aghast. 'What do you mean? You're not planning on coming with me, are you?'

Phillips flashed a thin smile as she locked eyes with Bailey. 'Oh yes. I'm afraid it falls to me to keep you safe until we can catch the killer. So wherever *you* go, *my team* goes.'

'I really don't think that will be necessary,' Bailey protested. 'I mean, my security team is more than capable of protecting me.'

Phillips stood, and Jones followed her lead. 'Well, you'll have double the protection now, won't you?'

Bailey opened her mouth to reply, but Phillips turned on her heels and headed for the door before she could say anything. 'We'll be in touch soon with the arrangements,' she said as she pulled it open. Glancing back at Bailey, she nodded, then stepped out into the corridor without waiting for a reply.

'She's nuts,' muttered Jones, attempting to catch up to Phillips as she marched back towards to reception.

'Bloody greedy, more like,' she huffed. 'All Bailey cares about is the money. It boils my piss that I have to put *my* people in danger, not to mention spend a bloody fortune in overtime to try and keep *her* from being shot.'

They soon reached the reception area. As they strode through it, neither said a word to the sullen woman behind the desk before they stepped out into the sunshine and headed for the car.

As soon as Phillips arrived at her desk forty minutes later, she put a call in to her opposite number in London's Metropolitan Police Major Crimes Unit, DCI Tahir Khan – nicknamed T. She had worked with him a few years earlier as part of task force, and seen for herself just what a brilliant detective he was. The perfect man for the current job, in her eyes.

As soon as the call connected, she wasted no time in bringing him up to speed on the situation they found themselves in.

'*So, how credible is the threat to life?*' asked Khan when she was finished.

'Well, the suspect is an expert marksman and was spotted on CCTV carrying what we believe is a long-range hunting rifle. The gun which we suspect was used to shoot and kill David Nelson a week ago.'

'*Ok, well, that's a worry.*'

'Yeah, it really is, because this guy's beef is personal and deep-rooted. We cannot underestimate how far he may go to kill Bailey.'

'*And what makes you think he's going to try anything down here?*'

'Instinct, T. Plus, Lesley Bailey's upcoming trip to London is in the public domain. She's been boasting about it recently in the business pages of the local rag, as well as a host of online articles. And if he knows we're watching her closely in Manchester, he might think he has a better chance of success in London.'

Khan remained silent for a moment on the other end of the line. '*The main issue we have is location. Cavendish Bank is in the heart of the business district. Every rooftop round there could be a potential vantage point for him. If we're to stand any chance of catching him, we're going to need TFU snipers as well as helicopter support, which won't be cheap. And I'm afraid the costs will have to be covered by the GMP.*'

'I was worried you were going to say that. How much are we talking?'

Khan sucked his teeth for a long moment. '*Anything from fifteen to twenty grand if the helicopter's in play.*'

'Jesus, T. At least bank robbers wear masks when they're robbing people!'

'*Sorry, Jane. It's an expensive operation with specialist units, and my gaffers won't carry a bill like that when it's not our case.*'

Phillips sighed. 'I understand, but I can't say I'm looking forward to breaking that news to the top brass here. I can already hear the knives being sharpened.'

There was a pause on the line for moment. '*So, do you want me to go ahead and organise the teams?*'

'I don't think I have much choice, T. I'd rather get a bollocking for spending too much money than for allowing someone to get murdered on my watch.'

'*So that's a yes?*'

'Yes. It is.'

'*Ok. I'll get straight onto it,*' said Khan. '*You mentioned earlier that Bailey has hired a private security firm. Can we expect any complications from them?*'

'Good question,' replied Phillips. 'They reckon they're ex-military, but one of my guys, DC Bovalino, thinks they're wannabes and may not be what or who they claim to be. I haven't seen enough of them yet to make my mind up.'

'*Right, well, we'll keep an eye on them as well. The last thing we want is this op turning into amateur night.*'

'Exactly.'

'*Ok, Jane. I think I've got enough to be getting on with,*' said Khan. '*I'll give you a shout if I need anything else.*'

'Thanks, T. See you Monday.' Phillips put the phone down and sat in silence for a long moment as she mulled over the cost of the London trip. Chief Constable Fox would no doubt go ballistic when she found out, but, thankfully, she wouldn't be the one to break it to her. That would be down to her boss, Chief Superintendent Harry Carter.

Picking up the phone again, she dialled his office.

His PA, Diana Cook, answered promptly, '*Chief Superintendent Carter's office, how can I help?*'

'Di, it's Jane. Is he free for a quick update?'

'*He is, actually, but only for about half an hour.*'

'Right. Don't let him leave. I'm on my way up,' said Phillips, and ended the call.

Five minutes later, Phillips strode into Cook's office.

Cook looked up and frowned. 'Sorry, Jane. The chief constable beat you to it. She's just gone in with him.'

Fox was the last person Phillips wanted to see just then. 'It's fine. I can come back later.'

Cook scanned her computer screen for a moment. 'He's free this afternoon at three, if that's any good?'

'Yeah, that'll be fine.'

Just then, the door to Carter's office opened. 'I thought I heard your voice, Jane,' said Chief Constable Fox, peering out. 'Perfect timing. You can give me an update on the Ardent cases.'

Phillips's heart sank as she nodded and followed Fox into the office.

Inside, Carter took a seat behind his desk, with Fox pulling up a chair opposite him and adjacent to Phillips.

'So, where are we?' asked Fox. Her thin, veneered smile could not hide her black, soulless eyes. Her cheaply cut and coloured blonde hair gave her the appearance of someone from a long-past decade.

Phillips glanced at Carter for a split second before clearing her throat and spending the next ten minutes bringing Fox up to speed on the hunt for Daniel Meyer, plus the logistical challenge of trying to keep Bailey out of harm's way during her trip to London in a few days.

Throughout the briefing, Fox stared in silence, a slight snarl fixed at the corner of her mouth. When Phillips had finished, she inhaled sharply through her nose, before exhaling loudly. 'And how much is this lot going to cost us?'

'Somewhere in the region of fifteen to twenty thousand pounds, Ma'am.'

Fox recoiled. 'For *one* day's policing?'

Phillips nodded solemnly. 'Yes, Ma'am.'

'That's all we need as we approach the half-year review.' Fox turned her attention to Carter. 'MCU is already well over budget.'

'I'm aware of that, Ma'am,' said Carter in a low voice.

'You said Bailey has hired a private security firm. Can't we leave it to them? I mean, it's her bloody choice to go to London. You've explained the risks she's facing.'

'That is one option, yes,' replied Carter, 'but it does come with considerable risk. If anything were to happen to Bailey – should she be injured, or worse still, killed – and it came out that we chose not to protect her just to save money, then the fallout could be career-ending for all of us, Ma'am.'

Fox remained stoic for a long moment as she processed the information, then nodded reluctantly at Carter. 'Looks like I have no choice, doesn't it? Ok. You've got your funding, but MCU will need to make up the saving in the second half of the year.' She turned her attention back to Phillips. 'Talk to Khan again and ensure he's only using *essential* officers, ok? Just because he's not paying for it, I don't want the costs of this op to get out of control.'

'Of course, Ma'am,' replied Phillips. 'Was there anything else?'

Fox shook her head. 'No. You can go. I'd like to catch up with Chief Superintendent Carter separately.'

Phillips needed no further encouragement to leave, and just a few minutes later she walked back through the door to MCU, relieved to have survived the meeting in one piece.

Bovalino met her at the entrance to her office and handed her a file. 'I've done some digging into Bailey's security firm. I can't find anything that proves any of them served in the military.'

Phillips took the file and began scanning through it. 'You said they alluded to the fact they were Special Forces. Could their records have been sealed?'

Bov blew his lips. 'Maybe, but you'd still expect the military service *before* that to be on file.'

'So, what are we saying? They're really just faking it?'

'I think so, Guv.'

'Jesus. That's all we need right now.' Phillips closed the file and handed it back with a heavy sigh. 'Unless...'

Bovalino raised his eyebrows. 'Unless what?'

'Maybe this is just what we need to get Bailey to cancel the trip to London. If she thinks the guys protecting her aren't up to the job, she may finally realise how much danger she's putting herself in.'

'I guess that could work,' said Bovalino.

Phillips patted the big man on his shoulder. 'This could be just what we need, Bov. Good work.' With that, she headed into her office, pulled out her mobile and dialled Lesley Bailey's number.

37

When Monday morning finally arrived, and, despite further pleas from Phillips to cancel her London trip, Lesley Bailey remained totally committed to presenting in person to the brokerage team at Cavendish Bank. In fact, when Phillips had called the previous week to share her concerns regarding the pedigree of her security team, Bailey had swatted them away. As far as she was concerned, they were a team of ex-Special Forces soldiers, which more than explained their lack of military service history on file. All of which meant that the day ahead would be as pressure-filled as they came.

She knew only too well that, in the hours ahead, there was a realistic chance she could find herself in the line of fire, thanks to an expert marksman hellbent on exacting revenge *eight years* in the making. And, having been shot once already in her life, she had no desire to ever go through that again.

The day hadn't started well, waking as she had in a shitty mood. As much as she tried to deny it, she was really missing Adam. She wondered if she'd been too hasty in ending it all the other night. Lying in bed thinking about him, she had started to compose a WhatsApp message hoping to find out how he was doing, but had stopped herself midway through. Who was she trying to kid? She knew the total commitment required to do her job was never going to change, which meant trying to fit a relationship in and around her work was pointless. So, with a heavy heart, she had deleted the message and thrown her phone on the bed, then taken a shower.

As she dressed, her house felt oppressively warm, the air already sticky on what was set to be another scorching day in Manchester. The forecast suggested London was in for record temperatures, which would only add to the difficulty and intensity of the operation ahead.

As they were paying a small fortune for what appeared to be half the Met police force, there was no sense in taking the whole MCU core team to London and incurring any additional overtime costs. That said, knowing the trouble that could be waiting for them in the capital, she'd requested that the man-mountain, Bovalino, accompany her today, leaving Jones and Entwistle back in Manchester to continue the investigation.

Because they had little intel on Meyer's whereabouts, they had no idea where he might strike, if at all. But, along with DCI Khan, Phillips had prepared for the worst and was hoping for the best. With that in mind, the armed police escort assigned to protect Bailey would begin at her home in Bramall, which was Phillips's first destination of the day.

Arriving just after 7 a.m., Phillips, standing alongside Bovalino, briefed Bailey – and her so-called protective detail – on the travel plans: leaving the house in the next thirty minutes, Bailey would travel in the Range Rover provided by her private security team. The procession would ride in formation with one TFU car taking the lead while a second TFU car, containing Phillips and Bovalino, would bring up the rear.

Once at Manchester Piccadilly Station, Bailey would be given an armed escort to the train, where they would take their seats in the first-class carriage next to the catering team – a space that would be out of use to the public. Upon arrival at London Euston, the Met Police's tactical firearms team would take over, driving once again in an offensive formation, delivering Bailey to Cavendish Bank safe and sound, and in plenty of time for her presentation. That was the plan on paper, at least.

'Don't you worry, Mrs Bailey,' said Harper, one of her security team. 'We'll make sure nothing happens to you.'

'Piece of cake,' added Dexter, his chest proud.

Phillips felt her eyes roll. The last thing she needed today was their egos getting in the way of protecting Bailey. 'Right,' she said, standing. 'I think we should get going.'

Five minutes later, just before 7.30 a.m., the motorcade rolled slowly out of Bailey's drive and onto the street as they began their journey into the city. In normal rush hour traffic at this time of the morning, it would take well over an hour, but under blue lights and sirens, they would be there in thirty minutes.

Sitting next to Phillips in the back of the TFU's mercifully air-conditioned BMW X5, Bovalino reiterated his concerns around Dexter and Harper, as well as the driver and third member of the team, Chappman, or Chappers, as they called him. 'Did you hear them in there, Guv?'

Phillips nodded without looking at him, her eyes fixed on the world shooting by the window as the procession picked up speed.

'It sticks in my craw. Bailey's trusting her life to a bunch of amateurs.'

Phillips's eyes remained fixed outside. 'It's her choice, Bov. We tried telling her, but if she won't listen, there's nothing we can do.' She turned to face him now. 'Except, that is, to stay alert, stay on point, and try and catch Meyer before he gets a chance to try anything. Ok?'

'Ok, Guv,' Bovalino said firmly as the procession accelerated past Cheadle Hulme train station.

Arriving at Manchester Piccadilly station without incident thirty minutes later, the motorcade slipped in through the side entrance and pulled to a stop. In a flash, Harper and Dexter were out of the black Range Rover and a second later Bailey appeared, briefcase in hand. As Phillips opened the back door to the BMW X5, she grabbed her lapel-radio, demanding the TFU officers immediately surround them and ensure they remained in that position throughout the short walk along the platform to the train.

A couple of minutes later, Phillips stepped into the small first-class carriage at the front of the train, where Harper and Dexter had already taken their seats at a table alongside Bailey. She and Bovalino dropped into the bank of four seats across the aisle, with two TFU officers taking up positions in seats situated next to the automatic door.

As everyone made themselves comfortable, a smartly dressed steward appeared and flashed a wide smile. 'Good morning, everyone. My name's Katie Finnon, and I'll be looking after you today during our short trip to London Euston.' She handed out small menu cards. 'Once we're out of the station, I'll come back and take your order for breakfast. You can choose from a Full English, or bacon and sausage sandwiches, as well as smoked salmon and scrambled eggs, or cereal and fruit.'

'This is the life,' said Dexter with a wide grin.

Bovalino caught Phillips's eye. He silently mouthed the words, 'Fucking idiot,' before he resumed looking out of the window.

'Now. Would anyone like a tea or coffee?' asked Finnon brightly.

A chorus of yes's filled the air and she set off towards the galley in search of her quarry, returning a few minutes later with two steaming metal pots, one in each hand. She spent the next few minutes serving up drinks, then left with the promise of returning soon to take their breakfast orders.

A moment later, the train began to creep slowly out of the station.

For the next hour, nothing of any consequence was discussed between the group as they worked their way through the various breakfast dishes they had ordered, along with refills of tea and coffee.

With their bellies full and the plates cleared away, Harper turned in his seat. 'So, we understand you think we're not up to the job?' he said, staring at Phillips and Bovalino in turn. Evidently Bailey had shared their concern about her security team.

'Nobody said that,' Phillips replied.

'Sounds like it to me. Why else would you be looking into our military records?' said Dexter.

'It's our job to investigate everyone connected to someone we believe could be in imminent danger. In this case, Mrs Bailey. It's standard procedure.' said Bovalino, clearly struggling to hide his contempt for the pair.

'Well, let's be clear from the outset, shall we? We're the best in the business at close protection, and the reason you couldn't find our records is because they're *classified*.'

'Oh yeah?' Bov shot back. 'And why is that? Or do I even need to ask?'

'Special Forces soldiers' records are strictly confidential.'

Bovalino exhaled loudly. 'How convenient.'

'It's true,' replied Harper. 'Because the work we do is on a need-to-know basis, and you don't need to know.'

'What about your time *before* the Special Forces? Why is there no record of that on file?'

'For our protection. There's a lot of people out there who would pay handsomely to slot us,' said Harper.

'Is that right?' Bovalino said.

'Yeah, it is.'

Bovalino sat forward now. 'Ok. So, when we met back at Ashton House for the first time, you both claimed to be ex-2 Para, right?'

'That's right,' said Dexter.

'And that's where you met, is it? In the Paras?'

Dexter nodded. 'Correct.'

'All three of you? Chappers as well?'

'Yes.'

'And you all passed selection at the same time and went into the SAS together, did you?'

Dexter nodded again.

Bovalino blew his lips loudly. 'Wow! That's impressive. I mean, as I understand it from the veterans I've spoken to, SAS selection is brutal, and the success rate for each intake is less than five percent. So, for *all three* of you from the same regiment to pass at the same time? Well, that's gotta be a first.'

'It was,' Harper shot back. 'And that's why we're so good at what we do.'

Bovalino offered a thin smile. 'Of course you are.' He turned his attention to Phillips now. 'Would you excuse me, Guv,' he said loudly. 'I need to get some air. Something stinks in here.'

Phillips stifled a grin. 'Sure thing, Bov. In fact, I'll come with you. We can have a walk through the train, see if there's any sign of Meyer.'

With that, they stepped up into the aisle. A moment later, Bovalino activated the automatic doors and led the way into the next carriage.

38

D aniel Meyer stared at his reflection in the small mirror hanging on the wall of the tiny en suite bathroom and took a long, deep breath. Today was the day he would deliver vengeance, the ultimate retribution for the deaths of his mother and father. Today would also see the destruction of his own life. After attacking a police officer, then fleeing his sister's home, he had no doubt the police were now looking for him. Did they suspect he was the man behind the deaths of Rice, Howard and Nelson? Was that why they had come looking for him that day? He had considered using his unregistered mobile phone to call his sister and ask what they knew about him, but had decided against it. The reality was, he had no idea who could be listening at the other end, or how quickly they could trace his location. Something he had to protect at all costs. Because the unlikely location of his chosen kill zone was probably his greatest weapon, and one of the reasons he had decided to strike outside of Manchester.

Moving back into the bedroom, he dropped down onto the bed and picked up the letter to Meghan that he had

handwritten an hour earlier. He wanted to read it to himself
one more time.

Hey sis,

*By the time you read this letter, I'll be long gone, one way or the
other. I'm truly sorry it had to be like this, but it was the only way I
could ever have peace. No doubt people will say I am a bad man
for what I have done, and maybe they're right. After all, I have
taken three lives so far and, God willing, will take a fourth today.
Matthew Rice, Cherie Howard, David Nelson and Lesley Bailey
destroyed our family with their greed and deceit. They took away
everything that mattered in our lives, all in the name of profit. For
eight years I've tried to make sense of it all, to find a reason for
what happened to Mum and Dad, but I can't. The cold, harsh
truth is that life is cruel and unfair. Good people die and bad
people live on unaffected.*

*Well, I made up my mind a long time ago that the bad people who
killed Mum and Dad would NOT get to live on, and they would
certainly NEVER profit from the idea they stole from Dad. That's
why I've done what I've done. And that's why I'm going to finish
the job today. Some people say God will send me to hell for this,
but the truth is, I'm already there. I have been for the last eight
years.*

*The pen drive included with this letter contains proof I've found
that Ardent stole Dad's patent. Whatever happens today, people
need to know what those bastards did to Mum and Dad, and to
our family. Tell the papers, tell the police, tell whoever you want.
Just make sure people know the truth.*

*Take care of yourself and Billy and the kids, and know that I'll love
you forever, my beautiful twin, Meghan.*

Always in my heart.

Dan xxx

Swallowing the lump in his throat, he folded the letter

twice, then slipped it into an envelope he'd already stamped and addressed to his sister, along with the tiny pen drive. Putting it to one side, he checked his wallet. He had just shy of fifty pounds in cash. Next, he checked the condition of the fake passport he'd used to get into the country just over a month earlier. The last thing he needed was to be stopped by immigration because of a curling page or peeling sticker. With everything seemingly up to scratch, he inserted his plane ticket to Dubai at the back of the passport and slipped it into his small red rucksack.

Finally, he checked the loading action on his Winchester 100 one more time. Rather than carry it in the leather gun bag he would normally use, he slipped it into the fishing rod bag he had bought the previous day. It was far better people think he were a fisherman than a sniper.

Leaving the laptop behind – he had no use for it now – he slipped on a black Nike baseball cap, threw his rucksack over his shoulder, then picked up the fishing rod bag containing the rifle. Checking the room one last time, he headed for the door and made his way downstairs.

As usual, the cramped hotel reception desk was unmanned, which suited him just fine. After dropping his key on the counter, he made his way outside onto the noisy street. The sun was shining, the air humid and thick with pollution from the heavy traffic. Slipping on a pair of polarised hunting sunglasses, he set off towards the main road at the end of the street. He mailed the letter into the red post box located on the corner.

As it dropped inside, he stopped for a moment to think of his sister. Guilt flooded him at the knowledge she was about to lose yet another member of her family. She was better off without him, he told himself. Pushing the pain for his sister to the back of his mind, he exhaled deeply as he attempted to steel himself for what lay ahead.

It was time to go.

Turning back to face the road, he stepped to the kerb and scanned the street for a minute or so until he spotted what he was looking for. Raising his arm, he shouted, 'Taxi.' A moment later, a black cab pulled up in front of him.

The cab's window was already open. 'Where do you wanna go, mate?' asked the driver in a thick Cockney accent.

'Albany Street, please.'

'Near the park?'

'That's the one,' said Meyer.

The driver pointed to the back with his thumb. 'Jump in.'

Meyer pulled open the heavy black door and took a moment to place his luggage on the floor inside before climbing in himself. He dropped heavily into the seat as the central locking clicked loudly shut and the cab pulled out into the early morning traffic.

39

T he train arrived in London just after 11 a.m. The plan was to wait until the rest of the passengers had disembarked before alighting.

As the staff busied themselves resetting the tables for the return journey to Manchester, DCI Tahir stepped into the carriage. He was short and stocky, with salt and pepper hair and a cheeky smile that belied his formidable investigative brain. He quickly introduced himself to everyone in turn, then briefed the room on the protocols in place for the short drive from Euston to the City of London's commercial district and Cavendish Bank. Once again, they would travel in formation under blues and twos, and expected no roadworks or traffic delays along the way. He assured them that if everyone did as instructed by his team, Lesley Bailey would be making her presentation to the investors on time and without incident.

'We'll be with the principal at all times, won't we?' asked Harper.

'Of course,' replied Tahir. 'The only exception being if we

run into trouble. If that situation arises, then my firearms unit will take the lead as Mrs Bailey's primary protection.'

Harper frowned and opened his mouth to protest but Tahir expertly cut him off. 'But we don't imagine that will be the case, so she'll more than likely remain with you throughout her visit.'

This seemed to placate Harper, who nodded and puffed his chest out.

Next, an armed officer stepped forward and passed out stab vests which Bailey, Phillips and Bov readily accepted, but Harper refused.

'We don't need those,' added Dexter.

Phillips and Bov exchanged dead eyes, a symbol of their shared contempt for Bailey's chaperones and their bullshit bravado.

A few minutes later, with the vests securely in place and the train now empty of all passengers, it was time to make the short walk to the police vehicles waiting in the loading area. Tahir led the way as they stepped out of the cool, air-conditioned carriage onto the platform. The air outside was oppressively hot and humid, the smell of diesel engines pervasive. A raft of burly firearms officers made it their job to surround Bailey, Harper and Dexter as they moved along the platform. Phillips and Bovalino brought up the rear.

'You'd think we were transporting the bloody Queen with this lot,' said Bovalino in a low voice. 'No wonder it's costing an arm and leg.'

'Don't knock it, Bov,' said Phillips, her eyes scanning the surrounding platforms for any sign of Meyer. 'I'd rather leave it to the firearms boys than put you or me you in the line of fire.'

'Fair point, Guv.'

Soon after, Tahir guided them to three waiting police vehicles, which included an armoured security truck –

normally used for moving dangerous criminals to and from court – to transport Bailey and her security team to their final destination. Parked in front of it was the ubiquitous Tactical Firearms vehicle, a BMW X5, which would carry the lead armed response team. Positioned behind the van was a second X5, allocated to Tahir, Phillips and Bovalino, and driven by another armed officer.

Finally, with everyone in their allotted vehicles, the motorcade set off, heading south towards the City. As ever, traffic in the capital was nose to tail, but with lights flashing and sirens blaring, the procession cut through the glut of cars like a hot knife through butter.

Tahir, sitting in the front passenger seat, turned to speak to Phillips and Bov in the back seat. 'There's little chance of anyone being able to get to Bailey while she's in the armoured vehicle, but she will definitely be vulnerable getting in and out of the bank. Based on your intel, I have snipers positioned on four of the rooftops surrounding the entrance to Cavendish Bank.'

'Is it worth us taking her in through the back door?' asked Phillips.

'We did look at that,' Tahir said, 'but there's more firing positions on that side of the building and significantly less visibility.'

Phillips nodded. 'What about security inside the bank. Has that been taken into account?'

'Of course. The bank has installed X-ray machines for Bailey's visit, and no one can get in today without being frisked and having their bags scanned. I checked it myself last night, and I have to say, they've got it locked up nice and tight. If Meyer's going to get to her, I doubt it'll be in there.'

Phillips sat back in her seat and stared out of the window; her mind's eye filled with the image of Meyer carrying the rifle from the storage facility. She wondered where he was right now and what he might be planning. Was he even in London? Were they being over-cautious? Was all this extra security and money being spent for nothing? They'd soon find out, one way or the other.

Two minutes later, the motorcade began to slow down.

'We're just a few minutes out,' said Khan into his radio. 'Everybody, stand by.'

As the vehicles came to a stop, Khan, along with the TFU officers, jumped out first to secure the area. Phillips and Bovalino followed them out into the sunshine and moved towards the front door, where they turned to face the armoured vehicle. On Khan's signal, the two armed officers allocated to protect Bailey exited the armoured truck, then proceeded to open her door. A second later, she stepped out onto the street before being marched towards the front door, Harper and Dexter in tow.

At that moment, Phillips watched as a cyclist mounted the kerb and raced towards Bailey, a large bag on his back. His face was shielded by sunglasses and a helmet, so she couldn't identify the rider.

Before Phillips could open her mouth to speak, Khan bellowed, 'Contact! Man on a bike to your left!'

Without flinching, the armed officers escorting Bailey surrounded her and bundled her at speed through the massive revolving front door of the bank, while a solo member of the TFU tackled the cyclist. Stepping into his path, he thrust the butt of his MP5 machine gun into the man's chest, knocking him clean off his bike.

The cyclist landed heavily on the ground, and appeared dazed and confused as he rolled around on the pavement, groaning in pain, his bare knees covered in blood. In a flash, more armed police officers were on top of him, pinning him face down to the pavement as they removed his helmet and sunglasses.

Phillips's pulse raced as she stepped forward, expecting to see Daniel Meyer's face, but her heart sank when she realised it wasn't him. 'Shit!' she said loudly.

'I'm just a bloody courier!' the cyclist shouted.

Khan appeared now and took a long look at the man. 'It's not our guy. Let him up.'

As instructed, the officers released their grips and stepped up, before helping the man to his feet.

'Run his name through the system and make sure he's not connected to Meyer,' said Khan to his men, then turned on his heels and headed towards the bank at pace.

Phillips and Bovalino followed him inside, flashing their IDs in order to bypass the X-ray machine and security search teams.

In the belly of the bank's main reception, they found Lesley Bailey, flanked by her armed police escort, looking ruffled but otherwise unharmed.

'Are you ok, Mrs Bailey?' asked Khan.

Bailey nodded in silence, and Phillips noted that for the first time since this whole investigation began, she seemed genuinely frightened.

Khan flashed a warm smile. 'Well, you'll be pleased to know it appears to be a false alarm. Looks like some idiot cycle courier rode straight into the middle of our operation.'

Bailey remained silent, unlike her so-called security team who appeared now, clearly agitated, and unhappy at having to pass through security to get this point.

'What kind of a shit-show are you running here?' said Dexter, squaring up to Khan. At well over six feet tall, he towered over the much shorter DCI. 'It's our job to protect the principal. How the fuck are we supposed to do that if we're treated like bloody civvies and made to go through security?'

'I did explain earlier that in the face of any threat, *my men* would become Mrs Bailey's *primary* protectors, which is exactly what happened. As for security, the only way to bypass that...' Khan pointed towards the big machine in reception, then held up his Police ID '...is to have one these.'

Dexter's eyes appeared to dance in his head as his nostrils flared. He was almost ready to blow.

Phillips glanced at Bovalino and noted his satisfied grin. She had to admit, she felt the same way.

At that moment, a tall, slim, middle-aged man in a perfectly fitted suit approached.

Bailey evidently knew him, as her eyes lit up when he she spotted him. 'Mr Cavendish,' she said, offering her hand.

'Mrs Bailey,' the man replied, shaking firmly. 'It's good to see you.'

'Likewise,' said Bailey.

Khan presented Cavendish with his credentials. 'DCI Khan, and this is DCI Phillips from the Greater Manchester Police. Thank you for being so accommodating with us today.'

Cavendish flashed his perfectly straight white teeth and offered his hand to them both in turn. 'Charles Cavendish. It's our pleasure. Anything we can do to support Mrs Bailey and our investors.' He turned his attention to Bailey, and gestured in the direction of the lift. 'They're ready for you, Mrs Bailey. Shall we go up?'

Bailey let out a sigh of relief and smiled. 'Yes, please.'

'Excellent,' he said, and set off towards the lifts.

Once again, Harper and Dexter assumed their close-protection roles, following behind Bailey as she walked alongside Cavendish. When the lift arrived, they made a huge fuss of stepping in and checking it was safe before signalling to their client to step inside.

'Jesus,' Phillips muttered under her breath as she, Bovalino and Khan followed them in.

The doors closed behind them, and everyone stood in silence for the minute or so it took to reach the trading floor at the top of the building. Phillips turned to face the doors as the lift slowed, and as the doors opened again, she stepped out into the plush hallway.

Cavendish made his way to the front of the group, then, with Bailey in tow – along with Dexter and Harper – marched towards a large smoked-glass door ahead of them. 'We're in here,' he said as he opened it and ushered them all inside.

As the door closed behind them, Phillips turned to Khan and Bovalino. 'Well, that's the first test passed.'

Khan flashed his trademark grin. 'Now all we have to do is keep her alive on the trip back to Euston.'

Bovalino clapped his hands together. 'Well. I wouldn't worry. At least we've got Harper and Dexter to show us how it's all done,' he said, his tone laced with sarcasm.

Phillips punched him playfully on the arm, then turned to Khan. 'Ignore him, T. He's got a thing for soldiers.'

Khan chuckled. 'Whatever floats your boat, big man.'

Bovalino laughed too.

'Right. Shall we head back downstairs and run through the plan for the return journey?'

'Good idea, Jane,' replied Khan. 'And while we're at it, let's get some coffee too. I spotted a small kiosk in the lobby. My treat.'

Phillips flashed a wry grin. 'Well, it's about time you paid for *something*, T.'

'Ouch, Jane, ouch,' said Khan, pretending to be offended, as they made their way back into the lift that would take them back to the ground floor.

40

M eyer paid the cab driver in cash, then stepped out onto the frantically busy London street. The temperature appeared to have risen significantly in the last hour, and the humidity was now so overbearing it reminded him of Bali. There were people everywhere, which was both good and bad: a lot of bodies made it easy for him to blend in, but any one of them could decide that today was their day to be a hero and attempt to stop him when he made his final attack.

Doing his best to avoid CCTV cameras, he made his way along the back streets, arriving at his destination in a little over fifteen minutes. Despite having been there just a couple of days previous, he remained awe-struck by how much the area had changed since the last time they had visited as a family, long before his father's fight with Ardent. It had been a special twelfth birthday treat for the twins – an overnight stay in a swanky hotel as they took in a London show, The Lion King. He remembered being shocked at how dirty, dingy and downright threatening the place had felt as they walked through on their way to the theatre district in Soho. It couldn't be more different. Gone were the concrete slabs and small shops selling touristy bric-a-brac; instead, a host of food trucks put out delicious aromas from around the globe, and pop-up bars placed on wooden decking alongside communal tables and benches, as well as colourful oversized deckchairs facing the sun.

As it was approaching 1.30 p.m., the lunch crowd was still out in force, long lines of people waiting to sample their favourite dish from their chosen food truck. With an hour or so still to go, and conscious of the fact this could well be the last meal he ever ate, he decided to order one of his favourite foods, seekh kebab in a pitta bread. He had adored them since taking his very first bite during a trip to Goa, just a month or so before he arrived in Bali. In prison, he had fantasised about eating them, once freed, every night for the rest of his life. After placing his order, he waited patiently, savouring the aromas while all the time taking in the faces and snippets of conversations of the people passing by. When his order was finally ready, he collected it and carried it across to one of the deckchairs on the grass. Placing his quarry on the chair for a moment, he removed his rucksack and fishing bag from his shoulders, dropping them to the ground, then picked up the food and sat down on the canvas seat.

For a moment, he almost forgot where he was and what he was there to do. His mind's eye was suddenly filled with fantasies of the different lives he could have led, had he made different choices; bringing his own children to see a West End show in London, just like his mum and dad had done. Sadness and regret washed over him in equal measure, only to be replaced a split second later by his ever-faithful and unflinching companion, hatred. He chastised himself for allowing sentiment to distract him from the job in hand. The truth was, it was too late for him to have any sort of normal life now. He'd made his choices, and in doing so had become a criminal on two continents. There was little point torturing himself, wishing for an outcome that could never happen.

Pushing all thoughts of what might have been to the back of his mind, he sat quietly in the sunshine, taking his time over the kebab and ensuring he savoured every mouthful of the delicious meal. It tasted just like the one he remembered from Goa. The only thing missing was an ice-cold beer. That would have made it perfect. But after eight years of sobriety, he knew that even the slightest amount of alcohol would diminish his aim, and he'd come much too far to let that happen.

When the kebab was finally finished, he squashed the wrapping in both hands, then stepped up out of the deckchair and headed to the nearest rubbish bin and dropped it inside.

At that moment, two armed police offices moved into his peripheral vision, stopping him in his tracks as adrenaline surged through his body. Careful not to make any sudden moves that would draw attention, he slowly turned away from them, then dropped down onto one knee as he pretended to tie his shoelaces. Staying in that position, he glanced towards his bags, next to the deckchair. Having grown up in an era where acts of terrorism could happen at any time in any British city, he knew only too well that a collection of abandoned bags could quickly become a security issue. The last thing he needed right now was people poking around in his stuff.

Satisfied they had yet to cause any concern, he turned his attention back to the armed officers, who had moved on past his position and, thankfully, showed no signs of stopping. Standing, he continued to watch them intently as they moved away. Several moment later, he walked back to the deckchair to pick up his bags.

That had been way too close for comfort.

He checked his watch; 1.35 p.m. Bailey would be on the move again soon. It was time to go.

41

Phillips and Bovalino had spent the last hour standing in the lobby of the bank, just a few feet in front of the lift that had carried them to and from the trading floor. With her back to the elevator, she had quietly observed the people passing through the X-ray machine, desperate for any sign of Daniel Meyer. But to no avail. She felt a mixture of relief and disappointment; relief that Bailey was still in once piece, but disappointment that Meyer remained at large, and she still had no idea where and when he might show up.

The static of her radio caught her attention, and she listened intently as the armed unit positioned up on the trading floor updated the team.

'Bailey is on the move. She's coming down now,' said one of the officers.

Phillips and Bovalino turned to face the metal doors as the digital floor display began counting down from 50. Khan re-joined them a minute later, just as the display reached G and a loud ping echoed around the space.

If Phillips had hoped for a more subdued approach from

Bailey's security team for the return journey back to Euston station, she was out of luck. As the doors opened, the loud voices of both Harper and Dexter filled the air.

'Stand back, stand back,' said Dexter, stepping out first.

'Here we go again,' Bovalino said under his breath.

Phillips nodded, but remained silent as Bailey, alongside Charles Cavendish, moved out into the lobby.

Bailey appeared visibly lighter, her posture strong, her face bright and content. Cavendish too was in good spirits, a satisfied grin etched on his face.

They stopped for a moment and, much to Phillips's surprise, Cavendish drew Bailey into a light clinch, complete with a double-cheeked air kiss, before stepping back to look at her like a bridegroom staring at his new bride. 'Well done, Mrs Bailey. That really was splendid. I have no doubt we'll be able to launch the share offering at the agreed price.'

Bailey flashed a smile. 'Thank you. That's wonderful news. And please, call me Lesley.'

'Thank you, *Lesley*,' beamed Cavendish.

Khan stepped forward now. 'Are we ready to go?'

Bailey turned to face him and chuckled. 'I don't suppose we could stop for a celebratory drink on the way?'

'I believe they offer Champagne on the train,' said Khan, without missing a beat. Turning to Phillips, she spotted a mischievous twinkle in his eye. 'And you never know. If you ask nicely, DCI Phillips might add it to her tab.'

Phillips raised her eyebrows. 'I think you'll find this trip has cost Manchester tax-payers quite enough already.'

'Spoilsport,' replied Khan with a wink.

Phillips shook her head and smiled as Khan radioed instructions to the snipers and armed response teams outside the building, telling them to be ready for Bailey coming out, and requesting location and status updates from each of them.

As the volley of responses crackled over the radio in turn, Phillips took a long, silent breath, attempting to calm her jittery stomach. The reality of what they may be faced with outside of the bank's doors had caused a surge of adrenaline to rush through her body, and she was suddenly very apprehensive and a little nauseous.

Satisfied everyone was in position, Khan gave the order to move out. Once again, armed officers formed a protective shield around Bailey, Harper and Dexter as they passed through the lobby and moved out through the revolving door.

Bovalino followed close behind, with Phillips at the very back, scanning every single face she passed as she strode through the lobby.

Stepping out into the sunshine, Phillips squinted as her eyes adjusted to the bright light, and her heart rate rocketed in anticipation. For a long moment, she held her breath as everything seemed to slow down, the noise and heat of the street a stark contrast to the serenity of the air-conditioned bank at their backs. When she could finally focus properly, her eyes darted between the windows of the surrounding buildings. The reflections on the glass playing tricks on her, and she saw potential shooters at every window.

But no shot came, and before she realised it, Bailey had been safely returned to the belly of the armoured truck.

A few moments later, as she approached the X5 that would carry them back to Euston station, Bovalino stood waiting for her. His face was crumpled, and he looked bemused. 'No sign of him anywhere, Guv.'

'No.'

'So, have we done all this for nothing?'

Phillips felt her brow furrow as she scanned the surrounding area. 'Maybe, Bov. But let's not get complacent.

We're not out of the woods just yet, so stay on your toes, right?'

Bovalino nodded emphatically, then opened the car door to get in.

Khan appeared next to her. 'Well, that went as smoothly as we could have expected.'

'Yeah, it did. And that's what's puzzling me.'

Khan frowned. 'You seem disappointed, Jane.'

Phillips shook her head. 'Not disappointed. More like unnerved. If Meyer was going to hit Bailey anywhere, it would have been here, out in the open.'

'Maybe he saw my guys and thought better of it?'

'Yeah, maybe,' replied Phillips as she continued to search the faces on the street for one she recognised.

Khan glanced down at his watch as he pulled open the front passenger door. 'Well. All I have to do is keep you lot out of trouble for the next forty-five minutes and my work here is done,' he said as he jumped into the front seat.

Phillips walked round to the opposite side and pulled open the rear door. Her guts turned, and her mind raced. 'What are you up to, Meyer?' she whispered before climbing in the back next to Bovalino.

42

As he stepped inside Euston station, Meyer's heart was beating so loudly in his chest, he could hardly hear himself think. All around him, people rushed, staring straight ahead, desperate to avoid all human contact. Londoners are famous for moving around the city in a permanent state of ignorance, which was yet another good reason he'd chosen London for the final kill. Manchester was quite the opposite. A city full of inquisitive people – nosy, even – keen to know everything that's happening and bursting with *have-a-go heroes*. It was the last place a man needing to make a quick escape wanted to be.

Taking a few deep breaths to help steady his jangling nerves, he reached into his pocket and pulled out his wallet. Inside, he located the ticket he had paid for in cash a couple of days ago, which allowed him access to his chosen kill zone. Retaining the ticket, he replaced his wallet in his pocket and joined the line of people waiting to pass through the automatic barriers. He'd not been back in the UK long, but already he appreciated the fact so much of the world was now managed by machines as opposed to people. It had allowed him to move around the country a lot easier in the last few weeks than he could have imagined. That said, the proliferation of CCTV cameras at every turn had shocked him. Big Brother really was watching.

A few minutes later, when he reached the front of the line, he placed his ticket in the machine and waited, but instead of releasing the barriers, the ticket was thrust back out with a loud beep as the red X remained stubbornly on the digital display. He tried again, with the same result. A backlog of commuters instantly began to build behind him as he repeated the process over and over without success. A uniformed train guard appeared on the other side of the barrier, his attention drawn to the grumbling of the travellers stuck behind Meyer.

He felt like his heart would explode as the guard approached, staring at him quizzically. Without saying a word, the guard reached over, grabbed the ticket from the machine and inspected it closely. 'This is your seat reservation, where's your ticket?'

Meyer was so consumed by panic he didn't hear him at first, and instead gazed at him open-mouthed.

'You need your ticket to get through the barrier,' the guard repeated, slower and louder this time, apparently assuming Meyer didn't speak English.

With the protests from the stranded travellers behind him growing in volume and venom, he came to his senses. He reached into his pocket and pulled out his wallet. Rummaging through it, he found what he was looking for and presented it to the guard without saying a word.

'That's the one. Try that in the machine.'

Meyer did as instructed, and to his considerable relief, the ticket was accepted and the barrier opened.

Evidently satisfied his job was done, the guard turned on his heels and walked away.

With beads of sweat running down the length of his spine and dripping from his nose, Meyer shuffled through the barrier as quickly as he could, carrying his fishing rod bag and rucksack, then quickly moved to one side to get out of the way of the glut of people who had been stuck behind him as they rushed to catch their trains.

He took a moment to compose himself once more, then waited for several trains to depart and a subsequent lull in the number of commuters. After some minutes, satisfied he could move more freely, he set off in the direction of his sniper's nest.

Wandering casually along as if he hadn't a care in the world, he kept his eyes peeled, checking for anyone who might be watching him. But as far as he could tell, no one could care less who he was or why he was there.

Then, with the area suddenly deserted – something he had witnessed during his initial site recce – he stopped next to the maintenance ladder and took one last look around. He was alone now, but it wouldn't be long before the area refilled with more trains and yet more passengers trying to get somewhere quickly. With the rucksack on his back and the fishing rod bag over his shoulder, he climbed the ladder in double-quick time until he reached his elevated position above the kill zone. Climbing onto the corrugated metal roof twenty feet above the platform, he removed his bags, then lay down on his back, out of sight. Next, holding the fishing rod bag to his chest, he released the straps that held it shut, reached inside, and pulled out his rifle.

Rolling onto his front, he removed the four-round magazine from the rucksack, then shoved the bag ahead of him so it could act as a rest for the rifle muzzle. Slamming the box magazine into the base of the gun just in front of the trigger, he pulled the bolt action back and armed the chamber. Finally, he adjusted his sights, taking his time to get them right, compensating for the relatively low light within the kill zone.

Satisfied everything was ready, all he had to do now was wait.

43

The motorcade made light work of the mid-afternoon traffic as they raced north through London back to Euston station. From her position in the back seat of the trailing vehicle, Phillips could see the armoured van ahead of them but not the lead car, which made her nervous. Agitated, she couldn't help but wonder where Meyer was going to strike. Was that even his plan, or had he already gone to ground and used his fake passport to get back out of the country? The reality was that, right now, she didn't have any answers to go with the three dead bodies of Rice, Howard and Nelson lying in the mortuary. Their lack of progress, added to the enormous operational costs of this trip to London, meant a bleak future. Chief Constable Fox demanded results, and unless Phillips could come up with a breakthrough in the investigation, there was a strong chance Fox would follow up on her threat to replace Carter as head of Major Crimes, which would be a disaster. He was a great boss, and she didn't want to lose him. Neither did her team.

As they approached Euston, Phillips leaned forward to

speak to Khan. 'My firearms guys will meet us at the drop-off point and escort us to the train from there.'

From his position in the front passenger seat, Khan turned his head towards her. 'Sounds like a plan.'

She patted him on the shoulder. 'Thanks for your help today, T. You've been brilliant.'

'My pleasure, Jane,' he replied with his customary grin. 'Always happy to help.'

Phillips continued to sit forward, staring out through the windscreen, eyes fixed on the armoured truck ahead as they turned off the main drag and into the loading zone at the side of the station, which had already been secured by armed officers.

As the motorcade came to a final stop, Phillips and Bovalino jumped out of the X5 in unison and quickly made their way to the side of the armoured truck. Two armed officers approached – half of her Manchester firearms team – including Sergeant Matthews, a man she'd worked with many times and trusted with her life.

'Are we good, Sergeant?' asked Phillips.

He nodded. 'Yes, Ma'am. We have a team in place on the train. Jennings and I will escort Bailey and her security team from here.'

'Good,' Phillips said. 'Well, let's get them out of the truck, shall we?'

Dexter stepped out first, followed by Bailey. In stark contrast to her confident demeanour when leaving the bank, she now appeared tired, shoulders sagging, eyes dull as she stepped out of the truck and down onto the loading bay. The stress of the day looked as if it was finally taking its toll on her. Harper stepped out last, and positioned himself next to her.

After a quick briefing from Sergeant Matthews, explaining the protocols to be used for the short walk to the train, the team set off towards the platform. Matthews took point in front of the group, while Jennings held the rear. Phillips and Bovalino followed at a short distance, scanning the surrounding area.

As they reached the platform, a train came to a stop on the adjacent platform, and as the doors opened, bodies swarmed all around them.

'I thought that platform was supposed to be out of use for the next hour?' asked Bovalino.

Phillips frowned. 'So did I. Just like it was this morning.'

Up ahead, the group was making steady progress against the throng of passengers rushing past them. Suddenly a woman stopped in front of Bovalino, causing him to jump out of the way to avoid bumping into her. She was clearly in a rush and frustrated by the fact her little boy – who appeared to be around six years old – was rooted to the spot just a few feet behind her.

Phillips chuckled to herself as she recalled her niece Grace at the same age. 'Stubborn as a mule,' she whispered as she passed them both.

It appeared the boy was not moving, though his mother continued shouting at him to follow her or risk missing their connecting train. What Phillips heard next, stopped her in her tracks.

'But Mummy, why is that man lying down up on the roof?'

Spinning on her heels, Phillips locked her eyes on the back of the boy's head and followed his line of sight. To her horror, ahead of her, lying on the roof that covered the platform, was a man with a rifle in his grip. 'Bov! Shooter!' she screamed, before grabbing her radio to warn Matthews.

Before she could open the link, the ear-splitting sound of a 308-calibre round being fired from the rifle exploded around them.

Instinctively, Phillips hit the deck about twenty yards

from Bovalino, who did the same. All around them, panicked passengers, fearing they were in the middle of a terrorist attack, screamed as they clambered over each other to get to safety. Everything seemed to slow down, and Phillips felt suddenly helpless as she cast her eyes on an elderly lady who had been knocked to the ground. Close by, a young mother on her knees cradled her tiny baby, crying with fear. Adjusting her position on the ground, Phillips could see that Matthews and Jennings had both taken a knee and pivoted in the direction of the shot. Lesley Bailey was nowhere in sight, but a second later Phillips spotted Dexter peeping out from behind one of the huge circular pillars positioned at intervals along the platform. She hoped to God Bailey was with him.

As Bovalino crawled closer to Phillips's position, she grabbed her radio. 'Matthews. This is Phillips. Do you have eyes on Bailey?'

She watched as Matthews grabbed his lapel mic before his voice crackled through the speaker.

'Yes. She's positioned to my right, behind the pillar, along with her security team.'

'Make sure they don't move until we secure the area.'

'I've already made that clear, Ma'am.'

A second shot boomed though the air, causing Phillips and Bovalino to lie flat once more. Looking up again a moment later, she caught sight of Dexter and Harper pushing Bailey from the behind the pillar towards the train carriage. 'No!' she screamed.

A third shot rang out, and Phillips watched in horror as Bailey's body jolted. Blood splattered across the platform as she dropped to the ground with a thud, alongside Dexter. Phillips fixed her gaze on a panic-stricken Harper who stood, rooted to the spot, as he looked down at his principal and partner lying motionless on the platform. As quick as a flash, he turned on his heels and rushed headlong onto the train.

44

With one shot left in the chamber, Meyer stared through the scope, trying to take his final shot to ensure Bailey was dead. However, with people running in all directions, his view had become obscured. In between the terrified commuters that rushed through his line of sight, he caught a glimpse of Bailey lying motionless on the platform, dark red blood pooling under her torso. Then he spotted the armed police making their way carefully towards her with their MP5 machine guns trained on him. He debated whether to try for one last shot, but knew that more armed officers could arrive at any moment. If he had any hope of getting away, every second counted. He decided it was time to go.

Leaving his rifle and bag behind, he rolled to the edge of the canopy, swung his body over the edge and dropped down to the platform some twenty feet below. As he hit the ground hard, he took a moment to compose himself before surveying his surroundings, checking for the armed reinforcements he was sure would arrive imminently. People continued to race away from the bleeding Bailey, rushing past him, screaming and shouting. As his gaze darted to the left, his eyes locked on Phillips's – the detective who had been hunting him. Climbing to her feet, she shouted at the huge man next to her, pointing in his direction. The big man spun around and stared at Meyer, then nodded as he too jumped up from the ground and raced towards him.

Spinning on his heels, Daniel set off at top speed.

THE PLATFORM WAS PACKED with panicked passengers as Bovalino gave chase with Phillips in tow. Meyer was running at pace, weaving and ducking his way through the throng of people fearing for their lives, all trying to exit the packed station ahead of the person next to them.

The barriers at the end of the platform had been automatically disabled soon after the shooting started as part of the station's terror attack protocols to enable people to move away from the danger zone as quickly as possible. This allowed Meyer to charge straight through into the main station concourse, where utter confusion reigned; the panic that had started on the platform had filtered through to the rest of the station in a matter of seconds. Bovalino still had eyes on Meyer, but with so many bodies running in all directions, maintaining it would not be easy. He could hear Phillips behind, shouting at him not to lose their shooter.

Up ahead, Meyer appeared intent on trying to make his escape through the double doors that led out to the outdoor food court, but stopped in his tracks as armed police rushed through from outside. Changing direction, he ran headlong towards the entrance to the underground station, pushing people out of his way as he disappeared down towards the trains.

Bovalino followed suit, and soon had eyes on Meyer

once again, watching as he took the stairs two at a time. When he reached the bottom, Meyer ran at full speed towards the ticket barriers which – unlike the overground station they'd just come from – were still in place. Bov continued down after him and stared open-mouthed as – without breaking stride – Meyer leapfrogged the barriers and rushed towards the escalators that led down to the trains.

A ticket guard, determined to stop any fare dodgers, began shouting at Meyer, and stepped in front of him, trying to block his path. But Meyer made light work of him, swinging his elbow into the guard's face and knocking him to the ground with a thud.

Bovalino reached the barriers a second later, but at six feet four and eighteen stone, there was no chance he could jump them. Instead, he flashed his badge to a second ticket guard, who eventually let him through. By then, though, he'd lost sight of Meyer.

Charging through the sea of people making their way to the underground trains, Bovalino arrived at the top of the escalator just in time to see Meyer leap off the bottom, then duck left towards the northbound Northern Line platform.

Barging his way down the left-hand side of the escalator, shoving people out of the way with his broad frame as he went, Bovalino finally made it to the bottom and ran at full speed onto the packed platform.

Meyer was nowhere to be seen.

Bovalino suddenly sensed the atmosphere change around him as word filtered through about the shooting in the overground station. The tension heightened further as shouts of 'Armed police!' echoed down the escalator behind him.

Up ahead, at the far end of the platform, a second armed police unit arrived, shouting at everyone to exit the platform. And that's when he saw Meyer, jumping from the platform down between the tracks. He was heading towards the tunnel.

PHILLIPS ARRIVED on the platform alongside the armed police, just in time to see Bovalino jumping down onto the track. What the hell was he doing? If he so much as touched the live electric rail, he'd be dead in an instant. Looking beyond him, his intentions soon became clear. Bov was chasing down Meyer, who was now running towards the tunnel.

She set off along the platform as she attempted to catch them up, which was easier said than done. All around her, panicked passengers were screaming and shouting as they rushed past her, trying to get away from whoever and whatever the armed police were chasing down. In the melee, she lost sight of Bov and Meyer until eventually she found herself in a small clearing at the edge of the platform. She screamed Bov's name, causing the big man to stop and face her.

'Be careful!' she shouted.

Just then, a gust of wind rushed out from the tunnel and along the platform, followed by the rumbling of metal on metal; a train was arriving.

'Get out of there!' she screamed at the big Italian as lights appeared deep within the tunnel.

He didn't need telling twice, and launched himself towards the platform.

Pushing people out of the way, Phillips rushed towards him and grabbed his out-stretched hand. But it was no good. He was too heavy for her, and the distance from the platform down to where he stood was too great. Phillips screamed for help, but everyone around her seemed hellbent on saving themselves.

The noise of the oncoming train grew louder and louder

by the second, as she continued to shout for help. All the time, Bovalino's hands were scrabbling for grip, his eyes wide with panic.

Just then, two armed officers rushed from within the crowd, expertly dropping to their knees as they attempted to haul Bov up.

'We've got you, big guy,' said one as they grabbed him by the elbows and dragged him upwards.

Taking her eyes off Bovalino for a split second, Phillips caught sight of Meyer standing at the entrance to the tunnel, arms above his head and facing the platform. A team of firearms officers had their guns trained on him, his chest illuminated by four little red dots emanating from their laser sights. They were shouting at him to move towards them urgently so they could get him off the track before the train arrived.

'Get him out of there!' Phillips shouted to the officers at the top of her voice as the noise and the wind rushing in from the tunnel crescendoed around them.

Meyer must have heard her. Turning his gaze towards Phillips, his eyes locked on hers. Everything seemed to slow down again.

She was aware of the armed officers shouting instructions at Meyer, the screams and shouts of the terrified commuters as they fled the scene, the train screeching along the rails, ploughing towards the station, but it was almost as if she was removed from it all. Her entire focus was now on Meyer and the sad eyes that stared back at her, oozing pain and regret. In that moment, he reminded her of Adam the night she had sent him away.

As if staring straight into her soul, he nodded, then turned to face the train as it filled the tunnel to his left. A split-second later, he disappeared under it as if he'd never existed.

45

L ater that night, lying in bed at home in Manchester, Phillips replayed the events of the day in her mind repeatedly. Despite being physically and mentally exhausted, she couldn't sleep. She struggled to comprehend that, less than twelve hours earlier, she had watched a man die. The utter sadness and resignation etched on Meyer's face just before he went under the train haunted her whenever she closed her eyes. She felt totally conflicted. Of course she knew he had murdered three people and had attempted to kill a fourth, but in some ways, she understood why he had done it. Bailey and her partners had not just stolen his father's invention; they'd effectively stolen Daniel and Meghan's parents from them, and destroyed their faith in the world. She could only imagine the anger Daniel must have felt each day of the eight years he had been locked away in that Balinese hellhole. She found herself wondering if, had she been in his position, would she not want some form of revenge too?

After tossing and turning for several hours, she gave up the fight for sleep and headed downstairs to the kitchen, where she made herself a large mug of sweet tea, then perched on a stool next to the breakfast bar, staring out of the window at the night sky. Dawn was not far away.

When she'd finished her tea, she picked her phone up and, for some reason unknown to her, clicked open the photo app on the home screen. The last picture she had taken flashed up, the one of her and Adam, sitting in the sunshine outside the Horse and Jockey. They both looked so happy together, smiling for the camera. God, she missed him. Zooming in, his beautiful face filled the screen. He was probably the most handsome man she'd ever dated, but he was so much more than that. He was smart and funny, caring and strong. An honest man with so much integrity. The perfect catch. Yet *she* had pushed him away for making one stupid mistake. But deep down, she knew it was more than that. She was scared. Terrified, in fact, of how being with Adam would change her life. She couldn't handle that. The truth was, she'd been on her own for so long she had become conditioned to it. Adam's surprise visit had spooked her in more ways than one.

Staring down at his photo, she was reminded of the devasted look on his face when she had ended the relationship, and she was suddenly consumed by guilt and regret. He had deserved better. He had wanted to talk it through, but she had cut him off at the knees because her fear of getting hurt further down the track was just too much to bear. 'You bloody coward, Jane,' she whispered as she placed the phone back on the bench.

Turning her gaze back to the window, the sun was rising, filling the sky with beautiful pink and orange hues, signalling the start of another day; a slate wiped clean. In that moment, she realised she had a choice: carry on living in fear of what might go wrong, or take a chance and live the life she had always felt was beyond her.

Glancing at the clock on the wall, she could see it was 4.30 a.m.

She nodded to herself as she slipped off the stool and headed upstairs; she knew what she had to do.

After freshening up and dressing, she returned to the kitchen, picked up her car keys and made her way into the hallway, where Floss sat staring at her from the doormat. 'Wish me luck,' she said as she stooped to stroke the little cat, then opened the front door and stepped outside into the fresh early morning air.

The drive to Liverpool from her home took just forty-five minutes. The traffic was as light as she'd expected at 5 a.m., and the traffic lights gods were on her side all the way. Parking up outside the emergency department, she turned off the engine and took a few minutes to steady her nerves, closing her eyes and breathing deeply in through her nose and out through her mouth. It was a technique she had discovered during the many hours of therapy she had under-taken to help combat the PTSD triggered by being shot in the line of duty. She had never imagined she would use it at a time like this. When she finally felt ready, she stepped out of the car and made her way past the bank of yellow and green ambulances stationed at the front of the hospital, and took up a position on a bench just outside the emergency room. The sheer volume of cigarette stubs that littered the ground under her feet, as well as empty coffee cups and soda cans bursting out of the overfilled wastebin next to her, suggested it had been a busy night for the team in A&E.

She checked her watch; 5.57 a.m. Adam would be off shift at 6.

For the next ten minutes she sat in the cool morning air, listening to the sounds of a city gradually waking up; cars passing by on the adjacent road, trains running in the distance, and lorries beeping as they reversed into the loading bays situated around the corner from her position. Her stomach wound up tight with nerves as she waited. She was terrified of how he might react, and hoping beyond hope that he would let her say what she had come to say.

Every time the automatic doors whooshed open behind her, her heart jumped into her mouth as she turned, expecting to see him, only to be disappointed when it was someone else.

As the time approached 6.25 a.m., she began to wonder if she had made a mistake. Was he still actually on night shifts, or had he moved back onto days already? The tension in her body was unbearable. Fishing her phone from her pocket, she stepped up from the bench and walked away from the building as she called Adam's number. A second later, she stopped in her tracks as the sound of 'Are You Lonesome Tonight?' wafted through the air from behind her. Her heart skipped a beat as she turned to see Adam, dressed in his blue scrubs, standing in the doorway to the hospital, a rucksack slung over his shoulder, staring down at the phone in his hand. *Their song was still his ringtone.*

'Adam,' she said softly, ending the call.

Looking in her direction, his eyes suddenly widened. 'Jane. What are you doing here?'

'I need to talk to you.'

'What about?' he replied, still rooted to the spot.

Her legs felt like jelly as she moved slowly towards him. 'I wanted to say I'm sorry for the way it ended.'

Adam nodded, but said nothing.

She was right in front of him now. 'I messed up. I got scared and I freaked out.'

He produced a faint smile. 'Well, don't beat yourself up over it. Like you said, I did break into your house.'

Phillips closed her eyes and dropped her chin to her chest before looking up again. 'My job has made me jumpy, Adam.

During our time together, I deliberately didn't talk to you about it because of the way it consumes me. I wanted to keep you separate from it. But I've realised in the last few days that that was a big mistake. If I had shared some of the stuff that's happened to me over the years, you'd have understood that surprising me at home was never going to get the reaction you wanted.'

'Yeah. Quite the exact opposite, actually.'

Phillips smiled softly. 'What I'm trying to say, Adam, is, I'm sorry for the way I reacted and I'm sorry that we're not together anymore.'

'Me too,' he replied with sad eyes.

'And if it's not too late, I'd like to...well...'

Adam's eyes narrowed. 'You'd like to what?'

Phillips swallowed hard. 'I'd like to try again.'

'I see.' He nodded thoughtfully, before standing in silence for a long moment. 'And, what? You think I'm just going to take you back?'

Her stomach churned as she stared into his eyes. A tear rolled down her cheek. 'Maybe...'

'There's no maybe about it,' he said through a wide grin as he stepped forward and drew her into a long, tender kiss.

46

Ten Days Later

Phillips woke to the sound of the shower running in the bathroom on the other side of her bedroom wall. She checked the bedside clock. It was almost 8 a.m. She couldn't quite believe it. She would normally be at her desk by now, and for a split second felt guilty, before reminding herself she had more than earned a lie-in – and a late start. A fact Superintendent Carter had attempted to impress upon her on more than one occasion. "Try and get a better work-life balance, Jane." He had said it again only a few days previously.

Luxuriating in the pillow surrounding her head, she lay motionless for a while until the shower stopped. A few minutes later, Adam walked into the bedroom, a towel wrapped around his waist, his taut, muscular body glistening.

'Hey,' he said softly as he padded over to the side of the bed and sat down next to her.

'Why didn't you wake me up?' she asked.

'Because you looked so peaceful, babe. And like Harry

has been telling you, starting at 9.30 every now and again won't kill you.'

Phillips smiled and nodded. 'So, what have you got planned for your day off?'

'I thought I'd wander into the village this morning and grab some breakfast, then head to the shops and get the ingredients for my home-made Beef Massaman Curry, along with a couple of bottles of wine for tonight. That sound ok?'

Phillips leaned up on her elbow and kissed him firmly on the lips. 'Sounds like heaven.'

Adam smiled widely. 'Good.'

She patted him on the chest. 'And if I want to be back in time to enjoy them, I'd better get my arse in gear and get to work.'

Thirty minutes later, after a quick shower and a cup of coffee, Phillips kissed Adam goodbye and set off for her first meeting of the day, an impromptu visit to the Manchester Royal Infirmary to check in on Lesley Bailey. Five days earlier, she had been moved out of the intensive care unit at St Thomas's Hospital, on the banks of the River Thames in London, then transferred to the Manchester Royal Infirmary where, by all accounts, she was making rapid progress as she recovered from the gunshot wound that had almost killed her. As it was, the bullet fired by Meyer had ricocheted, causing extensive damage that included the loss of her spleen, as well as one of her lungs.

When she arrived at Reception, Phillips was not surprised to hear that Bailey was staying in a private room. As she stepped through the door, she noted that the small flatscreen TV attached to wall opposite the bed was switched on and playing at a low volume, but Bailey wasn't watching it. Instead, she had her nose stuck in the distinctive orange pages of *Financial Times*.

Phillips cleared her throat to let Bailey know she was there.

Bailey appeared to be her usual dour self as she dropped the paper and peered over the top. 'Oh, it's *you*.'

Phillips forced a thin smile as she moved to the side of the bed. Despite the massive trauma Bailey had experienced over the last few weeks, she really couldn't warm to the woman. 'How are you feeling?'

'Do you really want to know?'

'Of course,' lied Phillips, but the truth was, she really didn't care much.

'I'm totally pissed off.'

Phillips frowned. 'And why's that?'

'Well, let me think. I've been shot, half my organs have been removed and my share-offering has been put on hold thanks to police incompetence.'

As much as she wanted to, Phillips didn't bite. 'I think you'll find it was those same incompetent coppers who saved your life.'

'Pah!' scoffed Bailey. 'If you lot had done your job properly, I wouldn't have been shot in the first place. As it was, you walked me straight in front of a sniper's rifle.'

Phillips folded her arms against her chest. 'If I recall, it was your private security team that did that. And I did try and warn you before we went to London that they weren't who or what they claimed to be.'

A snarl appeared on Bailey's lip.

Phillips continued. '*And* as I understand it, the IPO has been suspended pending the outcome of the ongoing investigation into who owns the rights to the patent on your flagship foam.'

'Which is a farce! That patent is mine by rights. I paid Joseph Meyer a hundred grand for it.'

'After you stole it from him and forced him into near bankruptcy. At least, that's what his daughter claims.'

'She can claim what she likes. I paid a fair price for the work he put into its inception, and in turn he signed it over to Ardent. It was Ardent that turned it into a commercial offering and made it profitable.'

Phillips pursed her lips. 'Well, it seems his daughter thinks otherwise. And if what she claims is proven – that you, Rice, Howard and Nelson all conspired to steal it from him – then she has a very strong legal case to claim significant damages. Just think of that; retrospective payments going back ten years. That could cost you millions, and I doubt Charles Cavendish and his pals from the City would be quite so happy to reinstate your public offering anytime soon.'

'Well, I'd like to see her try and make a case. She has absolutely no proof that the patent was stolen from her father. Nothing whatsoever. She won't be getting a single penny out of me, I can promise you that.'

Phillips said nothing as she stared at Bailey's mean, twisted face. She really was a piece of work, and she'd spent more than enough time in her company for one lifetime. 'Well, as lovely as this has been. I really should be getting back to the office.'

Bailey didn't reply, choosing instead to return to her newspaper in silence.

Phillips shook her head and left the room.

———

LATER THAT AFTERNOON at Ashton House, she received an unexpected visit from Carter. 'Knock, knock,' he said as he stepped into her office.

Phillips looked up from her laptop and offered a weak smile. 'Hello, sir.'

Carter's brow furrowed. 'Everything ok, Jane?' He took a seat opposite her.

Phillips reclined in her chair and let out a frustrated sigh. 'I made the mistake of visiting Lesley Bailey this morning in hospital to see how she was doing, and let her get under my skin.'

'How so?'

'Well. You know what she's like.'

'Only from what you've told me. So, what happened?'

'As soon as I turned up, she started throwing all sorts of accusations around about my team being incompetent and almost getting her killed.'

'That's ridiculous!' Carter protested. 'She's only alive because of you and your team.'

'I know. And that's what pissed me off so much. I decided to poke the bear and started winding her up about the fraud claim made by Joseph Meyer's daughter, Meghan. And how, if she can prove it, she'd be entitled to millions in back payments.'

'Which of course she would be.'

Phillips nodded. 'But Bailey was adamant that there was no truth in the claims and that Meghan would get nothing. *Not a penny*. Honestly, sir, it took all my strength not to walk over and slap the vileness out of her.'

Carter chuckled. 'I'd have paid to see that.'

Phillips frowned. 'Seriously though, sir. Six people are dead because of that woman and her wretched lust for money. And yes, ok, she got shot herself, but *she* gets to walk away from all this scot-free. *And* if Meghan's claims do come to nothing, the IPO will inevitably be reinstated. As the only surviving partner, she'll end up richer than ever. It's just not right.'

'No, it's not.' Carter produced a smug grin. 'But I'm pretty sure Lesley Bailey won't be walking away from this one scot-free.'

Phillips's eyes narrowed. 'What do you know, sir?'

'Well. Let's just say, I have it on good authority from a mate in the Fraud Squad that, as well as staking a retrospective claim to Ardent's patent in the civil court, Meghan Butler has also presented *them* with evidence she claims proves Bailey and her partners did in fact steal the patent. And I'm told it's compelling.'

Phillips sat forward in her chair, eyes wide. 'You're kidding me?'

Carter shook his head. 'I'm not. In fact, apparently the evidence is so clear, the Fraud Squad will be launching a full investigation into Ardent's practices in the coming days. That should put a dent in her hopes of launching her IPO.'

Phillips clapped her hands together with glee. 'That's the best news I've had in ages.'

Carter grinned. 'I thought you might like that. And based on how she was with you this morning, it sounds like it couldn't happen to a nicer person.'

'No, sir. No, it couldn't.'

'By the way, where are we at with the Liam Bush assault on Bailey?' asked Carter.

'He's pleading guilty. Once we found CCTV footage of him disposing of a baseball bat on the night she was attacked, and his DNA and fingerprints came back as a match on the threatening letters, he caved. I think the chance of a reduced sentence made the decision for him.'

'How long will he get?'

'Three years instead of seven. If he behaves himself, he'll be out in eighteen months.'

'Excellent work again, Jane. First class. Another one off the list.'

'More ticks in the green column on the spreadsheets for Fox,' said Phillips sardonically.

Carter didn't reply. Instead, he shifted in his seat and cleared his throat. 'Look, Jane. One of the reasons I called in is that I wanted to say thank you for saving my arse on this one.'

Phillips waved him away. 'Don't be daft, sir. I was just doing my job.'

'Yes, you were. And because you did it so well, I get to keep mine.'

'Seriously, sir, it's me who should be thanking you. I know what kind of pressure Fox will have put on you over the last month, and you never once fed that down the line to me or the team. Instead, you protected us from it and gave us your complete support so we could get on and do what we do best. I can't tell you how much that means to us as a team. You've got our backs, sir, and please trust me when I say we've got yours.'

Carter smiled and said softly, 'Thanks Jane.'

Phillips returned his smile.

Carter clapped his hands together. 'So, can I treat my star detective to a celebratory drink after work tonight?'

Phillips felt herself blush. 'Er, I can't tonight, sir. I have plans.'

Carter's eyes betrayed his disappointment. 'Plans? I see. Anyone special?'

Phillips couldn't stop the Cheshire Cat grin spreading across her face as Adam flashed into her mind's eye. 'Yes, sir. Yes, he is.'

ACKNOWLEDGMENTS

This book is dedicated in the loving memory of my sister-in-law, Lisa Eve, who died suddenly while I was writing *Deadly Caller*. She was just 44 years old.

As an award-winning radio presenter known on air as Lisa Shaw, she was a huge support to my career as I moved from the corporate world to take on the challenge of becoming a full-time author. She interviewed me on her show several times and was an avid reader of my *Deadly* series. In fact, I know from conversations we had in the weeks before she died that she was very much enjoying *Deadly Obsession* at the time. It saddens me greatly to know that she never finished it.

And it breaks my heart to see how much she is missed by the loving family left behind. In the last few months, I have been truly humbled by the enormous strength and dignity demonstrated by her husband Gareth, her little boy Zachary, as well as her mum, Doreen, her dad and step-mum, Bill and Jean, and her sisters, Kim, Joanne and Emma. I must also pay tribute to Lisa's nieces and nephews, Jack and Gracie and Leo and Ivy, as well as my own little boy, Vaughan. Your smiles and cuddles have been an incredible tonic for the whole family.

And thank you to Lisa's amazing friends and colleagues who have shown us nothing but love and support.

I'd also like to make special mention to my publishing team of Brian, Jan, Garret and Claire. Thank you for your understanding of the challenges faced during this difficult time.

My coaches Donna Elliot and Cheryl Lee, from 'Now Is Your Time' and Fabio at 'Fabio Mazzieri Coaching' have been instrumental in helping me finish the story as our world was turned upside down.

I must also mention the people who gave me the gift of their experience and expertise this time round; Carole Lawford, ex-CPS Prosecutor; Joseph Mitcham, former para-trooper; Keith James, retired firearms officer; Julian McBride, close protection specialist; and my nephew, Hamish Profit, who guided me through the complexities of using a hunting rifle.

Thank you to Jo Robertson, the person I trust to read my manuscripts before anyone else.

Laurel, my editor. Your attention to detail is second to none.

Finally, thank you to my readers for reading *Deadly Caller.* If you could spend a moment to write an honest review on Amazon, no matter how short, I would be extremely grateful. They really do help readers discover my books.

Best wishes,

Owen

www.omjryan.com

ALSO BY OMJ RYAN

DEADLY SECRETS

(A crime thriller introducing DCI Jane Phillips)

DEADLY SILENCE

(Book 1 in the DCI Jane Phillips series)

DEADLY WATERS

(Book 2 in the DCI Jane Phillips series)

DEADLY VENGEANCE

(Book 3 in the DCI Jane Phillips series)

DEADLY BETRAYAL

(Book 4 in the DCI Jane Phillips series)

DEADLY OBSESSION

(Book 5 in the DCI Jane Phillips series)

DEADLY CALLER

(Book 6 in the DCI Jane Phillips series)

DEADLY NIGHT

(Book 7 in the DCI Jane Phillips series)

DEADLY CRAVING

(Book 8 in the DCI Jane Phillips series)

DEADLY JUSTICE

(Book 9 in the DCI Jane Phillips series)

Published by Inkubator Books
www.inkubatorbooks.com

Printed in Great Britain
by Amazon

20374201R00164